Francis Selwyn (pen name of Donald Thomas) (1926–)

Donald Thomas was born in Somerset and educated at Queen's College, Taunton, and Balliol College, Oxford. He holds a personal chair in the University of Wales, Cardiff, now Cardiff University. His numerous crime novels include two collections of Sherlock Holmes stories and a hugely successful historical detective series written under the pen name Francis Selwyn and featuring Sergeant Verity of Scotland Yard, as well as gritty police procedurals written under the name of Richard Dacre. He is also the author of seven biographies and a number of other non-fiction works, and won the Gregory Prize for his poems, *Points of Contact*. He lives in Bath with his wife.

Mad Hatter Summer: A Lewis Carroll Nightmare
The Ripper's Apprentice
Jekyll, Alias Hyde
The Arrest of Scotland Yard
Dancing in the Dark
Red Flowers for Lady Blue
The Blindfold Game
The Day the Sun Rose Twice

As Francis Selwyn

Sergeant Verity and the Cracksman
Sergeant Verity and the Imperial Diamond
Sergeant Verity Presents His Compliments
Sergeant Verity and the Blood Royal

Sergeant Verity and the Swell Mob
Sergeant Verity and the Hangman's Child

As Richard Dacre

The Blood Runs Hot
Scream Blue Murder
Money with Menaces

Sergeant Verity and the Hangman's Child

Francis Selwyn

An Orion book

Copyright © Donald Thomas 2000

Previously published as *The Hangman's Child*

The right of Donald Thomas to be identified as the author of this work
has been asserted in accordance with the Copyright, Designs and Patents
Act 1988.

This edition published by
The Orion Publishing Group Ltd
Orion House
5 Upper St Martin's Lane
London WC2H 9EA

An Hachette UK company
A CIP catalogue record for this book is available from the British Library

ISBN 978 1 4719 0421 9

www.orionbooks.co.uk

To Louis B. Chandler
a salute from another stretch of the trenches

Author's Note

Jack Rann's Newgate climb was performed in reality by Henry Williams in 1836. Walker's Cornhill Vaults were entered by Thomas Caseley during the weekend of 4–5 February 1865. James Sargent's micrometer of 1857 is illustrated on p.157 of Vincent Eras' *Locks and Keys Throughout the Ages*, Lips' Safe & Lock Manufacturing Company, 1957. With the exception of these debts to reality, the characters and incidents of the present novel are entirely fictitious.

ONE

THE HANGMAN'S CHILD

1

'Handsome' Jack Rann shivered in the cold May morning of his
dream. The windows of tall London house-fronts flamed with
summer dawn, where Snow Hill curved up past The Saracen's
Head and entered Newgate Street. The rooms of the Magpie and
Stump, ablaze with gaslight until dawn, were blank and dark. An
aproned potman was clearing the picked carcasses of cold fowl and
rabbit, the debris of kidneys and lobsters. Scraps and cigar butts
littered the sand of the wooden floor.

A low anthem of voices rose from the mass of men and women
wedged between the walls of Newgate Street. Uniformed consta-
bles stood at the rear of the crowd, among the taunts of a dozen
stunted and sallow youths. Dandies at the upper windows of the
tavern stroked their moustaches and twirled their cheroots. Not a
head among thousands turned from the sight before them.

High in the blank wall of Newgate Gaol was a tiny door, used
only on such mornings as this. A temporary black-draped platform
stood out from it. Carts carrying posts and planks had rattled up
Snow Hill as late as four in the morning to complete the work. The
carpenters had erected two black-painted posts on the platform
with a stout cross-beam between them. A dark iron chain dangled
from the centre of the beam. The hammering died away.

Last of all, a coach carrying the Sheriff of Middlesex and his
guests made its way through the crowd and the doors of the great

prison closed behind it. The clock-hands on the square medieval tower of St Sepulchre stood at ten to eight. The onlookers shivered expectantly in the early chill.

An elderly man, his frock-coat and cloth hat faded by rain and sun, wandered the fringes of the crowd with a tray of pamphlets round his neck. He stared reproachfully at each group, pausing to offer his goods in a mournful chant.

'A Voice from the Condemned Cell! Being the last confession of Handsome Jack Rann, who suffers today for the barbarous murder of his friend and accomplice, Pandy Quinn. See Handsome Jack in his earliest years, took from his orphan home to be made a climbing-boy! But the poor infant was never taught to shun the broad way leading to destruction! He that had no parents to guide him becomes today the hangman's child!'

'Hurrah!' shouted a drunken subaltern, his arm round a laughing woman at an upper window. 'Hurrah, then, for Handsome Jack!'

The patterer glanced up, frowned, and resumed his dirge.

'Jack being a thief from infancy, the demon that ever haunts the footsteps of the vicious seduced him to spill the blood of Pandy Quinn in a tap-room of the Golden Anchor off Saffron Hill at Clerkenwell, with a cowardly Italian stiletto-blade! See him on the gallows trap! Hear him in his own confession! Printed for six pence with two cuts and a set of verses!'

At the climax of the old man's chant, the minute hand on St Sepulchre rose to a perfect vertical and the bell of the dark tower tolled eight times. Stillness held the crowd. The patterer with his tray of yellowed pamphlets shuffled on. In the press-yard of the prison, the iron had been knocked from the legs of the fourteen men and women who would now be led out, one by one, to die. Only a husband and wife, who had poisoned their lodger for his clothes, were to be hanged side by side at the end of the morning's ritual.

The little door opened, high in Newgate wall. A man's head appeared briefly and vanished. He reappeared, distinctive and self-assured in black suiting and dark cravat. A group of young officers on a balcony of the Magpie and Stump jeered him. Their hooting faded into silence. Four more men followed the black-dressed figure in a close group. Jack Rann was russet-suited, like a countryman visiting the city, but with his shirt-collar open for the hangman's convenience. His hands were strapped together in front of him and, as he stood there, he opened his palms once or twice in a helpless little gesture.

A group of apprentices at the rear of the crowd, their view obstructed, shouted, 'Hats off! Heads down in front!'

A voice from the platform drifted high across the crowd. The condemned who were still alive and in full health heard the opening of their own burial service.

'Man that is born of a woman hath but a short time to live . . . . He cometh up and is cut down like a flower . . . .'

In the silence of the great crowd, the governor of the gaol turned to the hangman and consigned the victims to him.

'Your prisoners, Mr Calcraft!'

Jack Rann placed himself quietly beneath the beam. The hangman, who had first come alone on to the platform, pulled him round to face the crowd, took a white night-cap from his own pocket and drew it down firmly to cover the murderer's face. The onlookers packing Newgate Street wall to wall held their breath. The executioner stepped back and gave a signal to his assistant below the platform by three taps of his heel on the planking. The wags on the tavern balcony shouted the count.

'One ... Two ... Three!...'

Jack Rann, in the daylight of his dream, wondered why he could still see the balcony of the Magpie and Stump when the night-cap was already drawn down to veil the bulging eyes and starting tongue, the portrait of a 'Hangman's Child'.

While there was time, he cried out that he could still see, that he was also a figure in the crowd, watching himself up there on the gallows trap.

5

The bolts of the trap thudded, the hinged wood banged against the frame. The hooded figure felt himself stumble into the dark drop as it opened under him. His cry choked, as he first went down and then shot upwards again, sitting tall and awake on his plank bed in the depth of night. His tongue was sticking out between his teeth, as if in obedience to the dream.

The sky beyond the barred window was black, yellowed here and there by fire on a dark cloud of London smoke. He was not hanged at all. He had all that to come.

Jack Rann's heart thumped like a trip-hammer as reason returned. The thud of the trap had been only the warder's hand on the sliding spy-hole as the Hangman's Child cried out in his shallow sleep.

Then, as at every waking for the last two weeks, his heart's beating filled his breast and his throat with a swelling dread. Eight mornings from now the midnight dream was to be reality. Tomorrow would be the last day allowed for visits. Three days later the warders, who watched the corridor of death-wards, would move into the cells of those whose sentences had been confirmed, for fear they might harm themselves in their despair.

No one had entered in answer to his cry, such sounds were too common along the death-wards. A warder's voice from the stone corridor said, ''e's himself again now.'

A yellow oil-lamp glimmered through the open slot into the whitewashed oblong of the cell.

'You still there, 'andsome Jack?' He knew the warder's voice now. William Lupus, the worst of them. 'Dreaming your dreams again? A man'd think you couldn't get there fast enough. Monday week. Then it's "Over the water to Charley" for you, my lad.'

Handsome Rann lay back under his blanket, hands folded behind his head. He was not handsome, even his nickname was a joke. The narrow head, the starved build, the bony shoulders and the lantern jaw that suggested humorous vacancy were nature's gifts to him. For a while, he had tried to impersonate the gentleman he had never become. The pose had served him well in his trade as thief. But in the previous autumn, Rann and Quinn had trespassed on the preserves of Bully Bragg and the Swell Mob. Not a trick in the world would save him after that.

It was chance that Pandy Quinn fell first into their hands. A knife had slipped while Pandy was held down for questioning, but Bully Bragg and Strap Mulligan had turned even that accident to profit by casting Handsome Jack as Pandy's killer. A trickster and an artist with a lock, he fitted every item on their bill.

He shivered, hearing again the voices of the ragged children who ran after the pauper hearse, as it carried the body to the riverside mortuary.

> 'Pandy Quinn! Pandy Quinn!
> Lived by evil, died in sin!
> Robbed the rich and poor as well,
> Lied on earth, and lies in hell!'

'You was my friend, Pandy,' said Jack Rann softly in the dark. 'You taught me everything. I could never hurt you.'

His murmuring roused the turnkeys.

'Tell you what, Handsome Jack.' It was Lupus again at the spy-hole, the warder whose very name sounded like a disease. 'You was lucky over eating your grub. Sometimes, when a man knows he's to hang, it touches him in the throat. We had a cove as couldn't swallow for fright, not food, not even water. His gullet was that tightened up, getting ready for the noose. So we told him the Home Office was that worried he might famish before the day, they'd agreed to have him beheaded, under some old law. And you know what, Mr Jack? All of a sudden he could eat hearty as a hunter and drink like a whale. Only thing was . . . .' The voice broke into quiet laughter in anticipation of its own good humour. 'Only thing was, Jack, he couldn't put a razor to his gill no more to shave himself. Shy of the blade, he was. You been lucky, Handsome Rann, all things considered.'

7

'I never so much as touched Pandy Quinn,' Jack Rann spoke quietly again. 'Let alone did I kill him. I never so much as hurt anyone, let alone bled 'em to death. And where would I get one of them Eye-tal-ian blades to do it?'

But Lupus heard him.

'You ain't half a caution, Handsome Jack!' he said humorously and slammed the metal spy-hole shut.

Rann stared up into the darkness, wide awake, fearing what he must dream if he slept again. Close by, St Sepulchre chimed the single hour after midnight. Greyfriars followed it. Then the boom of St Paul's further off.

The fastidious little brain in the narrow skull assembled facts, divided them and divided them again. After tomorrow he would be allowed no more visitors, no news of the world beyond Newgate's massive walls. Three days more, when his sentence was confirmed, they would set a guard in his cell. Until then, Lupus and the turnkeys would keep a common watch on the block of death-wards from the end of the corridor. There were too many men and women waiting their turn on the gallows-trap for the warders to guard them individually before their date of execution was decided.

He let out a sigh and blinked at the darkness above him. With the fatalism of a professional thief, he had always known that he would sometimes escape punishment for his crimes and sometimes be punished for those that were not his work. Informers, rivals, and policemen would see to that. This lottery of punishment was the nearest thing to justice in his life. Murder was different, however. The lottery had no right to mark him for death without an explanation.

Three men watched the death-wards, two at a time. Lupus was the most vindictive. Jessup, the senior man, was stern but not unkind. At dawn on the first day, he had shown Rann how the mattress on the plank bed must be rolled and fastened with a strap after use, the two blankets folded squarely on top of it.

'And I shan't show you twice, my lad,' Jessup had said. 'You do as you're told and we shall get along like Box and Cox.'

Listening to the gruff kindness, Jack Rann had almost believed they would not hang him after all. He gave no trouble, not even to a brute like Lupus. Once he had asked a medical officer with whiskied breath what it would be like to die in such a manner.

'Be a sensible fellow,' the doctor had said, 'and, if the time comes, you'll go sweet as a nut and never feel a hurt. There's nothing to the noose but a wry neck and a pair of wet breeches. A man will piss when he cannot whistle, as they say.'

Never feel a hurt. Pain was defined for him at seven years old, when the parish union apprenticed him as climbing-boy to a master-sweep. It was explained to him that in wider chimneys a boy must hold his position by elbows and knees. The harder his skin, the easier he would find it.

In front of a hearth that shone white with heat, his master held the child, while the master's wife scoured the skin from his elbows and knees. The strongest brine that the pork-shop could provide was applied to the raw patches before holding them to the heat. Neither his master's promises of baby's sugar-cake nor the cane flourished by his master's wife would check the child's screams.

Set to work next day, Jack Rann the climbing-boy came down with such blood running from the four sooty joints that the sweep's wife quite thought his kneecaps were hanging off. The dangerous state of his wounds convinced the couple that the amount of brine and the time before the fire had been too little. Rann remembered those weekly rituals as the heat of hell, the sweep growling, the harridan screeching, the child screaming. He thought he might rather be hanged than endure such torment again.

He dismissed the past and thought again of the future. Tomorrow the watch would include Baptist Babb, the prisoner's friend. Rann had no time for 'uprighters' and 'white chokers', croaking of repentance and salvation. Baptist Babb would save his soul but not his neck. Still, with his quiet Scots voice, the freckled balding head, the heavy skull that caused forehead creases by its weight, Baptist Babb was a figure of interest. A weak link in the chain of retribution.

He closed his eyes. There was a time after midnight when the great city around him fell silent. The last drunkard had gone shouting homeward and the first cries of the market-traders with the crash of their iron-rimmed wheels on the cobbles of Newgate Street and Snow Hill had not begun. That deep stillness lasted only a little while, but he heard it now.

Silent as the tomb. The phrase described the great prison at that moment. Newgate was no ordinary gaol. Men and women were not brought here to be judged, only to feel pain or death. They came to be hanged or flogged, according to the pleasure of the court, at one time to be branded or maimed. Yet for that short hour of night, the cursing and the weeping, the anger and the pleading, fell quiet. The massive fortress of despair was briefly at peace.

Jack Rann listened again. Somewhere close to him he heard a slow but regular drip of water on stone. It held his attention. He frowned and tried to calculate where the drops were falling. With hands still clasped behind his head, he measured the rhythm and counted two drops in every minute. They were falling in the yard outside, dripping from an iron cistern high in the angle of the wall. He was sure of it now. Handsome Jack closed his eyes as he tried to visualize it. Then he smiled at a new thought in the darkness, unfolded his hands, and went to sleep.

2

A hollow-cheeked medical officer examined him in his cell next morning. A pale snub-nosed young chaplain followed and talked of Kingdom-Come. Fingering the white tie of his clerical dress, he avoided the prisoner's gaze, his eyes on the high heaven of frosted window-lights. The chaplain had many visits to make before noon and was anxious to be on his way. Jack Rann watched him and knew what the Home Secretary's clerk had decided.

That afternoon, Jessup came in with Lupus and Babb behind him.

'Prisoners' consulting-room, Rann! Look alive!'

The chaplain had said nothing about a visit. In any case, the consulting-room was kept for interviews with a lawyer or a clergy-man, unlike the breath-stained wire grille through which he might have spoken his last words to his family or friends. Jack Rann had no family. Nor would his friends have shown themselves in Newgate. But he had no priest, no lawyer except the compliant hack whose 'poor prisoner's defence' at the Old Bailey sessions had put him where he was now.

He sat on the plank bed while Lupus locked iron shackles on his ankles and drew out a thin chain to connect these with the steel cuffs on his wrists.

'Who'd want to see me now?' he murmured, as if to himself.

'Workhouse missioner,' said Jessup briskly. 'Brought your little girl. One visit you get. This is it.'

Rann concealed his curiosity. He had no little girl nor a woman who might have been the mother of one. His lust, when it became a trial to him, was soothed by the likes of Maggie Fashion from the Cornhill Mourning Emporium or Miss Jolly, dancer at the penny entertainments of Smithfield or Shoreditch.

Jessup and Babb waited in the corridor, away from the odours of confinement in the cell. Lupus tightened the shackles on the prisoner's ankles until Rann gave a choked gasp of pain. Lupus looked up and grinned. He shook his head.

'You ain't half a caution, 'andsome Jack,' he said amiably, tightening the shackles a little more.

With Lupus and Babb following him, Jessup leading the way, Rann walked in shuffling steps. At every movement the iron anklet scraped the skin of his bony leg. He clenched his teeth. Now, of all times, he must give no pretext for cancelling the visit.

The low-vaulted prison corridor ran to the centre of the great building. There it was crossed by another, like the nave of a cathedral meeting its transepts. The space where the two stone-paved corridors crossed was a square of four low arches. Joined by wooded panels to waist-height, glass-paned above, they formed the consulting-room.

Prisoner and adviser were divided by a broad oak table, the full width of the room, with chairs on either side. The warders stood several yards outside, respecting the privilege due to a lawyer with his client or a clergyman comforting a sinner. The respect did not extend to turning away their eyes. Nothing would pass from one hand to another, over or under the broad table.

Rann looked towards the glassed-in space and swore to himself. Two figures stood on the far side of the table. Any man with pretensions to charity might offer himself as a workhouse missioner one day and vanish the next. If such a visitor chose to bring a prisoner's child to see him on a magistrate's authority, it was nothing the law could prevent.

Rann knew this missioner as 'Orator' Hawkins, an attorney's

clerk dismissed over a probate embezzlement. It was not brought to court for the sake of the firm's name. Hawkins had been Bully Bragg's mouthpiece for the past two years. Rann wondered what a lord of the Swell Mob like Bragg could want with him now.

The visit would not have been difficult to arrange. Bragg boasted of two or three justices among the clients of his 'French Introducing House' off Drury Lane. No magistrate would doubt the good offices of such a figure as Hawkins. The close cut of dark hair, the precise lines of formal suit and pearl-grey choker, the kid gloves, gave him the air of a fashionable preacher from a Kensington or Marylebone chapel. The broad forehead diminished to a narrow trimly bearded chin, the small and high-pointed ears were like architectural features. At closer range, the light-blue eyes were hooded and dead. They held steady while the 'Orator' read a man his sentence of execution on Bully Bragg's behalf.

The 'Little Girl' was a figure of dark but rather sullen good looks who appeared by her dress to be about sixteen. A slim and agile figure, she was costumed in a plain mourning-gown of black merino wool. The dark hair usually worn down her back was entirely contained in the lining of a black hood. Her cheap gown and bonnet resembled the uniform of an orphanage or workhouse. No doubt she had snatched at sixpence or a shilling from Bragg to act the part of a snivelling child.

Rann knew this vision of hardened prettiness and dispassionate brown eyes as Suzanne Berry or 'Lambeth Sue', one of the mudlarks who scavenged at low tide between Westminster and Southwark. Boys and girls collected coal, wood, bottles, bones and rags for the 'dust contractors'. By dark they stole from the barges moored at wharves above London Bridge. Most girls with Suzanne's prettiness were soon apprenticed to an adult pickpocket or sold themselves for their 'fancy-men' to sailors or dockers in the raucous streets of Wapping or Shadwell. Someone had soaped and scrubbed her well for her present appearance.

Prisoner and escort entered the glassed-in space, where Hawkins dry-washed his hands, anxious to proceed with his duty.

As the warders went out and Jessup closed the door, Hawkins raised his right hand, two fingers together in an ambiguous sign of greeting or benediction. He thought better of the gesture and lowered his arm. Suzanne glanced quickly at Rann, then lowered her face and sobbed a little into a folded handkerchief. Rann guessed it was fright at the place she found herself in. He scowled at Hawkins.

'So what does Bragg want? If I was to see anyone, I'd as soon have had Mag Fashion or Miss Jolly. I was to have one visit. What use are you to me?'

Hawkins dropped his voice. 'Don't shout! They may hear you through the glass.'

Rann shifted his chains and stood awkwardly at his side of the table. Hawkins sat opposite. Suzanne kept her profile hidden in the dark hood. Yet her brown eyes watched the man who was to die, staring as if at a fairground freak.

'Let them hear,' said Rann with soft contempt. 'You think I'd help Bragg? Or you? Bragg's voice is all you are, my son. When he talks from his backside.'

Hawkins' face changed as little as if Rann had not spoken. The insults were like blows deflected or received with meek indifference. He looked at the prisoner like a head clerk surveying a bankrupt tradesman.

'Mr Bragg is sorry for the situation in which you find yourself, Mr Rann. Truly so. But he has a proposition which may be to your advantage.'

Rann stared at him. He spoke slowly, as though to the feeble-minded.

'Eight days from now, I'm to be stretched. You think Bragg knows different?'

Hawkins' bony nose tightened, as if catching some prison odour.

'Mr Bragg can do nothing about that.'

'Do nothing!' Rann hoped the warders could hear him but he

14

doubted it. 'Bragg's the reason I'm here! Him and Policeman Fowler swore my life away. I want to know why. Even if I'm to be stretched, I've a right to know why. I didn't put a knife in Pandy Quinn. I couldn't a-done. I'd nothing to cut him with.'

'Jury thought otherwise,' said Hawkins suavely. 'End of the case.'

The fetters jangled as Rann shifted forward a little.

'You listen,' he said. 'I got a message at the Three Tuns in Hatton Garden. Come to the Golden Anchor in Hatton Wall, off Saffron Hill, quick-sharp. Pandy in a tap-room fight. When I went in, Pandy was bleeding on the floor. Someone cut him, well before that. All they needed was me. Bragg and his boy, Moonbeam, jumped me from behind a door. That old bastard Catskin Nash wipes me with blood off something. They pushed me down on Pandy. Held me till Flash Fowler come from upstairs, where he so conveniently happened to be with one of Bragg's girls. Now you tell me why.'

Hawkins looked quickly aside at the warders, who assumed expressions of indifference, and then back at Rann.

'Now you sit down and listen, Handsome Rann. Your brief had his say down the sessions. No one believed you then, no one believes you now. As for no knife, that's where you're wrong. Since yesterday, my friend, you're trussed tighter than a sirloin for the skewer. They found the knife you say you never had.'

The impossibility briefly knocked the fight from him. He sat down awkwardly and glanced warily at Hawkins and the girl, dark eyes flicking side to side.

'How could it be found?'

'By looking,' said Hawkins calmly. 'Policeman Fowler was called by the man that found it. Yesterday morning. Down a drain on Saffron Hill. Just below Hatton Wall and the Golden Anchor. Where you run out and dropped it the minute after you cut Quinn. Mr Fowler never stopped looking for it, being anxious to see justice done to all concerned. Hurtful things having been said in court about Mr Bragg and Moonbeam and poor old Mr Nash. Hurtful allegations about the police too. But Charley Fowler found your Italian cutter down a drain on Saffron Hill. Twenty yards from the Golden Anchor, where the slop must've carried it.'

'Then he put it there himself!' said Rann furiously.

'Whether he did or not, Handsome Rann, he's believed, and you're not. And Mr Bragg and Moonbeam, and their witness Mr Nash, are believed now, for all your slanders. And it's certain-sure what'll happen to you. You'll be confirmed for the rope in a day or two. So, you want to hear Mr Bragg's proposition or not?'

Rann said nothing. For the first time since his trial, he felt sick with fear. It was not the promise of the rope – he had always expected that – it was the care taken by his enemies to destroy him that took his strength away. Hawkins drew a gold hunter from his pocket and checked the time.

'Bragg and Flash Fowler swore my life away,' Rann said helplessly.

For a moment he feared he might weep. Hawkins' mouth tightened.

'You had Pandy's blood all down your shirt.'

'Course I had. How should I help it? Me held down on him by Bragg and Moonbeam, while Catskin Nash wiped it everywhere!'

'And before he died, Pandy told Policeman Fowler you stabbed him,' Hawkins said firmly. 'After that you were bound to swing.'

'Gammon!' said Rann in quiet anger. 'All Pandy Quinn said when I was standing there was, "My hat! Oh, my hat!" like he was surprised at something. Then he said, "My hat'll be the death of me!" And that was all.'

'His hat?' Hawkins looked up at him, impatient no longer. 'What about his hat?'

'How should I know? Even Policeman Fowler didn't know at the inquest. Twice that useless brief of mine asked him, and he didn't know. I was Pandy's friend. He wouldn't say I stabbed him when I never did.'

The 'Orator' shot his crisp white cuffs, his interest in the hat at an end.

'Mr Bragg is concerned about your legacy.'

'What legacy?'

Hawkins' mouth extended in a muscular spasm that might have been taken for a grin in a better-natured man.

'First off, there's your young women. Miss Jolly and Maggie Fashion. Mr Bragg got no special use for 'em, but they can't be left. Who's to protect them?'

'Protect them from what?'

Hawkins cleared his throat and dropped his voice.

'There was some scheme you and Pandy was working on. Something rich. Six houses you entered on dark evenings last October, Soapy Samuel first acting as a parson collecting charity subscriptions. To spy out the land.'

'Gammon,' said Rann miserably. 'Ask Soapy Sam, if it interests you so much.'

'We would,' said Hawkins evenly, 'if he could be found. He'd be asked in such a manner as he'd never forget.'

Rann said nothing. He guessed what was coming next.

'Thing is, Jack Rann, not one house ever complained of being burgled.'

'So they was never entered, or there was nothing taken.'

Hawkins sat back, stuck his thumbs under his lapels and drew a deep breath at the hopelessness of it all.

'West End,' he said patiently. 'Two in Portman Square, one in Audley Street, one off Park Lane. One in Belgrave Square. A furrier's rooms in Regent Street. Nothing worth taking? Don't play games with me, Jack! You and Pandy was after something bigger than pictures on their walls or jools in the safes. You were investing time – and money. And it ain't come to the boil yet, has it? I want to hear about it. Then we'll see about protecting your young women.'

Maggie Fashion and Miss Jolly were to be the sacrifice. He

stared at Hawkins and knew he was done for. The Orator eased one soft hand with the other.

'Trouble is, Handsome Jack, you and Pandy were up to some lark you never should have been. Hunting other men's game.'

'Hunting?'

'Call it poaching. You must have known you were working where no one works without Mr Bragg or Mr Nash allow. So Mr Bragg and Mr Nash want to know two things, as your side of our bargain: what's the lark and who's the putter-up?'

'There's no lark and no putter-up!' said Rann grimly. 'Houses ain't apt to complain when they lose something they shouldn't have had in the first place.'

Hawkins nodded as if he understood.

'So the Bishop of London's hiding stolen goods, is he? And old Lady Mancart's got a collection of saucy paintings, has she?'

'You might put it the other way round,' said Rann hopefully.

Hawkins flicked dust from his cuff and glanced at Rann with ineffable contempt.

'Don't fuck me about, Jack. You're time's up, one way or t'other. But when you step off, the job you and Quinn planned won't be forgotten. If you won't tell, others must. Mr Bragg's a gentleman, always has been, but others is less refined. When you've swung, we'll ask Mag and Miss Jolly, for a start. Much the same as they might have asked Pandy, if he'd been fortunate enough to live a bit longer.'

'Those girls got nothing to do with it.'

'Won't stop Mr Bragg asking. Them not knowing, if that's true, would be most unfortunate for them and a bit of a pleasure for him. I daresay you'd recall Mr Mulligan that's called "Strap?" Old Strap might think Christmas comes early if the sorrowful task was given him. But you let us take all the care about this business of yours and you'd save those young persons a world of grief when you depart.'

Hawkins broke off and made a gesture, as if the possibilities were limitless. Rann sat up and stared at him, but it was Hawkins who broke the silence.

'And here's the little bit of a bonus, Mr Jack. Little bit of a bonus, eh? Of course, Mr Bragg can't save you being turned off. No one can. But you might have better living the next week or so than you'll otherwise get. Every comfort might attend your remaining days.'

'I'm in here, aren't I?' He felt again that he might weep in front of Hawkins and the girl with the new intensity of despair.

'And will remain,' said Hawkins reasonably, 'but you may eat the best, brought in from the London Coffee House, instead of slum-gullion for the cells. And a man may visit a female relative if she happens to be on the women's side of the prison. You could remember a young cousin, I daresay. Several might claim that right with you.'

'You never were in Newgate,' Rann said. 'Things like that can't be done in here. Not by you, nor by Bully Bragg!'

Hawkins examined his perfectly clipped fingernails.

'Not by me nor Mr Bragg,' he agreed reasonably, 'but for a pocketful of chinkers, you could not begin to imagine what Mr Lupus might do.'

'Warder Lupus?' Rann stared into the dead blue eyes. 'He's the brute of them all!'

'And who more likely to take gold for favours than the brute of them all?' Hawkins sat back with a self-satisfied smile. 'Therefore of greatest use and value.'

Rann stared at him again.

'So when I'm gone, Bragg and Catskin Nash and the rest are going to protect Mag Fashion and Miss Jolly if I tell you a story now?'

'Why should they not?'

'And Soapy Samuel? He's to be protected, is he?'

Hawkins almost checked himself, but for the slightest movement of the eyes.

'No!' said Rann, his whisper little more than a hiss. 'He's dead and at the bottom of the river, I suppose! A knife slipped, like it did when Bragg was asking Pandy! And Mag Fashion and Miss Jolly'd go the same way, once he had his answers. You think I'd trust a man that put me here? Him and Flash Fowler?'

But Hawkins had regained his poise and looked again at the gold hunter-watch. Rann struggled to his feet.

'Bloody crawling Judas! You can't help me and never meant to! You go back to Policeman Fowler and Bully Bragg! I'd sooner see them and you in Hell!'

Hawkins favoured him with a wry, wan smile.

'But you'll be there first, Jack Rann. Next week, as it happens. Still, if you got further to say, I'll be back to say a prayer with you. Easy, now they know me. You might have a week so agreeable you'd hardly concern yourself with what was to come at the end. Respited even for a week more till sessions ends and they have the last gallows. You got to swing. That's the law. But next week might turn into the week after if you slipped down the list. So long as you're hung this sessions. You got no business to be around after that. Until then, sweet and savoury. Glass of wine of an evening; muzzle cocked by a young lady on the other side with an arse like a marchioness. You don't have to suffer now and hang prompt, do you, Jack?'

But Rann turned to the door and waved the turnkeys towards him.

'You always were a stupid little squirt, Handsome Rann,' Hawkins said, moving his lips in a mimicry of benediction. 'Never anything but a fool to yourself.'

He turned away and took the girl by her arm. Rann thought he saw a significant glance exchanged between Hawkins and Lupus, at a distance through the glass. The 'Orator' looked back as the warders began to move.

'One other thing Mr Bragg'd have to know. Where's your box of tricks? Bars and wedges. Steel picks. And Pandy let on about a

Jack-in-the-Box to bust any safe. And Mr Bragg would want the micrometer Pandy put together. Especially that. They reckon it opens a lock soft as a spring breeze passing. All that'd be part of the bargain, Mr Bragg says. You think about it, Handsome Rann.'

Jessup came in on the prisoner's side. He slid his hands into Rann's pockets and patted him down. Anger and despair teased the Hangman's Child as he shuffled back to the bleakly furnished cell. They took his shackles off and the cuffs from his wrists. Lupus was alone with him, standing beside him, last to leave. William Lupus had understood Hawkins' final glance.

'You ain't half a caution, 'andsome Jack,' he said bitterly, driving his fist hard into the narrow back above the right kidney.

James Babb, known familiarly as 'Baptist' Babb, had kept watch with his colleagues on the glass square of the prisoners' consulting-room. Like the others, he stood back to respect the privacy of a man's last sight of his child. Through the glass, the exchanges between Rann and his visitors were so much dumb-show.

Unlike his colleagues, Babb had spent some time as a policeman until an infection of the lungs reduced him to the role of turnkey. And among his legacies from childhood, with a deaf cabinetmaker for a father, was a knack of reading lips. In his short career as a constable, it was admired and envied for the use it might be.

He had caught a little of what passed between Rann and Hawkins. It was enough to trouble him. It troubled him the more for its hints at corruption among his colleagues. To speak of that among them now was impossible: to keep silent would be to condone it. And what if, after all, the accusation proved untrue?

That evening, he sat alone at the stained table in his Newgate lodging. The remains of a veal and ham pie with a glass of water half-drunk stood to one side. He was a solitary man, unlikely to be visited at this hour. As the white gaslight bubbled and flared in the corner-bracket above him, he took an 'ink-and-dip'. In his mind he saw a man who might be broken but would never bow, stubborn

21

and valiant, faithful to justice. Dipping the steel nib in the evil-smelling ink, Baptist Babb adjusted his cuff and addressed himself to Sergeant William Clarence Verity of the Private-Clothes Detail, 'A' Division Metropolitan Police, Scotland Yard.

3

Sergeant William Clarence Verity of the Private-Clothes Detail, Detective Division, Whitehall Place, presents his compliments to Chief Inspector Henry Croaker. Sergeant Verity begs leave to bring to Mr Croaker's attention certain facts respecting the case of James Patrick Rann, alias 'Handsome Jack' Rann, now under sentence of death in Her Majesty's Prison at Newgate for the murder of a confederate, William Arthur Quinn, commonly known as 'Pandy' Quinn.

Sergeant Verity is in receipt of information from an officer of Newgate Gaol. This witness was on supervision when Rann received his last visit from a person claiming to be a workhouse missioner, accompanied by a second person alleging herself to be the prisoner's daughter. Sergeant Verity has the honour to request that Mr Croaker will read the enclosed report upon this incident.

Sergeant Verity believes the first impostor to be Edward Warren Hawkins, familiarly known as 'Orator' Hawkins, dismissed from his position as an attorney's clerk three years since, following allegations of fraud. Prosecution of this case was dropped on the complaint being withdrawn. The young person now acting as his confederate appears to be one Suzanne Berry, formerly detained at Tothill Fields House of Correction for six months under the vagrancy laws. The means by which two such persons gained access to the prisoners' consulting-room remain to be investigated.

From further information which Sergeant Verity has the honour to present, gathered by a prison officer present at the visit, a criminal conspiracy of importance appears to be in contemplation by those who sought the deaths of Quinn and Rann. The identities of Bragg, Mulligan, Nash and 'Moonbeam', are known to Sergeant Verity from previous inquiries. Though not lately convicted, Bragg is a violent criminal who served seven years' transportation in his youth for warehouse burglary. Alfred 'Catskin' Nash is known as a 'putter-up', though acquitted for lack of identification in the trial of those indicted for the robbery of Acutt's Linen Drapery, Westminster Road. William Mulligan has been twice convicted of living upon immoral earnings and once for assault and battery. Henry Jenks, a fairground prize-fighter known as 'Moonbeam', was convicted with Mulligan on the last of these charges.

In the light of the enclosed information, Sergeant Verity further requests that consideration may be given by the Home Office to a stay of execution in the case of James Patrick Rann, while the evidence given against him by Bragg and others is further investigated. Though Detective Sergeant Fowler was able to arrest Rann while the suspect was restrained by Bragg and Jenks, no weapon was found at the time with which the accused could have stabbed the victim. The blood upon Rann's clothing appears solely the result of having been held down upon the wounded man. The information which is now to hand may point to Quinn being murdered by others and the prisoner Rann being victim of a conspiracy to pervert the course of public justice.

Sergeant Verity has the honour to remain Inspector Croaker's obedient humble servant.

W. Verity, Sgt., 12 May 1860

From Deputy Commander Detective Division, Whitehall Place, SW

Chief Inspector Croaker is in receipt of Sergeant Verity's memorandum of the 12th inst. Mr Croaker takes this opportunity to remind Sergeant Verity that it is not his place to address his superi-

ors as if he knew the business of the Division better than they.

Inspector Croaker is dismayed that Sergeant Verity is party to the unauthorized passage of confidential information from the prison service. Mr Croaker is communicating his misgivings to the Prison Commissioners for consideration and action. Mr Croaker understands that Officer Babb has been suspended from his duties while disciplinary charges are considered. Should Mr Croaker learn that Sergeant Verity has passed such confidential information to other persons, he will unhesitatingly follow the same disciplinary process.

Mr Croaker cannot determine why Sergeant Verity should calumniate a missioner who sought to bring the prisoner Rann to repentance. On inquiry, Mr Croaker finds the visitor to have been the Reverend Lewis Maybury, who sailed by appointment on the following day to join the chaplaincy to the English colony in Montevideo. The fact that Mr Maybury can no longer answer for himself in the circumstances is no reason why he should be defamed in his absence. Mr Croaker trusts that Sergeant Verity will think of this.

The criminal conspiracy which Sergeant Verity alleges appears no more than a chimaera. The characters and records of Bragg, Nash, Mulligan, and Jenks are sufficiently documented in the files of the Detective Police, as they are in 'H' Division, Metropolitan Police, an area in which these men remain under the scrutiny of Detective Inspector Fowler and his colleagues.

In this connection, Sergeant Verity will have the goodness to familiarize himself with Mr Fowler's promotion and substantive rank before making any further communication.

Mr Croaker need scarcely remind Sergeant Verity that the prisoner Rann was convicted upon what the trial judge described as the plainest and most conclusive evidence. His Lordship informed the prisoner, upon conviction, that he could offer not the smallest hope that the sentence of the law would not be carried into effect. That advice was tendered to the Home Office. In such circumstances, it is not the policy of the Home Secretary to interfere with the process *of the law nor the decisions of the courts.*

In conclusion, Sergeant Verity will oblige Mr Croaker by pursuing his present detachment to the river police with more diligence and effect than has been evident heretofore. The smuggling of tobacco and other contraband from vessels moored at the Thames wharves remains an affront to the commercial probity of the City of London and a criminal assault upon the finances of Her Majesty's Treasury. Sergeant Verity will look to this matter forthwith.

H. Croaker, Insp. of Constabulary, 13 May 1860

4

The dawn cloud broke into a mackerel sky, a blue vault above smoke-grey drifts. Jack Rann looked up at this distant square of light, high above the soaring granite walls of the airing-yard.

Outside each death cell was a walled space, where a man or woman might walk without supervision. Escape through these yards was the first thought that crossed the minds of the condemned and the last hope that died. In a hundred years none had escaped from Newgate's airing-yards. Three had injured themselves in brief but futile attempts.

From dusk until dawn, the door from the cell to the yard was locked. By daylight, Rann might walk in the paved area as he pleased. He had learnt every angle of it, every crack in the York paving, like a schoolroom map. It was twenty feet by thirty, the bottom of a towering shaft of polished stone, sixty feet high with its square of London sky. He laid his hand on the surface of the wall. Smooth as glass. No crevice nor crack, not so much as a chip in the stone that a man might work upon, even if the interval between sentence and execution allowed him time. No mortar-gap for the searching fingers, no ledge for the toes.

He had walked here, day by day, head lowered as if resigned to death and eternity. They would like to see him penitent, if they bothered to look. The pasty chaplain might smile on him. To the turnkeys, he seemed safe enough where he was.

Lupus had been sure to tell him a tale that Rann had heard long ago. How a poor fool, maddened by his fate, flew at the walls of the yard a few hours before they came to fetter him for the gallows. The terror of the noose, aided by smuggled hessian tied under his boots, briefly defied the implacable sheen of granite. Somehow, the poor devil had got up the angle of the corner to ten, almost twenty feet. He was not halfway to the top, where the razor-honed steel of a *cheveau-de-frise* would cut his hands to pieces. Defeated, beyond all help, he braced himself in the angle while they watched from below. His strength and resolve failed. He fell back down the shaft on to the stone paving. Perhaps he thought they would never hang a man shattered by the impact.

An hour later, crying in pain, the bones of his legs splintered, he was carried to the noose on a chair, jeered by the crowd for his lack of pluck. Rann thought of the poor fellow in the cold air of early morning and shuddered.

A water drop, heard in the quiet night but scarcely audible now, fell by his foot. He kept his head down and smiled. Only when he reached the far side of the sunless yard did he lean his back against the wall. He gazed up at the city sky and knew the dice had rolled. Other men might allow a day or two for making plans. For Handsome Jack, it was now or never.

Suppose, somehow, he could climb the polished height? Fifty feet above the ground, twenty feet higher than the roof of the death-wards whose wall formed one side of the airing-yard, the revolving *cheveau-de-frise* ran round the granite. There was no way over it, under it, or round it. It was a stout wooden pole set with unbroken lines of razor-edged steel blades that would slice off the fingers that clutched it. The blades on the inner side came so close to the wall that they almost scraped the surface. No man would get between them and the slippery stone.

The device revolved freely. Sometimes in the night he had heard a distant mouse-screech of metal as the wind caught the blades. Even if there were gloves thick enough to clutch its razor fineness, the steel would revolve downwards at the first touch, throwing him fifty feet on to the paving below.

The builders had done their job well. What then? There was a wooden support for the *cheveau-de-frise*, running round the wall several feet below it, set as thick with spikes as a hedgehog's back. A man would skewer his hands or tear his fingers on it but he might hold there. Even then, he would still be below the *cheveau-de-frise* with no way past it.

Small wonder that the condemned looked at such fortifications and trusted instead to a reprieve. But when the reprieve was refused, a death-watch entered the cell and all hope was gone.

As he gazed upwards, a seagull glided across the brightening sky and the clocks began to strike. Rann thought of the ocean, the sea-bells that warned of rocks, and longed for such freedom as the white bird's.

How would a man with nothing but the clothes he wore climb fifty feet of sheer, polished granite? Until that was accomplished, the *cheveau-de-frise* and the support with its iron spikes scarcely mattered. Small wonder that his gaolers allowed him to 'air' as much as he pleased.

Like the gleam of a steel-tipped arrow, the morning light struck another falling water-drop. It vanished into the dampness of the paving in the far corner of the yard. High in that narrow corner angle, the commissioners had installed an iron cistern. When Newgate was modernized it acquired a fresh-water supply. Rann measured the height to the cistern with his eye and thought it nearer forty feet than thirty-five. Ten feet more and there was the spiked support rail. A few feet further and the blades of the revolving *cheveau-de-frise* blocked all progress. Ten feet above that, if a man had wings, he would still find himself marooned on a high wall in the centre of the prison.

He walked another circuit, trailing his hand on the chill of smooth granite. Where the cistern had been installed, the surface was a little grazed. No more than that. No toehold, no fingertip crevice. Shoe-leather would slip like a skate on ice. In case they were watching him, he walked on. Only one substance might cling to that lightly grazed surface. Shoe-leather would never do it.

Rann had no wish to be the fourth man crippled by Newgate's walls but his heart beat faster. The judge at his trial, a cadaverous, thin-blooded amateur of pain, had killed all hope of reprieve. Tomorrow, perhaps today, they would put a guard in his cell.

He stood upright from the wall. Before the mackerel sky had cleared to summer blue, he would be free – or he would be dead.

The sooner the better. He walked back into the cell and listened. The warders might be in the passageway, though he could not hear them. Lupus and Jessup exchanged little conversation. He sat down on the wooden bed whose mattress he had rolled at dawn and whose blanket he had folded. The spy-hole was shut. Slowly, in case they were watching, he unlaced the stiff prison boots, drew them off, and eased his insteps with his hands. It was not the act of a man planning an escape; only a fool would attempt it in bare feet. As it happened, Rann had known all his life that it was the one way in which it might be done.

He listened and still caught no sound. Perhaps they were not there. With each death-ward so securely locked and bolted, there must be times when neither guard was present.

He drew a deep breath, walking slowly and barefoot into the shadow of the yard. Speed would come presently. In the course of his life he had grown wise in the ways of officials and authorities. Escape from Newgate was known to be impossible. Therefore, if Lupus or Babb unlocked the cell and saw him neither in there nor in the yard, the warder would first suppose that he had been taken away by higher authority. The delay while they checked might give him his chance.

From the tight corner of the granite walls, above which the cistern hung, he could see the cell interior through the open door. If they entered in the next few minutes, he was done for. Better to wait until they had come and gone – or go now? Go now! Go now!

His skull rang with the thought like a bugle-call.

He thrust his back into the angle of the wall, hands behind him, testing and moulding against the slight roughness of the stone, grazed by the installation of the cistern above.

He raised his left leg, braced one bare foot and then the other against the adjacent side of the narrow corner. The softer soles and heels of his bare feet moulded themselves to the surface as boots would never do. Rann had known the knack of it for almost thirty years. For all their cleverness, his captors never considered that the orphan thief had first been a sweep's boy. To climb with hands behind him on one surface, bare feet on the other, body pressed into the corner, was one of the oldest tricks of childhood's trade. The twisting and distortion of the body in such angles made cripples of those who outlived their childhood. Jack Rann had saved himself from that. Put up factory chimneys and domestic flues, he had climbed at last to the very top of an engineering stack, slipped down the far side, and left his master-sweep for an apprenticeship in picking pockets.

Another deep breath of courage. The moulded suction of the hands and feet held him in the corner of the wall, his feet clear of the ground. His heart stopped as a foot slipped. He lost purchase and found himself standing again. He began once more, lost footing on glacial granite, and tried a third time. Lodged in the narrow corner, he moved one hand cautiously upwards behind his back, took the pressure on it and slowly moved the other. The art of the feet was to move them like claws, one by one. Inch by inch, he was climbing now. The yard was three feet below him at a guess, the cell door still unopened. His hands sweated but held. The York paving was four feet down ... five ... and six. Once he thought he heard the metal ram of a key in a lock. Pressing the bruised granite with all his strength he waited motionless, as though this would make him invisible, but he heard no more. It was another cell, not his. His might be next.

The art of it was to find patches where the hauling up of the iron tank had roughened the stone. Once, fifteen feet above the yard, he found only a sleek and chilly surface. His hand slipped an inch but he pressed hard and checked it for a vital second, heart beating in his throat.

He paused to wipe away the sweat from his hands, one by one, on his shirt. Shirt and trousers were all that he wore. He looked down steadily. Twenty feet? Glancing up, he thought the metal square of the cistern was nearer now than the paving of the yard. The narrow features contorted with energy and concentration, as he struggled in the stone angle. For a moment he lost his breath and held still with the practised self-discipline of a roof-top thief. All the same, at thirty, he was already an old man playing a young man's game.

Beyond the prison, a clock chimed the quarter. Rann was surprised that only fifteen minutes had passed since he stood in the airing-yard, gazing up to where he now writhed for his life against the granite.

Another breath and a cautious movement of one hand. Thirty feet surely? Above him, an iron rim round the base of the cistern would be in his grasp if only he could stand upright.

Instead, he pushed his back hard in the angle and worked himself a few inches higher, one hand and then the other, fingers splayed to find the next slight roughness of the stone, right foot and then the left, keeping the pressure even, moulding the soles of his feet for purchase there. Despite the smoothness, he felt that his left foot was bleeding. The stone was chipped sharply here and there by the fixing of the iron supports below the cistern. But the roughness that broke his skin also gave him safety, as he closed his mind to pain.

At last, he reached up cautiously and touched the iron rim round the base of the cistern, above and to one side.

Rann breathed deep again. With his right hand, he held the cold iron rim, gritted by rust. He steadied himself, feet against the granite. With a sob of breath, he snatched upwards with the left hand.

His arms ached while he hung there, as though he had been hoisted on a strappado. To ease the pain, a fool would now try to pull himself up the iron flank – and would fall. Dangling from the bolted rim, praying that it had not at some point flaked away, he moved hand by hand to where the cistern met the wall. An angled strut supported it. Those who offered such a perch had thought a man must either fall before he reached the tank or would never get past the *cheveau-de-frise* above it.

He drew his left knee up and lodged his foot in the iron angle of the support, taking the weight that had tortured his biceps. Pushing up, he held the top rim of the iron cistern with the grip of one hand and then the other. Using the strength of his foot in the angle, he got his right forearm on the upper cistern-rim. He drew his foot cautiously from the iron bracket, snatched with his left hand and eased his second arm on to the upper rim. By a heave and a kick, he pulled himself on to the ledge of the cistern-cover. He stood on the flat, ribbed metal, his chest against the granite wall. Now he could reach up to touch the spikes guarding the support ten feet below the *cheveau-de-frise*.

He listened for movement in the morning stillness of the prison below him and still heard nothing. What had seemed like half an hour on the granite surface was perhaps no more than five minutes. Two sides of the yard away from him, the roof of the death-wards now appeared almost level with his feet. For the first time, he dared to promise himself that he might be free. He felt for the spikes of the support-rail and knew that there must be minutes of pain as the price of life. First, he tore a strip of cotton from the hem of his shirt, tore it again and wrapped half round each hand.

He checked his cry to a gasp of pain as he clenched on the wooden support. The spikes themselves were set with needle tips on every surface. With nothing else to cling to, dangling forty feet above the paving, he began to move hand by hand in a slow agony round the two walls of the yard. He felt sweat on his shirt-front and then saw it was not sweat but blood running from his hands, back down his arms. The shirt-cloth round his palms had become two blood-sodden rags. But to surrender now would allow the world to chuckle at his bravado, and then hang him just the same.

The blood-drops falling in the yard might betray him to the first person who noticed them. There was no help for that. Yet to come so far and be caught on the prison roofs was worse than letting go and smashing on the stone paving below. He would smash rather than let them take him again. He tried to hurry and almost lost his grip with one hand.

But he was at the first corner now. The second wall was the shorter side of the oblong yard. The leads of the death-wards lay only twenty feet along that flank of granite. Twenty feet more of blood that ran slippery on needle-sharp iron. He sobbed with the pain. But then it was ten feet, and five. He came to the end of it. To his right, a dozen feet below the support from which he hung, were the flat leads of the condemned block.

A rooftop-burglar's dead-fall was the only way. Throwing himself to one side, he let go of the support above him. Twisting and falling, he heard the brief rush of wind at his ears. He missed the roof but felt the stone ledge of it smack into his hands. One hand slipped but the other held. He snatched a second hold. Kicking and flipping like a fish in a net, Jack Rann pulled himself slowly on hands and knees to the flat roof of the condemned block, bleeding, and weeping with relief.

He was still at the centre of the prison and time was against him. The succession of flat roofs varied little in height, with gaps of eight to ten feet between each and a drop of forty feet to the passageways below. Where some of the roofs ended, a spiked rail marked the boundary of the prison along Newgate Street.

Blood still dripped as he gathered his strength, sprinted at the first gap, leapt with all his power, saw the drop flash beneath him, and landed sprawling on the next roof. A long chase down it, a narrower leap and a landing with a trip that gashed his ankle.

How far until he was safe? Even as the question occurred, he knew that he could never be safe. Sooner or later, the nightmare was to come again – unless he could cross an ocean to a new continent; unless the legacy of Pandy Quinn's genius might save him.

He took another leap and made a landing that was easier. Now a wider gap. Ten feet, he guessed. He drew back, ran with all his might and hurled himself across it. He missed the flat roof, caught the ledge and pulled himself up.

His strength was gone for another jump like that. Then, a dozen feet ahead of him, he saw a smoke-stack at the edge of the roof he was standing on, its black lettering weathered almost to nothing. 'Tyler's Manufactory'. He had lost all sense of time and distance on the roofs but now he knew that he must be somewhere beyond the prison, above the first commercial premises of Newgate Street.

From this moment any man or woman might be his enemy. The first encounter might betray him. He edged forward and saw, several yards from the chimney, a woman in a grey woollen shawl and white apron gathering washing from a line between two posts. Such homeliness after weeks of the condemned cell gave him hope that she would not refuse him. From the shelter of the stack, he watched her carry the washing-basket to an attic well-ahead and go down into the house.

Rann waited a moment and then moved forward. There was an attic ladder inside the well-head, down which the young woman had gone. Easing himself through the opening, he went softly and barefoot after her.

It was a Newgate garret, built for extra rent on top of a shabby garment-warehouse. Through a half-open door, he saw the basket of laundry on a table, a grate of dead coals, a child in a wooden cradle. The woman turned as he stepped into the room, her young face round and florid, her arms bare and reddened from scrubbing the sodden clothes by which she earned her starvation wages as a street-laundress.

'Oh, God!' she cried, lifting the child in its linen shirt, holding it to her. 'Don't hurt us! Whoever you are, don't harm us.'

'I'm Jack Rann,' said Handsome Jack, sinking down on a plain rush chair, 'and I'm hurt worse than you could ever imagine. Help me, if you can. I've come this far, over the prison roofs. If I'm caught now, I must die on Monday. Let God be my judge, I never in my life did harm to any man or woman. But I won't be taken now, not if I have to die for it.'

She stared at him. She wanted to believe him, he could see that in her eyes, so that she might be sure of her own safety. There was a square of tarnished glass behind her which served as a mirror. Rann caught sight of himself, the grotesque figure of a make-believe murdered ghost from the stage of the Hoxton Britannia. A dozen downward paths of blood from his upstretched hands had streaked his face and matted his hair. His torn shirt-front was splattered red.

'The spikes on the wall,' he said quietly. 'That's what drew the blood. I want nothing from you. I must get to the street, that's all. I mean you no harm.'

'But not to the street like that,' she said. 'You'll be seen and took first thing.'

She still doubted him but must have seen how much greater his fear was than hers.

'Then how?' he asked.

The young woman shook her head.

'There's only what you see us wearing and the linen in the basket.'

Jack Rann looked about him and knew that she spoke the truth. Apart from the clothes she wore in her poverty, there was nothing but the laundered linen and no other room but this.

'Soot,' he said suddenly, 'let me have soot from the grate.'

He stepped to the hearth with its dead coals and the woman drew back a little, holding the child more firmly. Rann put his blood-streaked hands into the hearth and felt the searing coarseness of the black grit. He smeared his face and hair, his shirt and arms, until they shone with it, his eyes gleaming like the whites of boiled eggs, their sockets pale through the mask of blackened skin.

'Which way?' he asked.

Still holding the child, she led him down the stairs into a cobbled yard at the rear of the warehouse. At one end, was an archway. Beyond it he saw market-carts and a coster-girl selling apples from a basket.

Rann looked at her for the last time.

'I got nothing to give you. One day, I'll thank you, though. I don't know how, but I swear I will.'

She gazed at him, still doubtfully, and at last said, 'God bless you, poor stranger.'

Before he could reply, she turned and went quickly back to the stairs. Jack Rann walked, blackened and barefoot, towards the arch. He was now indistinguishable by his face or clothes from ten thousand men of his kind in the city.

The crowds almost obscured the market-barrows of the fruit-sellers and the fish-merchants along either pavement. A woman was singing for coppers outside a tap-room at the far corner, 'The Bird in Yonder Cage Confined'. Rann took it as an omen. Cabs, carts, and twopenny buses moved in a slow procession at the centre of the road.

The noise of the city, after so many weeks in the silence of his cell, almost overpowered him with jubilation. Now it was time to plan. He wiped the soot from his moist palms over his face for good measure and slipped quietly along Newgate Street.

5

'Eight a penny! Lumping pears!'

An old coster in a moleskin jacket and wide-awake hat laughed in his face at the startled eyes in the blackened skin.

Rann moved between the barrows and the stalls that fringed the butchers' slabs of Newgate Market, his bare feet raw on the paving-grit. He watched the congested traffic, edging from Snow Hill to Cheapside. To one side was a counter of pickled whelks, like huge snails floating in saucers of brine. On the other, children knelt by a sweet stall, gambling with marbles for 'Albert Rock' and 'Boneyparte's Ribs'.

A uniformed policeman was talking to an aproned coster-girl with her horse-pail of ice, as she scooped out lemonade the colour of soap-suds. ''ere's your coolers! 'aypenny a glass! 'ere's coolers!' The policeman, his hands folded on the truncheon behind his back, smiled and spoke close to her ear. Rann guessed they could not yet have missed him from his cell.

The cries of the market rose like a protective screen. He saw a donkey-cart coming slowly up the curve of Snow Hill from Farringdon Market. Behind the driver was a pile of empty, slatted flower-boxes and sacks. Rann moved forward and breathed a fresh earthy smell of potatoes as the wheels rumbled past him. The carter had made his deliveries and was on his way from the city, possibly south but more likely east, to market-gardens and fields beyond Bethnal Green.

The tail-board was down. Rann walked quickly after it, jumped and swung himself up to sit at the end of the cart without the driver knowing or needing to care. It was so neatly done that a coster holding a haddock on a toasting-fork laughed and called out to him, "'ooray for that! Let him laugh who wins!'

Rann waved back, like a man without a care. They would forget him more easily for that. Yet as the cart followed the prison wall of rough-hewn stone with its windowless recesses, he felt a terror of Newgate greater than when he hung from the spikes of its *cheveau-de-frise*.

Like a man in a dream, he saw Greyfriars and Christ's Hospital with its Bluecoat boys, the golden cross and upper dome of St Paul's above the roofs. To one side on the tail-board lay the empty potato sacks. A fool would have crept under them and hidden but Jack Rann knew better. He was concealed by the crowds and by his covering of soot more surely than by all the sacks ever made.

As the cart rattled eastwards, shaking and bumping, he felt the scales tilt to his side at last. He had never had his likeness taken by a camera. The only people who might recognize him were those who knew him before the death of Pandy Quinn, or Flash Fowler and those who had arrested him, or the court that had tried him, or the warders who had guarded him. They were not a hundred people in London's two million, but in time they might be enough. Yet, so long as he moved fast, perhaps only betrayal could hang him now. He pictured Miss Jolly, timid shopgirl and lynx-eyed dancer of the penny entertainments. Maggie Fashion, mannequin of the bereaved at the Mourning Emporium. Such young women would die for Handsome Jack more surely than another man might do. And, if the moment came, they might more easily destroy him.

Turning his head to glance down Cheapside, he saw the pillared spire of Bow Church, the gilt-figured clock that hung above the pavement, the Sultan Café with its sign that 'Smoking-Rooms May be Hired by Private Parties', dark little shops that sold snuff or tobacco, vintners with racks of green bottles displayed on the pavement. Square-paned windows caught the sun at a dozen different angles.

Beyond the Royal Exchange, the cart entered Cornhill. Not a head in the well-dressed crowds turned to look at him nor at the donkey-cart that carried him. In a city of a million fires and chimneys, there was no more common sight than a sweep on a cart-tail beside sacks that might soon be filled with soot.

Behind its plain brick fronts, Cornhill belonged to the wholesale premises of goldsmiths, jewellers, watchmakers and tailors. In its pillared banks, the wealth of the city slept undisturbed. Here and there rose a more splendid façade, canopied and balustraded with red brick and stone facing.

They passed Sun Court, a courtyard of Tudor brick within the arch of Walker's Vaults. Pandy Quinn's legacy. Jack Rann looked away, as if the passers-by might read the secret in his eyes. He gazed instead at the reflections of the vaults in the display windows of Trent's Cornhill Family and Complimentary Mourning Tailors, plate-glass framed by black marble, divided by corrugated brass pillars. But Mr Trent's funeral tailoring was as much part of Pandy's master-plan as the vaults themselves.

Rann jumped off at Aldgate pump, where the classical pillar under an iron-framed gas-lamp spouted water into a shallow trough for a poorer district of the city. Here the shops and houses were stained by weather and neglect, windows dusty and empty, the road almost deserted. With nothing in the world but the shirt and trousers that he wore, he slipped down as the cart slowed at the crossing.

His destination was a slum courtyard off Rosemary Lane, along the drab length of the Ratcliff Highway. Narrower streets faded into the distance of a noon haze. Provision merchants and gin-shops traded behind the plain shop-fronts, families lodging two or three to a room on the floors above. The long canyon of the street was crowded at this hour by labourers from the nearby docks, in round, wide-brimmed hats, canvas trousers and shirt-sleeves. Bells that might have tolled for a funeral were sounding from Wapping to the Isle of Dogs to call the gangs back to work from their dinner break.

Boys with trays of glazed cakes slung about their necks, and girls offering fried fish, mingled with the crowd. A thinly clad woman with a child on her back bought a piece of fish for a halfpenny. She walked in front of Rann, tearing at it hungrily with her teeth, eating the warm flesh covered in breadcrumbs and sucking at the bone before she threw it away.

From Rosemary Lane, he turned into a low archway, no wider than a house door. It led into the slum court known as Preedy's Rents.

Beyond this narrow tunnel, which lay under the upper floors of the building that fronted the street, rose a turmoil of voices. A crowd was packed into a courtyard, a hundred feet long but not twenty feet wide. Men and women shouted and jumped at the far end. Every window of the upper floors was filled with faces, watching a quarrel between two neighbours as it turned into a fight.

Even at noon, the yard was in deep shadow, wooden tenements rising like cliffs above it. Projections had been built out at random on the higher levels. Preedy's Rents had the air of a slum that might crumple at any moment in a cascade of rubble and timber upon the crowd in the courtyard.

Inside the tenements, a narrow hallway and wooden stairs were almost in darkness. He climbed slowly and with care. The unlit stairway creaked and trembled under the gentlest footstep. He came to an unpainted door at the top and listened. There was movement but no voices. Rann knocked sharply.

'At?' The reply sounded brisk and confident.

'You there, Lord Tomnoddy? That you, Short-Armed Tom?'

A chair-leg scraped. Whoever had been sitting down said something to himself as he got up. A bolt was drawn and the door opened by a thickset man with a florid face and dark hair, arms conspicuously long for his height. He was any age between fifty and seventy, his face lightly wrinkled like fruit dried on the branch. Lord Tomnoddy, or Short-Armed Tom, was a tosher or sewer-hunter. His trade gave him the only names by which he was known.

Before the sewerman could speak, Rann said quietly, ''s all right, Lord Tomnoddy. It's me, Jack Rann. And I ain't a ghost, 'cos I ain't been hung. Nor mean to be! Not if you'll help me now.'

'Christ Aw-mighty!' Tomnoddy stood back and opened the door wider to let out more light. 'You never been respited?'

Rann shook his head and stepped into a plainly furnished garret-room. Tomnoddy had been at dinner.

'If you ain't been respited, Jack . . . .'

Rann put his hand against the wall.

'I'm that famished ...' he said, and fell silent.

Tomnoddy helped him to a chair, as if caring for an invalid.

'Famished? You look like the Cock Lane Ghost, my son. 'Course I'll help you. What else would I do?'

On the bare table was a half-eaten plate of cold boiled beef, a saucer of red pickled cabbage and some dingy-looking pickled onions. The meat was profusely covered with mustard, ready to be eaten with thick slices of bread that had been cut into big mouthfuls by a clasp pocket-knife lying open beside the plate. A dented pewter pot contained half a pint of ale.

'I got your kit safe,' Tomnoddy said proudly, the worn face breaking into a quick smile. 'All in the carpet-bag. No one touched it. It's back of a wall in a Shadwell tunnel, well off the main drain. No one been there for years. Anyone looked for it'd have to choose from a couple o' million bricks! Old Samuel had to make himself scarce from Bragg and Catskin Nash. So he's with it. Flash Charley Fowler'd give a bit to know where your tools was. And Bully Bragg'd give as much to have Samuel with a fork through his gullet.'

The kindly smile returned to the sewerman's face but the smile and the words meant nothing to Rann. He sat on the plain wooden chair and could neither eat nor drink. He began to shiver, in the heat of the day and the stifling air of the garret. Once he had begun to shiver, he found he could not stop. And when he could not stop he began to weep, until he could not stop that either. For all his hunger and thirst, it was half an hour before he could eat or drink or tell his story. Tomnoddy listened. Then they sat in silence until the old sewerman spoke.

'Mind you,' he said admiringly, 'that was a swift dodge, that soot. Won't last but good enough for now.'

'Nothing can last me here,' said Rann thoughtfully. 'I can't stay. Not on the same manor with Flash Fowler and Bully Bragg. Elsewhere in London, my face ain't much known. But even then it's a chance someone'd spot me, next week, next month, next year. I never hurt Pandy Quinn, he was my friend. On my soul's salvation, I swear I never did. Pandy was like a father who taught me a trade. But so far as that court goes, judge, jury, Flash Charley, and the rest, that's past history. If I'm caught, I'll be stretched. And that's all about that.'

The lines of Tomnoddy's face deepened earnestly. The crowd outside had long since fallen quiet and the tenements were silent in the afternoon heat.

'You thought what you'll do, Jack? They'll look for you round here. First place.'

'I thought of nothing else,' Rann said. 'Lying there, waiting. I decided. There was a job Pandy and I was fitting up before he was cut. A real sweet job, Tom. It's what caused the trouble with Bragg and Catskin, 'cos we never asked them to be putters-up. We worked on it six months and more. It's a big one and it's still there to be done. So, my Lord Tomnoddy, it's what I mean to do. It's my way out.'

Tomnoddy stared at the debris of meat and pickles on his table.

'You ain't got Pandy now, Jack. You start on the rob again, you'll be took. Sooner or later. And when you're took, you'll be stretched. Sure as if they had you in Newgate now.'

Rann shook his head. 'I mean to finish, Tom, not start. What me and Pandy was fitting up might keep a man the rest of his life. Six men, even. Thanks to you, I've still got my kit. Give me three pairs of hands, I'll do that job. And then I'll be on my way. I can't stay here.'

The sewerman looked at him as a white cloud masked the sun and the light began to thicken.

'Where'll you go then, Jack?'

'A long way off. Where I can't be found nor fetched back. Somewhere not a living soul could know me. 'merica, p'raps. With those emigrants on the ships out of Liverpool, like peas in a pod. Might try 'stralia. Who's you, they say? Jack Rann? Never 'eard of him, I say. Merchant venturer, I am. And here's the cash to show it.'

Tomnoddy inclined his head and breathed out hard through his nose.

'Trouble is, Jack, it's now that matters. Not when you're in 'stralia nor 'merica. Now's when they'll catch you, if they do. This week, not next year.'

Rann shrugged. He looked round the garret with its bare walls, a cheap case-lock ticking, the sparse plain furniture.

'I'll live down the sewers, same as Samuel, if I must.'

The older man nodded.

'If you don't drown in the sluice or get ate by the rats. You don't even know the lie of the sewers, Jack.'

'No,' said Rann brusquely, 'but you do, Tom. If it comes to that. Which it won't.'

'Which it has,' said Tomnoddy glumly. 'And it's forbidden down there now as well. They won't let us in to hunt the sewers, 'cos there's a little danger. They fears as how we'll get suffocated. At least they tells us so. But they don't care if we get starved. No, they doesn't care nothink about that. But the police and the narks is always on the look-out for men going into 'em by the river tunnels. And they waits sometimes above the open street-gratings for any noise or light below. If you're took that way, Jack, you'll be stretched as sure as if you'd waited quiet in your cell for Mr Calcraft.'

'Get me in there, Tom,' Rann said firmly, 'I need that carpet-bag. It's got the kit. Jacket, trousers, shoes with rope soles. There's even a few sovs in the lining.'

'I can bring it.'

'And I want Soapy Samuel. You can't bring him.'

'But Samuel ain't no use to you, Jack. He never did nothing but dress up like a fancy parson and collect money at house-doors for poor missioners in Africa that never existed. Sam couldn't open a kiddy's money-box with a carvin' knife.'

'I want him, Tomnoddy.'

'And he won't come up, for mortal terror of Bully Bragg.'

Rann nodded.

'That's one reason I want him, Tom. I mean to show him it's the only way he can ever be safe.'

Tomnoddy sighed and shrugged. He gave it up.

'Tell you this, Jack Rann. You ain't going nowhere as you are. Not to the corner of the street, let alone the outfalls and tunnels. You get cleaned up, rested, healed. You stay here, understand?'

'I ain't got time, Tomnoddy!'

Lord Tomnoddy was unimpressed.

'You have got time, though you don't know it. The way they watch the outfalls, it means going by dark and low water. It's light at low water now, forenoon and afternoon. If I'm caught, it's twenty-eight days for trespass. If you're took, it's your death. End of the week, Jack. Almost dark at low water then. We'll go down the foreshore and in through the tunnels. There's thirteen lots of stairs down to the river between Execution Dock and Limehouse Hole. And there's Pelican Stairs in Wapping Wall. They can't see much by dark, so they don't watch.'

'You shan't be the poorer for this, Tomnoddy,' said Rann gently, but the old tosher ignored him.

'Another thing you'd best remember, Jack, in case you should ever go alone. The commissioners put iron doors on those tunnels a while back. Doors that close with the pressure of the flood tide against 'em and open again to let the sewage out with the ebb. A little before the ebb, they open the sluices higher up the drains. If you was in the main channels then, and if you couldn't get smartly into one of the unused branch tunnels, you'd be swept to death and found in due course on the river mud. But once the channels have run dry again and the sluices been closed, a man can get in that way without being swept off. It's safe from the ebb to the flood, until the river gets too high. Never safe when it's still on the ebb. Savvy?'

Jack Rann looked about him at the garret room with its sloping roof and the blankets on the floor that made up the old sewer-hunter's bed.

'Safe enough after where I've been,' he said quietly.

But Lord Tomnoddy had not quite finished.

'So long as you ain't seen and caught by the river police or the Customs or one of the sewage commissioners' men,' he said sternly. 'You might as well be swept away as have that happen to you now.'

6

Sergeant Verity sat on a tall counting-house stool and spread Inspector Croaker's memorandum on the slope of the high desk. He read it again. Above his head, at the level of the pavement, the iron-rimmed wheels of a coal-wagon from Whitehall Wharf crashed on the cobbled surface like an ocean breaker hitting a bank of shingle. The reverberation shook the basement room. Even with the ceiling-light closed, the office allocated to the sergeants of the Private-Clothes Detail rang like a foundry and reeked in the warm May evening with an air of horse dung and soot. Somewhere in the cells of Metropolitan Police 'A' Division, beyond the wall, a man was singing, a child sobbed, and an elderly woman let out arpeggios of screams in a nightmare of delirium tremens.

The cramped office seemed smaller for Verity's bulk. The tall stool seemed about to shatter like doll's-house furniture under his tightly trousered buttocks. As he gazed at the memorandum, a slight frown of concentration clouded the pink moon of his face with its black hair flattened for neatness and the moustaches lightly waxed at their tips.

He eased himself off the tall perch and stood with hands clasped under the rusty black tail of his frock-coat which, with dark trousers and stove-pipe hat, made up his Private-Clothes issue. In his mind he saw Henry Croaker's dark glittering eyes, the neatly pressed coat of the former lieutenant of artillery buttoned up tightly to its leather stock, a face the colour of a fallen leaf.

'Sour as vinegar and mean as a stoat!' he said decisively.

Sergeant Albert Samson, the other occupant of the office, looked up from the ledger in which he was entering his official diary. He grinned through a luxuriance of ginger mutton-chop whiskers.

'You heard from Mr Chief Inspector, then? I hope he saw the funny side of it. You bleatin' on about how Jack Rann wouldn't hurt a fly, much less kill an old fraud like Pandy Quinn. An' no sooner you tell Mr Croaker, than that little bugger Rann hauls hisself out of Newgate, shows his arse in all our faces, and bloody disappears. I do hope Mr Croaker had a laugh but I shouldn't think so.'

Verity's colour deepened at Samson's ginger-whiskered grin.

'Ain't you got no conception, Mr Samson, of how easy a poor rogue like Rann can be sewn up by villains like Bragg and Catskin Nash?'

Samson received the suggestion with a single hooting laugh and a clap of the hands.

'I got a conception of you, my son, on next quarter's roster. Three months on night-duty, supervising loaded sewage carts to see they don't splash the boots of their betters.'

Verity glared at him.

'You might laugh the other side of your face, Mr Samson, when you hear the rest of what Mr Croaker had to say. Flash Charley Fowler been made up to inspector.'

'Inspector? Charley Fowler? How'd he pull a stroke like that?'

At arm's length, Verity handed him Inspector Croaker's confidential memorandum. Samson read it slowly.

'Made up to inspector, Mr Samson. Not a sergeant any more. From now on, so long as you and me is on this smuggling detail, he's our superior officer.'

Samson shrugged.

'Still, Flash Fowler ain't likely to be hard. Better him than some. And so long as he lets the reins lie easy . . . .'

Verity looked at him grimly.

'He's a rogue, Mr Samson, and a lecher. And worse. It ain't just Bragg put Rann where he is. That whole business of Pandy Quinn got a smell about it like last week's bloater. If that knife wasn't found honestly a few days back, then Flash Charley is number one for being a necessary after the fact.'

'The word,' said Samson with quiet pedantry, 'is accessory.'

Verity glared again and shook his head.

'Oh no it ain't, Mr Samson. The word is murder. Even if done by the public hangman.'

Samson watched him clamber back on to the painful little roost of his high stool.

'You let the reins lie slack, Verity,' he said amiably, 'that's my advice to you. Once this smuggling caper's seen to, we'll be back to usual.'

Verity stared at him.

'I never was brought up at home nor in chapel to let duty lie slack, Mr Samson. Least of all when a poor wretch is being hunted to be took again and hanged.'

Samson picked up a cylindrical ruler to draw a line under the day's ledger-entry in his police diary.

'And when you and me was against the Rhoosians before Sebastopol,' Verity added accusingly, 'where should we all have been then, if we'd let our duty to Old England and the Queen lie slack? And suppose it wasn't Handsome Rann as coopered Pandy Quinn? Then there's a poor devil to be hung for nothing. And a murderer gone scot free.'

Samson gave a short gasp of exasperation at a blot on the duty ledger, which might not have been there had he been left in peace.

'Don't prose so,' he said without lifting his head.

Verity stared at the ceiling-light as a brewer's dray passed with a clatter of flagons.

'I'll do more than prose, Mr Samson. Mr Croaker made my mind up for me. Baptist Babb's a good man and he put his trust where it belongs. He's no business to be suspended, only doing his duty for conscience sake. If there's mischief over Pandy Quinn and Flash Fowler, what hope d'you suppose we got of putting the lid on the smuggling trade? You think Bully Bragg ain't behind that too? 'Course he is! I mean to see where the truth lies in all this, Mr Samson. And I ain't going to be put off easy.'

Ten minutes later, the two sergeants emerged into the twilight of Whitehall Place. The gentleman's town-house, which gave the side street its name, remained the centre of Scotland Yard. Verity drew a red handkerchief from his trouser pocket and dabbed his forehead.

'Mr Samson, what did he mean about his hat?'

'Whose hat?'

'Pandy Quinn. "My hat'll be the death of me". He said it when he was dying. What did he mean?'

'How should I know? Coves that's about to snuff it often rambles.'

'Funny thing, Mr Samson, I seen a few snuff it. Here and in the Rhoosian War. My poor friends at Inkerman. You know what? They talked more sense in the last few minutes, most of 'em, than in the rest of their lives. I want to know about a lot o' things to do with Pandy Quinn. And I want to know about his hat!'

Samson said nothing. They cut through the cobbled alley, past the wine vaults with their faded gilt lettering, the bootmaker's with its display of 'The Wellington Boots' in a bow window, and the little jeweller's on the corner with its discreet notice that "Ladies' ears may be pierced within".

Standing in the length of Whitehall, the gas-lamps burning against the last pale daylight of the city sky, the two sergeants took their separate beats on the night-patrol. Verity glanced at his watch.

'Right, Mr Samson. North of the river for you, south for me. I'll watch so far as London Bridge until midnight, then take the

Bermondsey wharves and streets till dawn. I'll cross after that and see you at the dock gates down Ratcliff Highway or in the hiring-yard after that. Seven o'clock sharp.'

'Don't prose!' said Samson again, looking a good deal more genial in the open air. He had replaced his dark stock with a sports-man's green cravat.

'Not prosing, Mr Samson. And what I don't want is you found, supposed to be on duty, in a riverside snug with a glass of rum-shrub. Or, worse still, found passing the time o' night with Fat Maudie or one of them. Land both of us in the cart.'

Albert Samson stared at the pink moon of a face under the brim of the stove-pipe hat, the waxed moustaches and flawless self-confidence.

'Gammon!' he said cheerfully, turning away towards The Strand, a promise of hot shrub and Fat Maudie.

Verity measured his pace towards Westminster Bridge. The pavements were hot and gritty under the worn soles of his boots. Smoke of the day's fires and wagons from the coal wharf had left a deposit of soot in the air, which gave the city the taste and smell of a railway terminus. He felt a hard black dust between his teeth.

To one side rose the gothic silhouette of parliamentary towers, on the other lay verminous tumbledown slums of Union Court and the Devil's Acre. Whores in shabby cloaks and feathered bonnets sidled out in the summer dusk, bearing disease and hunger in their looks. Whitehall was a good spec for a woman who might catch a rickety silver-haired captain from the Horse Guards, even a parlia-mentary gentleman. But such women knew Verity's type as well as he knew them. None approached him. A few shuffled further away. His threadbare 'private-clothes', his lumbering gait with hands clasped under his coat-tails, his habit of talking to himself alone on the night-beat, marked him out for what he was to the greenest bunter in the game.

A young girl on the opposite pavement called out, 'Ain't yer feeling frisky then, old crow?'

A shrivelled woman screamed with delight. Laughter rippled along the length of the pavement. Verity walked on. The sluggish flow of the river stank in the summer dusk, he could smell it a street's length away. Elegant folk rode over it, handkerchiefs to noses. A policeman's duty, he told himself, was to trudge through the miasma with the determination of the soldier he had once been. Wagons drawn by heavy ungroomed horses rattled past him as he reached the Surrey shore. Its blackened houses of London brick were painted with advertisements for the pleasures of the Big Ben Cigar Stores and Lumley's English Confectionery.

'You do not fit a murder to a man like Jack Rann unless there is a mighty tale he can tell, sir! Supposing you are Bully Bragg, which you ain't, sir!' Verity addressed the wraith of Inspector Croaker who rose mute and abashed against the darkening sky. 'No, sir! And you do not send a man to his death when he had nothing in his hand that could have coopered Pandy Quinn. And as for Handsome Jack having done Pandy Quinn and then dropped his cutter down a drain most convenient for Flash Fowler to find . . . . Just ask yourself, Mr Croaker, sir, how many murderers can you count who did their victims, went off to hide the weapon, and then came back special so's they could be found standing beside the body of the deceased?'

On the high brick viaduct over Westminster Bridge Road, the engine and carriages of a Waterloo train were stationary during the collection of tickets.

'Not one!' said Verity furiously, having given the ghostly chief inspector time to answer.

Faces at the carriage windows stared down into the deep canyon of the street with its public house and the long plate-glass windows of the monster linen draper's.

'Not bloody one!' said Verity, warm with indignation.

He emerged from the New Cut into the gaudy traffic of the Waterloo Road, fiery pillars of steam rising from the terminus of the South Western Railway. As he waited to cross the long thoroughfare towards the river again, tarpaulined drays and hansom cabs from the terminus jostled against horse-buses placarded with garish advertisements for Holloway's Pills and Reid's India Pale.

A boy of nine or ten with torn trousers and soiled shirt, clutching a broom taller than himself, waited to whisk a path for frock-coated or crinolined pedestrians through the horse-dung and the vegetable refuse of coster-barrows. Verity conveyed a coin in his open hand, a periodic transaction for information received. The little crossing-sweeper spoke from the corner of his mouth.

'Soapy Samuel gone, Mr Verity. Clean gone, sir. Folks think he might have took the same boat as Pandy Quinn. Mr Sam being of much that family. And Mag Fashion got a frightened look since Handsome Rann went down. She and that little wriggler, Miss Jolly the penny-dancer, rented a two-pair back off some widow in Houndsditch. Bully been askin' after 'em.'

It was unlikely that Bragg or his 'watchmen' could follow the boy in such a crowd as this but when the coin passed from Verity's hand, the child gave no sign of gratitude or receipt. He skipped out into an opening between the traffic at the road's centre, daring the cab-drivers and draymen to run him down. He whisked with his broom, eyes shielded by a greasy cap picked up from an old-clothes yard.

'Copper for a crossing, gents! Here's your chance and never say die! Copper for the orphans of the fleet!'

Under the midnight shadow of Southwark's square cathedral tower, Verity crossed the piazza of London Bridge station. Lights still burnt in bow-fronted little shops under the colonnade. Cabs waited outside, drivers nodding on their boxes, hats and whips askew, the warm tawny glow of the carriage-lamps glimmering like the riding-lights of distant ships.

He went down narrow steps from the station plateau into Tooley Street, warehouses behind the Bermondsey wharves rising high on either side, crowds at the doors of ramshackle oyster-bars and drinking shops with their grimy and uncurtained windows.

Outside the tap-room of The Green Man, two sparring 'snobs' in loud check jackets let him pass, grinning at him. Then they put their heads together and shouted with laughter. One of them entered the tap-room and touched Strap Mulligan on his elbow to draw attention. The sporting gent whispered in his patron's ear. And Strap's jaw dropped in a panting-dog grin that might have been mistaken for pure good humour. He beckoned a green-aproned pot-boy, dropped a penny in his hand, and gestured towards the street.

7

At the tall dock gates, off the commercial length of the Ratcliff Highway, a solitary figure sat on a bench by the high wall, a woman in shabby black. The new cooking-tins at her feet marked her as a pauper emigrant preparing for her voyage. The high wooden gates were bolted back against the walls. From the yard came a subdued murmur of many voices. Verity stood in the gateway, feet astride, one hand in the other behind his back, the stance of an officer on duty, scowling a little as he waited for Samson.

He had done duty at the hiring-yard a dozen times during his surveillance with 'H' Division. The high-walled space divided the steamer berths from a street of tall brick repositories and the attic workrooms of weavers or cabinet-makers. By half-past seven the yard was packed by 2,000 men. Most came from the unpaved alleys of Wapping and Shadwell, the tenement-courts or lodging-houses of Shoreditch and Whitechapel, some from the hovels under river bridges or embankment arches. As they pressed forward to the row of bookmaker-stands, where the 'calling-foremen' were ranged, the very number of faces made it impossible to pick one from another. Still the Private-Clothes Detail made regular visits at the morning call. The yard was a common refuge for thieves and fugitives, even for men who had killed by accident or intent. It was one of few places where a man could get work without a character or a recommendation.

The first men through the gate were close under the stands where day-labourers might be hired for eightpence or a shilling. The foremen opened their books and began to call names. Verity watched the scuffling and scrambling, the stretching of countless hands high in the air, to catch the caller's eye. Now and then a foreman would look up from his list towards the hungry strugglers and give one of them a nod. The man would break away and join the file of those collecting passes for a day's work.

As the number of waiting men dwindled, the names were called more slowly, no longer from the books. Men who were left jumped up on the backs of others, lifting themselves above the rest to attract notice. The shouting grew more intense as the chance of work ebbed. The shouts reached the level of a scream. Some called the foremen by surnames or Christian names. Others shouted their own names. Their eyes protruded grotesquely in the fury of their need to work.

After ten minutes the calling had stopped. The foremen had news of another ship that might need a gang of hands, if favourable wind and tide brought it to a berth. A few minutes later, they closed their books and stepped down. The gangs were complete. Several hundred men must wait until the following morning for their chance to work, eat, and feed such families as they had.

Verity turned away from a sight he never witnessed without despair on behalf of those who were left.

'Poor devils,' said Sergeant Samson close behind him now.

Before Verity could reply, an obscure struggle began in a far corner. One of the foremen was carried off his feet by a rush of labourers whose names had not been called. A group of stalwart onlookers moved towards the skirmish. There was shouting, the foreman stepped free of the mêlée, the labourers drew back. As Verity and Samson approached, a large smiling man met them.

'What's the trouble, then, Mr Bragg?'

Bully Bragg drew the curve of a thumb down the side of his face, as if in a humorous confidence. He swaggered a little, from the width of his hips and the shortness of his legs. With dark hair piled absurdly on his head, he looked like an overweight dandy of a century past, dressed in the suiting of a sporting gentleman. He grinned at them.

'Trouble? Bit of pushing, Mr Verity. No trouble. Men keen to work. Nothing for 'em just yet, but p'raps later. Dutchman waiting off Gravesend last night for a berth. Some'll get a late shift, if it comes up on this tide. Not that it's to do with me. Bystander, same as your good self.'

Samson had walked round the far side of the group.

'Who got hit?'

There was silence.

Bragg turned back to Verity, plump hands outspread, the pale softness of his face creased in pure amiability.

'Bit of harmless pushing, Mr Verity. Little bit of impatience. 'Cos, in reason, men want to work.'

Verity led Samson away.

'It ain't the tobacco smuggling that riles me most, Mr Samson, it's the way these poor creatures are treated. Assault on the finances of the Treasury, Mr Croaker says the smuggling is! Not much of the finances of the Treasury bloody come this way! As for Bragg . . . .'

'Mr Bragg got nothing to do with the 'iring,' Samson said firmly, 'just 'appened to be here, same as you and me. Don't try it on, my son. It won't work.'

Verity scowled at him.

'There's a lot of things I mean to try on, Mr Samson. Such as having a quiet word with Orator Hawkins. He never went to see Jack Rann in Newgate for his 'ealth!'

Samson groaned as they walked towards the waiting-shed, a wooden hoarding with a narrow sloping roof, running down one wall of the yard. Open to the weather along its side, it was wide enough to provide shelter overhead for a double row of wooden benches, back to back. Men not called by the foremen might wait out the day in the hope of another gang being required, its hands paid fourpence for a late shift.

''ello, Sloppy Dick,' said Samson cheerily. 'What you been doin' to yourself, then?'

The young man looked up, a round childish face on a muscular body. He was holding a bloodstained rag to his nose and there was the first colouring of a bruise on his cheekbone.

'Nothin', Mr Samson,' he said reasonably. 'Bit of a tumble. On'y in fun.'

'Well,' said Samson understandingly, 'if you was just to tell us all about this fun, p'raps it wouldn't happen again.'

The young man looked hard at him, as if he had not quite understood. Then his face cleared.

'Oh, no, Mr Samson! No! Quite definite! Nothing to say! A tumble's nothing. Not as bad as never having me name called again. I mind meself, Mr Samson, and do as told. I can't afford otherwise.'

''Course you can't,' said Samson encouragingly, 'but you might be treated more respectful if you was to tell—'

There was a rush past the two sergeants. At the opposite corner of the yard, a foreman had appeared to call an extra gang for the ship that had been off Gravesend. In the distance, the same fight for work began, the same jumping on backs, the same urgent thrusting of arms high above the crowd. This time Sloppy Dick was walking to the wharfinger's gate for his pass to work.

'Even Sloppy Dick,' Samson said. 'He'll take a noser and a black eye from Bully's men and thank them, rather than he'll say a word against 'em. And if he's told to slip a satchel of tobacco in his shirt, he'll start his nose bleeding again in his hurry to do as asked. And you still fancy Hawkins telling you how to get the noose off Rann and round Bragg instead? You ain't half got some imagination, my son.'

His duty completed, Verity wished Samson a good morning and walked back the way he had come. Along the wharves from Shadwell to London Bridge the air was first pungent with the vast stores of tobacco, then sickly with fumes of rum. Worse was the stench of hides and the huge bins of horn. Then the day was fragrant with coffee and spice. He picked his way among sacks of cork, yellow bins of sulphur and lead-coloured copper ore. A warehouse floor seemed freshly tarred, where sugar had leaked through great tiers of casks.

He thought of the Orator. Hawkins cared nothing for Scotland Yard, but he could be made to live in terror of Bully Bragg. Let Bragg believe that his Orator had turned coppers' nark. Mr Bragg had a way with a knife, and Hawkins knew it.

Thanks to Baptist Babb, Verity knew enough of the Newgate conversation between Hawkins and Rann. Suppose he promised Hawkins to repeat it word-for-word to Bragg, confiding to the Bragg that every helpful word came from Hawkins himself, in exchange for payments from the police informants' fund. Hawkins might yet know fear of a kind unique to Bragg's victims.

'And that's how we shall have a lever under you, sir,' Verity said to the imagined Orator, loudly enough for several passers-by to turn and stare.

By sunlit water, he eased his way among men whose faces were blue from carrying indigo, and Customs gaugers whose long brass-tipped rules dripped with spirit from the casks they had just probed. A group of fair-haired sailors, chattering German, stopped to watch him pass. A black seaman, red-cotton handkerchief twisted turban-like round his head, shouted a greeting. A broad, straw-hatted mate stopped him, offering green parakeets in a wooden cage. With measured stride, Verity passed the steam-wharf moorings, the fancy paintwork of paddle-boxes on the packet-boats for Belfast and Cork, Leith and Glasgow.

'Brothers, sisters, father, mother, never been a better friend to you than I mean to be, Mr Hawkins,' said Verity to his imagined victim. 'Only say the word, and I'm the man to save you being carved in your own juice, fine as a Michaelmas goose for Mr Bragg's table.'

Over London Bridge, covered drays with carcasses or barrels of fish rumbled to Smithfield and Billingsgate. Blue-smocked butchers bore trays of meat or cabbages on their shoulders, among street-sellers of pea-soup and hot eels, ginger-beer and Chelsea buns. In the recesses above the stone piers, the destitute had passed the summer night, huddled in formless bundles. They watched the traffic listlessly, staring at a world of which they had no part.

8

London Bridge was the first barrier to sea-going ships. Upstream, the river was busy with barges carrying coal, flour, or casks of beer. Their masts and sails were lowered as the oars carried them under the spans of Southwark, Blackfriars, Waterloo, and Westminster. Penny-steamers churned the sparkling water, thin stacks trailing banners of smoke. Pontoons and posts in mid-stream marked the progress of the new bridge carrying the Charing Cross Railway to the north bank.

Verity paused, scowling, by the pillared brick of the Red Lion Brewery. The ebb tide had uncovered a litter-strewn foreshore at King's Head Stairs. Its stone steps, at which watermen landed passengers from Temple Gardens, were deserted in the morning quiet.

A group of mudlarks scavenged among the small craft lopsided on the sludge. Their ragged clothes shone with the river's slime, so wet that the garments clung smooth as skin under the black ooze. A few wore dustmen's caps with flaps at the nape. Others had their hair in wet tufts, like black imps of damnation in the *Illustrated Family Bible* of his childhood. Stooping and pausing, they sifted for scraps of coal, iron, rope and bone. Copper nails which fell from vessels berthed or repaired along the shore were the most valuable item.

Several lighters lay moored to posts just beyond low-water,

among them a deep, iron coal-barge. A wooden cabin built into its stern accommodated the crew. The barge rode high and empty, brown sail furled, its stern swinging heavily in the current. There were hundreds of these vessels, supervised by police boats and excise cutters. They acted as tenders to steamers or gaunt black colliers anchored down-river, bringing cargo cheaply to the heart of Westminster and Southwark.

Only the master or watchman would be on board until the tide lifted the hull. At low water, it lay twenty feet from the tideline, where the mudlarks on the sleek brown flanks of river soil and in rivulets of sewage sifted the debris of kitchens and factories, slaughterhouses and gas-works.

Concealed by the corner of a wall, Verity watched the developing drama. The older scavengers had taken to the water, forming a chain several feet apart, from the water's edge to the barge. A tall youth of fifteen or sixteen was chest-deep in the river under the lee of the vessel's side. The lighterman, asleep in his cabin at the stern, had no idea that they were there.

A figure appeared from the iron hold of the barge, jumping up on the broad gunwale, moving deftly as an acrobat along it. Unlike the muddied imps, she had been rinsed clean by swimming round the far side and climbing up the mooring rope. Her dark hair, drawn back on either side of her forehead, lay in a well-soused tangle on her back. Yet the insolent sun-tanned profile, the sullen mouth and the agile limbs against which her tattered wet dress was plastered were unmistakable.

Verity had last seen her at the close of petty sessions, the committal of offenders to the Tothill Fields House of Correction in Westminster. Baptist Babb had since identified her, masquerading as Jack Rann's 'Little Girl' in the prisoners' consulting-room of Newgate Gaol.

'Why, Miss Suzanne!' said Verity softly. 'Though you don't know it yet, you and me shall stitch Mr Hawkins neat as Honiton lace!'

The robbery of the barge was carried out with quiet professionalism. Lambeth Sue stood on the gunwale above the youth who was chest-deep in the river. She dropped a cloth bundle. He caught it, felt it, then tossed it to the next member of the chain several feet behind him. The bundle sailed and bobbed through the air, hand to hand, until it reached a growing pile of booty on the shore.

Suzanne vanished, then reappeared, swaying nimbly along the high black side of the iron vessel. A paper package fell into the hands of the youth below. Next a small box, then a tin. Verity's eyes widened at the outrage. This was no scene of innocent mudlarks hungrily scavenging for a few scraps of coal or wood to warm their chilled bodies; these were experienced young thieves, looting the living-quarters of the barge, while its guardian slept.

He was outnumbered by seven or eight to one. But the heroine of the robbery would be his lever under Bully Bragg. Once she took to the water, it was the easiest thing in the world to cut off her escape.

At last there was a roar of fury from the barge. Suzanne scrambled on to the gunwale, teetering along its ledge, followed by a burly man in shirt and breeches. Some of his words were lost in the distance and tumult, but a shout of 'Thieving slut!' came clearly to shore. From his hand swung a doubled length of thin rope with which he thrashed the air behind the fugitive, never quite near enough to catch her.

Though she was nimbler, the lighterman walked the gunwale as easily as the pavement of a street. She leant forward to dive. With a shout of frustration, he swung the rope at her backside. There was a cry and a floundering splash on the far side of the hull. The human chain plunged towards the shore, Suzanne dog-paddling in the rear. The lighterman shouted from the bows to anyone who might hear, as the thieves snatched up their loot from the tideline and ran for the stone stairs.

She would be the last up the King's Head Stairs by ten or twenty yards, easily intercepted as the rest fled. They came in a rush, panting and laughing. Scattering down College Street, they were lost in the commercial bustle of Belvedere Road. Suzanne trailed well behind. Verity waited, hidden from her as she came under the stone quay and began to climb the steps. When she reached the top, he took her arm from behind and felt her start with shock.

'A word with you, miss!' he said magisterially.

She went limp in his grasp, winded and defeated. Alone among the thieves, she was carrying nothing.

'You needn't be handcuffed, so long as you act sensible,' he said reassuringly. 'You ain't got nowhere to run from here.'

She responded with a whimper of submission and despair.

'I'm so 'ungry!' she sobbed.

'Well,' he said encouragingly, 'if you was to be an evidence against the rest, you might have nothing to answer for.'

She looked up into his face, wanting to believe in his goodness and his promise. She even drew a little closer as if to confide in him, and then spat with great accuracy into his eye. Half-blinded for an instant, he felt her bony knee come up sharply between his legs.

'Stinking jack!'

Then, as she twisted away, there was a rending of cheap cotton. Verity, wiping his eye, held nothing but a wet and slimy rag that had been the sleeve and shoulder of her ragged dress.

He sprang after her. His hat had gone in the struggle, rolling on the edge of the stone stairs. He would find it later. Like many fugitives, Lambeth Sue underestimated his speed. He cornered her at a riverside wall of the Military Stores. In a pantomime dance, she made to dive past, first on one side, then on the other. Verity stepped left, guessing she would run for the alley on his right.

She did as he expected. The alley was formed by five storeys of the Red Lion Brewery facing a high wall that protected the unfinished railway bridge. At the top of the brewery wall was a wooden hoist with iron chains dangling from it. This was a side route into Belvedere Road. But it was the dinner hour and there were no drays entering or leaving the brewery yard. Plate-iron gates had been locked across the alley, turning it into a cul-de-sac. His fugitive was trapped.

For all her nimbleness, she was winded, hovering with the brick wall behind her, dodging from side to side. In a last trick of her trade, she bolted at him on one side, swerving at the last moment to the other. As she swerved she lost her footing and fell with Verity on top of her.

'That's enough!' he said furiously. 'Ain't you got more sense?'

A fist hit him on the eyebrow. She panted, clutching at his hair, gathering spittle. He had one arm pinned, her other waving free. He snapped a metal cuff on the captive wrist. Then, to his dismay, the fugitive began to scream. He gripped the arm that was still flailing.

'Dirty brute!' said a deep voice behind him.

He did not dare to take his eyes off the captive.

'Police officer,' he said breathlessly to whoever was standing over him. 'And if I should require your assistance, you'll be legally obliged to render same.'

'Dirty brute!' said the voice again. Someone scuffed a boot on the ground beside him but he snapped the second cuff on his captive's other wrist and got to his feet.

A large man in red plush waistcoat and knee breeches, his legs the size of balustrade pillars, stood behind him, feet planted astride and arms folded. A thin companion in a high battered hat was leaning against the brick wall, picking his teeth with a straw. The man in the waistcoat gestured at the kneeling girl.

'Get those darbies off her, you poxy jack!'

'You keep out of what don't concern you,' said Verity grimly, 'else there'll be another pair for you.'

But he was the one now trapped in the alley. With a chill at his heart, he knew there was only one way out.

'Right!' he said, facing the pair of them, 'oo's first?'

The man with the straw straightened up from the wall, as if

65

suddenly interested in the exchange. The large man in the waistcoat came forward, fencing for a grip. Verity side-stepped, caught his antagonist's right arm in a lock and spun the man by his own momentum. The large man hit the brick wall with a bellowing gasp. But he straightened up and came back, no more troubled than by falling on a feather mattress. His shoulders were hunched, fists moving. Verity clamped his teeth hard, knowing that a loose jaw more easily becomes a broken jaw.

His opponent lunged twice but Verity dodged back, so that the fists merely patted his cheeks. He kept his guard up. The man lunged again. Verity went back with the blow, then came forward with one knee going straight to his attacker's groin. The bruiser in the red waistcoat lost his balance, recovered, backed to the wall and picked up a short wooden spar. He advanced with it, driving Verity back by jabs to the face. At the next thrust, Verity grabbed the wood and hung on, twisting and bending with his assailant until both men lost their footing.

In a flailing of arms, clutching and snatching, they fought half-kneeling and half-standing. With a crash of glass they went sprawling over a crate of bottles by the brewery wall. Dogs began to bark. Suzanne was screaming again. They struggled to their feet, grappling, while the onlooker who had been picking his teeth with the straw fenced round them, for a chance to intervene. Snatching the fallen spar, he ran in and hit Verity behind the knees. Verity tried to face both men and tripped. He caught his foot on the stone edge of a deep gutter, an outlet from the brewery wall to the river. There was sufficient discharge in the drain to soak his black trousers as he fell, tearing the elbow of his frock-coat.

Shaken by the fall, he got to his knees, preparing for battle again. But his assailants now stood back and he saw a newcomer above him. Looking down was the soft smile and dark pompadour hair of Bully Bragg. Over Bragg's shoulder, stood the newly made-up Inspector Fowler, exquisite in fawn summer suiting and royal-blue cravat.

'Why, Mr Verity!' Bragg's quiet smile conveyed bewilderment. 'Whatever has happened? Let me give you a hand up, my dear fellow!'

'I'll thank you to stand out of my way . . . .'

'Mr Fowler! This way, if you please. My poor Mr Verity!'

The man with the straw and his companion with the red waistcoat had an unapologetic air. Bragg swung round on them.

'Mr Hardwicke! Mr Atwell! Can either of you explain this? Or the young lady?'

Fowler intervened, holding out his hand to Verity.

'We'd best have those cuffs off her. No call for them now.'

Verity handed him the key.

'She was on the ground and him on top of her,' said Hardwicke in the red waistcoat. 'Ravishing in an alley, it looked like.'

'You was told I was police!' said Verity ferociously.

'Told,' said Hardwicke reasonably. 'But telling and being is different things. You didn't look like police. You didn't act like police, neither. You fought like a brick. You could've been anyone. That's how misunderstandings d'come about.'

Fowler unlocked the cuffs. Suzanne set up a hooting cry. The dim light of the alley caught a slim, sun-tanned shoulder, where the dress had been torn from her.

'He tried to have me clothes off! See me dress!'

Fowler's enquiring glance at Verity invited an explanation, but Lambeth Sue had not finished.

'And he walloped me! Look at me arse!'

There was a respectful silence at the sight of a pink imprint.

'Indeed,' said Fowler quietly. He looked again at Verity.

'I never! What she got there come from the lighterman on the coal-barge and well deserved! You ask on the barge off King's Head Stairs. You'll see the truth!'

'Well,' said Fowler pleasantly, 'I'm glad of that.'

A few minutes later, Verity followed Fowler from the alley. The others walked behind. He sensed their hidden smiles at his humiliation. With Fowler and four known criminals in attendance, he left hatless, like a felon under escort.

When they were alone together, Fowler rested his thumbs under the lapels of his fawn summer suiting.

'Just 'cos a man's made up, Verity, he don't cease to be human. And I hope I don't.'

Verity said nothing. He noticed that Fowler now called him 'Verity,' rather than 'Mr Verity,' the familiarity of a superior with a former equal. Verity stood hatless in torn frock-coat and wet trousers. Fowler sat, or rather lounged, behind the duty officer's table, dressed more like the keeper of a Regent Street night-house.

The police ship was an old wooden frigate with masts cut down, moored just below Waterloo Bridge. Square stern-windows in its after-cabin reflected watery brilliance on low beams and white-washed ceiling.

Fowler gave him a leer.

'I hope I'm human, eh?'

Verity nodded. He could not bring himself to answer.

'Nothing personal,' Fowler insisted. 'Nothing vindictive.'

'I did what was right.' He felt that the words were being torn out between his teeth.

Fowler's hand gestured, as if waving an invisible cigar.

''Course you did, Verity. And that little slut who made the trouble, she's well suited. Or will be at the next sessions. You and the lighterman, that's two witnesses to robbery of the barge. Industrial school for her, or some such reformatory as takes the court's fancy. She thinks her backside's smarting now, wait till she finishes twelve months there.'

'I did nothing wrong, sir! With respect, sir!' He made 'sir' sound like a reprimand rather than a term of deference. But Fowler treasured it smilingly.

''Course you didn't, Verity. Not wrong, but most unfortunate. What you have done, see, is wipe out months of surveillance that'll have to start all over again. 'Course, you hadn't been told about barges off Lambeth, your beat being down Bermondsey and the wharves. The coal-barge that caught your eye this morning has been watched for some time. So have four others.'

'They never have!' The full extent of his tragedy was becoming clear to him. 'I was never told!'

'On my manor, Verity, a man gets told what he needs to know, not what he don't.' Fowler's thumbs were still in his lapels. He seemed to be rolling the invisible cigar in his lips. 'Your job was the wharves, not lighters nor barges. Five of them been suspected of bringing contraband from the big ships. Lighters can come in close, discharge cargo, keep the contraband on board. Then, at night, or when no one's watching, it's got just a few feet to travel at low water. They can toss the packets down to someone standing in the water. Easy as that. See?'

'Robbery!' said Verity firmly. 'That's what I saw.'

A fly landed on Fowler's immaculately stitched lapel and he flicked it away.

'You got no evidence, my friend, beyond the lighterman cursing Lambeth Sue for a thieving little bitch and taking a swipe at her. That don't necessarily have to be because of robbery. Look! You been on a smuggling detail two months. Then you see half-a-dozen young villains passing ashore packages from a lighter. Didn't it never cross your mind what else they might be doing?'

'Robbing!' said Verity, desperate for the first time in their encounter.

'And you recovered any goods to prove it, have you?'

'I couldn't hold her and chase them!'

Fowler shook his head, as if it were all beyond him.

'So, for all you know, each of the items stolen could have been stuffed with tobacco or anything else.'

Verity stood his ground.

'No alternative but what I did.'

'Listen, Verity. You tell me, an officer of your experience, it never occurred to you to get help?'

'I'd have lost the girl.'

'But you knew who she was, old fellow! We could have got her any time. According to you, she wasn't carrying anything! But the others who had the goods, you let 'em all get away. Suppose you'd grabbed one of those little brutes and we'd found contraband in his packages. We'd be halfway to court now. Whereas, it's only the evidence of a lighterman that's stood between you and charges of attempted ravishing of her and grievous bodily harm all round. You'd have been off the Force and in Horsemonger Lane lock-up before tonight!'

Verity said nothing. He loathed Fowler. But Fowler was right.

'Whereas,' Fowler said quietly, 'the master of that barge now knows that the police saw everything that happened today. And the reason they saw it, he'll think, is because they were watching. And by now he's told his four friends on their other barges that he's been watched. So what do you suppose they'll do?'

'Don't know, sir,' said Verity miserably.

'Don't you? They'll all tell their friends. And they'll start their scheme again all different. So that's half the river-police surveillance plan blown to smithereens.'

There was silence. The trap had closed so neatly that Verity could neither see a way out nor even guess who had sprung it.

'I hope I'm human,' said Fowler again. 'I'll put it to Mr Croaker as reasonable as I can. Make plain you did no wrong.'

Verity stared at him.

'What's it to do with Mr Croaker?'

Fowler looked surprised.

'I'm human, Verity, but human ain't the same as being stupid! You're done for on surveillance. Back to Division's the only way for you. I can't keep you here. Not now your face is known as watching the lighters.'

'My face is known anyway!' As he stood before the table, he sensed odours of malt and hops seeping from his clothes, after his fall into the brewery outlet. 'I'm known from walking a beat round

Bermondsey and the hiring-yard. Anyway, my face been known to Bragg and his two men for weeks past. So's Mr Samson's.'

Fowler's teeth touched his lower lip and his eyes narrowed, as if a thought had occurred to him.

'You suggesting some connection between Mr Bragg or his men and the smuggling of contraband? Are you, Verity?'

He saw the precipice in time.

'No, sir. Just that my face had been seen by a lot of people round the wharves and the docks for a long time.'

'So it has.' Fowler sat upright and shuffled some papers together, as if that decided the sergeant's fate. Then he looked up, surprised to find Verity still there.

'Division,' he said firmly. 'After all, it's where you and Samson belong. Make your peace there. Mr Croaker's all right, he's a reasonable man.' Fowler looked up from his papers again and gave Verity a wink. 'Reasonable man is Harry Croaker. Once you know him. P'raps not so human as I am, though. Eh?'

9

At dusk on Friday, the two men were dressed alike. Tomnoddy and Jack Rann wore toshers' velveteen coats with baggy pockets, trousers and aprons of dirty canvas, bags slung on their backs. Each carried a bull's-eye lantern and a seven-foot pole with a hoe on its end.

'Mostly,' Tomnoddy said, 'sludge in the channels is about a foot. In places, it's five or six foot where the brick's rotted away. When you feel it sink, use the pole. Catch anything with the hoe.'

They passed the bar-room windows of the Town of Ramsgate, Wapping Old Stairs and Pierhead Wharf. Iron bridges connected riverside warehouses by the upper floors. Tomnoddy turned by the Prospect of Whitby, a tavern door between elegant bow windows, following the alley to Pelican Stairs, a muddy foreshore scattered with stone and brick.

On its darkling mud, the tide had withdrawn to a luminous rim of froth. No movement showed on the sluggish water, except for a dozen little skiffs and wherries, dredgermen with grappling irons over the bows and nets hanging at the sides. A haul of bones, coal, and old rope was jumbled in the sterns. Each boatman hoped for the weight of a dead man or woman in his net, the emptying of sodden pockets, and the 'inquest money', to reward the landing of a corpse.

Tomnoddy ignored the lengths of wood, copper nails, and scraps of iron across the moonlit flanks of soft mud. Etiquette reserved them for those who understood nothing of the sewers. A shape in a coat or an old dress glimmered across their path in the thin moonlight, darted down and shuffled off with its booty.

The nearest outfall appeared at first to be bricked in. Then Rann saw the square iron doors, which hung from hinges at the top of the arch.

'Aladdin's cave,' Tomnoddy said, 'if a man knows how to look. There's ten thousand gold sovs lost down drains or manholes every year. Hold t'other side of the iron, Jack. This is how it shuts tight with the river against it at the flood. So's they don't have water up the sewer and in the streets.'

Rann took the cold flank of plate-iron and felt it move as Tomnoddy added his weight. The brick-lined tunnel was shaped like an egg upright on its narrow end. Rann had imagined something grander than a channel three feet wide and six feet high. A man trapped in it when the sluices were opened would have no chance.

'Open your bull's-eye.' Tomnoddy set the example. 'Take the shade off. It'll shine ahead while you're stood and light the ground when you stoop. When you see a roof-grating, shade it. Move like a ghost. They can see light up in the street and hear any word. When you see rats, shine it on 'em. They don't stay for that.'

The old sewerman went first, the sound of his boots splashing lightly in the ooze and the shallow ripple of water running over it.

'Rats is the worst,' he said philosophically. 'A man gets lost down here easier than in a maze. And he drops down at last and is ate to the bone by packs of brown Hanover rats like good-sized kittens. They mostly feed on waste from slaughterhouses round Whitechapel and Smithfield. But leave a dead man down here, next day he's skull and bones picked clean.'

The tunnel opened into a large cavern, where narrower drains converged. The vault of the roof was hung with stalactites of putrefying matter two or three feet long. Rann shivered.

'A man can't live down here!'

'Samuel can. He's that much in fear of what Bragg's knife can do. Watch yerself, Jack, it's low and narrow just there. Don't knock against them bricks! They're rotted from what grows on 'em. One tap brings 'em in like an avalanche.'

Lamplight showed a narrower tunnel, the flow running deeper. With a pang of disgust, Rann felt it wet his canvas trousers above his boots. The stench was worse: gas-factories and breweries, vegetable decay and stable dung, slaughterhouse offal and chemical waste. A heap of fallen brickwork blocked a channel to one side. Before it, dry ground was littered with tin kettles, ashes, broken jars, shards of flower-pots. Sewage stagnated behind it.

'Air's foul where the roof's low,' Tomnoddy said, 'fresher where the gratings are.'

The brickwork of roof and drain had fallen in ahead of them. Tomnoddy was stepping on transverse planks laid across the channel. A wooden beam, dark with rot, spanned the tunnel roof. The sewermen paused.

'Lombard's Tailoring rests on that beam. The day the timber gives, half the street'll come down with it.'

He paused and straightened up. Rann saw a faint light ahead, from an oblong recess in the roof. He did not need to be told that it was the shaft of a street-grating. His companion turned.

'Stay here,' he said softly, 'and don't move for nothink. Sam's lodging up ahead in a chamber that's wholesome and dry. It's up a bit, at the end of a side-tunnel. Ain't seen use for years. But if he starts a kick-up and row when he sees you, he'll be heard above. I'll go to him first.'

Rann watched Tomnoddy tread carefully from board to board, the pale lantern-ray fainter on a dark curve of rotting brick. At the overhead grating, the light went. The silence was scarcely broken by the ripple in the channel under the boards. He felt the loneliness of a man in his grave.

Scampering feet from a ruined side tunnel made his heart jump.

On the broken masonry, his lamp showed a breathing shape, the size of a black pony, curled in an indistinguishable heap. The light caused it to shift and break, a mound of more brown rats than he could count.

Oil-light glinted on eyes that were bright with hunger. But the lantern beam kept them back, half the pack staring into the brilliance, others fighting and squeaking. He put the lantern down and clapped his hands once. The pack scattered out of sight, into a warren under the planks and fallen bricks. Then he saw a glimmer beyond the street-grating and knew Tomnoddy was coming back.

'He's there,' Tomnoddy said wryly, 'seeing he got nowhere else to be.'

They followed the main channel, under the street grating, and into an old branch tunnel, long disused. It lay on rising ground, the brick dry underfoot, littered with broken earthenware and stone.

'Used to carry rain off above the Fleet Ditch,' Tomnoddy said. 'Now the water goes in the main. More wholesome up here, suppose a man's got to live like this.'

They were six or eight feet above the main sewer. Tomnoddy turned into another branch, blocked about twenty feet in. To one side was a makeshift door, vertical slats with two cross-braces. The old sewerman pushed it open.

'Cellar of the old King James – what they calls Jimmy's. The tannery took the building down to clear a yard for the hides and skins. Never bothered with filling in the cellars. Yard's above us now, five or six feet. There's no way in save this.'

Tawny light from three lamps lit the low vaulting of the cellar roof on which they hung. The racks and bins where wine had once been laid were transformed into a makeshift bed, table, and cupboards. The brick walls were dark, shabby, but dry. A few sacks contained Samuel's possessions.

'Handsome Jack? Jack Rann? That really you?'

''Course it's me, Sammy. And I ain't been hung. Not yet.'

Samuel stepped into the light, so bedraggled that Rann only

knew him at first by his voice. Even in fear, the voice had a rich confidential tone. With a few words of prayer, a phrase from Bible or liturgy, it had made men and women offer their lives and fortunes to such a friend. Soapy Samuel's best days were past, but he had seldom returned from a 'mission' to Wandsworth or Bayswater without a gold sovereign or two in his pocket. At a street meeting in Kensington, supported by Chelsea George dressed as a converted African pagan, the old pals had once taken up a collection of eighteen pounds from a well-dressed crowd.

'Hello, Sammy,' said Rann more formally, holding out his hand. Samuel took it limply. The sleek white hair that had given him nobility was unkempt. The blue eyes that warmed easily with love and persuasion stared in dismay. The sharp nose that had scented opportunity, now smelt peril and destruction. The smooth-shaven gill, the keen lines of the face, the profile of an amiable questing rodent, had grown sharp with hunger. His dark clothes were crumpled. Even in the odours of the sewers, the clerical impostor stank of spirits.

'Christ, Sammy!' said Rann, 'Look at you!'

Samuel drew back, as if he had been struck a blow. He moved unsteadily.

'Frightened,' he said with a downward shake of his head. 'Frightened I was, Jack, frightened I am.'

'Down here, I shouldn't be surprised.'

'Up there.' The old man pointed at the ceiling. 'I go up at night. I beg, if I can. There's a few give. Then I get back, quick-sharp. Bring me what you can, there's a chum.'

He sat down heavily on the makeshift bed, a study in defeat.

Rann took a step closer. Sour fear mingled with drink in the air of the cavern.

'You can't stay down here, Sam. Summer comes, this air'll be full of cholera. That'll kill you, if rats don't eat you first.'

The points of Samuel's bony cheeks shone as he shook his head.

'You don't see it, 'andsome Rann! They know you and Pandy

was up to something tasty. They meant to have it off you. They know I put up those houses for you, so they reckon I know too. Which I don't. They want to know who's the putter-up and what's the game. I can't tell 'em.'

Rann brought himself to sit down on the wooden bed. But Samuel looked away.

'You're out of it now, Sammy!'

'Don't be a fool, Jack Rann.' Samuel looked briefly at him. 'They didn't mean to do Pandy so quick. They was asking him things and hurting him when he didn't answer. The ways they cut him! He answered in the end, you bet. Then you was to be asked next, then me. Didn't you wonder why you were called to the Golden Anchor that afternoon? They'd have had you all right. But first, the knife slipped on poor Pandy. Seeing as he was bleeding away to a corpse, they couldn't do you the same. Not with Fowler upstairs, ramping some doxy of Bragg's. Flash Charley may be their man but he couldn't straighten two murders in one afternoon. So you was fitted for knifing Pandy Quinn. Two birds at one go.'

Jack Rann sighed.

'You got no cause to be ashamed of being scared, Sammy.'

Samuel had the look of a child about to cry at some injustice.

'Pandy must have spoke my name, Jack! I don't blame the poor devil, but where's that leave me? You and Pandy knew what you was up to. You could say, if it got too bad. But they'd hurt me to make me tell 'em things I don't know! I never was a schoolbook 'ero, Jack. I'd answer 'em straight off. But I couldn't, if I didn't know!' He shuddered. 'Bully Bragg, Moonbeam, Catskin, and a knife. I couldn't be naked under that knife, Jack. I'd drown in the river first. I'd live down here. I'd die down here, if I have to, not watch meself being cut bit by bit . . . .'

He bowed his head and covered his face with his hands. Rann thought he might begin to weep. But Samuel did not weep.

'Jack's right, Sam,' said Tomnoddy from the shadows. 'You can't live 'ere for ever.'

'You tell me where, then!'

'With me,' Rann said, ' 'merica, 'stralia, anywhere.'

Samuel looked up, the worn face showing humorous contempt.

'With you? You'll be stretched when they catch you – which they will, soon or late.'

Rann smiled at him.

'No, Sam. I mean to do what me and Pandy was going to do. I can't stay here, not in London, nor in England. So I mean to have enough to take me and you anywhere on earth. But I got to do it quick. And I can't do it without you.'

Hope glimmered in Soapy Samuel's eyes.

''ow much?'

Rann breathed deeply.

'It won't be more than twenty thousand golden sovereigns, split five ways. Enough to buy half Piccadilly.'

'How much!'

'Likewise, not less than ten thousand. Enough to buy one side of half Piccadilly.'

'There ain't so much . . . .'

'And just so there's no misunderstanding, Sammy, we whack the lot, equal shares for all. Like Pandy always said.'

Samuel looked at him, the bony profile torn between disbelief and longing. He gave it up.

'No, Jack Rann. Not me. I can gab, that's all. I can't climb roofs like Pandy. I can't tickle locks the way you do.'

Rann put his hand on the bony shoulder.

'You're more to me, Sammy. All you do is what you always do. A plum in the mouth. A smile in the eyes. A man o' God to charm the Devil hisself out of Hell – and then put him back again. And you don't need to take a penny from anyone.'

Despite his misery, Samuel chuckled at the absurdity. Rann held him by the arm.

'Sammy! I mean to have my way with all of them. Banks and vaults. Police and prisons. Bragg's magsmen and the whole bleedin'

Swell Mob. I'll screw them finer than they was ever screwed. Once it's over, they'll hurt like hellfire. But none of 'em will know who did it to 'em or how it could be done.'

Samuel wanted with all his soul to believe.

'You can't do it, Jack. No one could.'

Rann spoke carefully and finally. 'If I'm not up it, Sam, why ain't I still in the death cell? Getting into a vault is a sight easier than getting out of there.'

'All right,' said Samuel grudgingly. 'Who's in this, then?'

'There's Tomnoddy for looking after the kit, that's only fair. Otherwise four.'

'Who? I got the right to know before I say.'

Rann hesitated. Then he said, 'There's Tom, you and me. There's Miss Jolly, the penny-dancer. And Mag Fashion down Trent's Cornhill Mourning Tailors.'

Samuel gave a shout of outraged humour.

'Newgate done something to your brain, Jack Rann!'

'Newgate made me swear never to be took again,' he said quietly. 'Nor I shan't be.'

Samuel stood up. In his despair he became waggish.

'So you and me, and a little wriggler from the penny gaff, and a shop mouse that lives for gin. That's it, is it?'

'It's what's needful.'

'You, me, a shop mouse and a penny-dancer? To bugger the banks, and the police, and the Swell Mob – any one of which could have you strung up on sight! And then come clean away with ten or twenty thousand pieces of gold?'

'I don't have a choice,' Rann said meekly. 'No more do you.'

'Choice! You want your bloody head read, Jack Rann!'

In the same quiet voice, Rann said, 'Suppose you stash the gab a minute, Sammy, and just listen for a change?'

TWO

THE CHINESE SHADES

10

The windy light of a courtyard lamp cast a jagged shadow-play on his profile as Rann ducked through the archway of Preedy's Rents into the street. In dark jacket, trousers and cap, he felt as nondescript as under his covering of soot. Where the road opened out at Sparrow Corner, he found a cobbled crossing, crowded with dredgermen, ballast-heavers, and their women. A blind, dark-haired beggar sat against the wall, by a door lettered on frosted glass as The Wine Promenade. The last notes of *The Minstrel Boy* faded from the old man's bamboo flute.

''ello, Old Mole,' Rann said softly, squatting down. 'You ain't 'eard voices that might be Maggie Fashion, or Miss Jolly, the shop-girl that's turned penny-dancer?'

The beggar's eyes turned upwards, lids fluttering a little, showing nothing but the whites. He felt Rann's jacket with finger and thumb, as he spoke.

'See my 'ands? Tailor's fingers. Till that gas-light in the slop-shop killed the nerve of the optics. These fingers plays my flute now. And if someone was to smash 'em, I'd starve. *Comprendee?*'

Rann let him hear two coins rattle. The old man sniffed.

'Mag Turnball, with fair hair in a tail and a strapping bum, not heard of in weeks. Miss Jolly shows off down the new gaff. Monmouth Street. What they calls Chinese Shades. Gents goes to watch after dinner. Young fellows from the regiments too. Half-past ten or eleven. If she ain't hooked an harristocrat first!'

Old Mole's shoulders heaved in dry appreciation of his own humour. He pocketed the coins, and spat deftly across the pavement into the gutter.

'Now, you got what you paid for, my friend. An' if what you want is tail, you'd be best off elsewhere than them young shicksters.'

He knocked saliva from the mouthpiece, touched the flute to his lips and blew the first plaintive notes of *Villikins and his Dinah*.

Rann crossed the Minories and made his way through the little streets north of The Strand. He guessed the way she would come but knew better than to startle her where the world might see. At the corner of Monmouth Street, a stationary cart bore a tall crudely lettered board promising, THE CHINESE SHADES! A large black hand, roughly drawn, pointed down an alley to Seven Dials.

He found an unlit doorway between a slop tailors with its shutters down and the dusty windows of a stationer offering the adventures of Fanny Hill and the reformatory chastisements of Elaine Cox in photographs.

A little before ten, he saw her pass under a street-lamp, coming from the moonlit spaces of Trafalgar Square. Rann recognized the plum-coloured merino gown, the pork-pie hat with a white feather. In one hand she gathered up the skirts a little, holding them clear of the moisture that gathered by night on the paving. He pictured, rather than saw, the warm gold of Miss Jolly's complexion, the slight seductive slant of almond eyes, dark hair combed back from the clear slope of her forehead. He knew the neat little body like a map, the delicate whorls of her ears, the slim grace of her neck, the straight slender back and the trim legs. Her very walk gave her away. She would never be a conventional ballet-girl. Her legs were a little too short for her height, causing quick diminutive steps as she walked, a tight swagger of her hips that was inelegant and yet suggestive.

Across the darkness of the street, the alleyway by the gaff blazed with white fire. Gaslight streamed into a thin yellow fog of the summer night, glittering on the grimy windows opposite. Against this pale brilliance, Miss Jolly presented a composed, odalisque profile, features sharply defined, brows arched high over expressionless Turkoman eyes. He saw her slip into shadow and out again, then vanish through a doorway. There was a babble of voices, the cracked sound of an old piano playing *Pretty Polly Perkins of Paddington Green.*

A warehouse front had been taken out to make an entrance to the improvised auditorium. The crowd was pressing forward, pennies held out towards the money-taker in his box. Girls of fifteen or sixteen, in cotton-velvet dresses danced noisily with one another. There were dragoon officers and gentlemen more at home in the Carlton Club or the Naval and Military.

Rann judged it best to go in at the back, where he could get out quickly. When the last of them had gone in, he offered his coin. Between plain walls, a wooden stage stood on trestles across the far end of the warehouse. Double gas-jets flared with a harsh brilliance to provide a form of limelight. The gas at the rear of the benches dwindled to tall undulating flames, leaving all but the stage in semi-darkness. There were roars from the costers at the rear.

"ats off in front!'

In a ripple, the stove-pipe hats of clerks and the silk hats of club-men came off, among shouts of 'Dandy O'Hara!' 'Flash Chants!' and 'Pineapple Rock!' Rann knew O'Hara by sight, a man who drove a cart for a dust-contractor until the comic gaffs made him a hero. The costers shouted their approval as the Dandy came on in a green suit and battered hat, his face painted as bravely as a street-girl. Chords from a broken piano struggled through the tumult.

Rann waited until the song's end. In the half-light, four men were already moving a frame and a stretched calico screen for the Chinese Shades. O'Hara gave the audience a final flip with the end of his comic cravat and bowed from the stage. The men slid the plywood frame to the centre of the platform, its calico screen shining fiercely with gaslight. The pianist slipped into a rhythm of half-tones, conveying oriental promise, while the costers stamped and roared.

The features of the brick interior were dim by reflected light, like Thames landmarks in a winter fog. Between the black flats was a crack wide enough to see the fleeting shape of Miss Jolly moving to the screen, agile coppery limbs glimpsed in shadow. Then, in sharp silhouette, she crouched at the corner of the calico, hair piled in a hive-shape, the long forehead, the sharpness of her nose, the demurely receding chin.

Costers and subalterns sat in utter silence now. The Chinese Shades defied the law and seduced the audience. No magistrate could say the girl was naked and no onlooker could believe she was not. The calico showed in profile an enigmatic beauty of Pharonic funeral sculpture, a gloss of scented hair drawn back in its elegant coiffure from the line of the forehead and the nose. Miss Jolly rose, in a new silhouette of straight back and narrow waist, under-emphasizing the breasts, the thighs firm and trim.

A skinny wag in front of Rann shouted, 'Pull up that there winder-blind!'

There was a gust of laughter and then silence again.

The slender body moved through its sharply outlined phases. The warm tan, the delicacy of neck and ears, the cat-like almond eyes, were powerfully suggested. In the elusive two dimensions of her performance, the onlookers swore they glimpsed a third, slim young shoulders curving to a velveteen lustre of coppery skin in the small of her back, the smooth paler ovals of Miss Jolly's bottom narrowing to firm thighs and trim calves.

Rann stood up, stepped from the bench, and went quietly to the side of the auditorium. His back to the brick wall, he sidled to the stage. There was a door behind him, a green baize curtain. He turned the knob, and went through.

Miss Jolly's shadow made a courtly bow, she arched back in an elegant sickle-pose, then knelt with forehead to the floor. The

86

piano thumped a crescendo. Rann went through the doorway, heard the applause, and found the stage. Its gaslight was blinding on the calico but Miss Jolly was naked as the costers imagined. Only when she had reached her changing closet would the men appear to remove the screen.

She turned again, her silhouette still sharp, and saw Jack Rann. A thin cry of fright was lost in uproar from the audience. She covered her mouth and dashed from the stage. A bellow of coster approval greeted his shadow as he crossed the screen in pursuit.

But his penny-dancer was trapped. On this side, the passageway of the warehouse led only to an external door that had been barred against intruders. She turned, her back to the brickwork, resistance failing in the fear that slanted from her eyes. Before she could scream again, he caught her.

'If I was a spirit, my love, I'd be winter-cold. But I come back to you. Jack Rann, alive and warm!'

'Jack?' It was a lilting whisper. 'They said you was to be hung! The Hangman's Child, you're called!'

'I don't feel cold as a spirit, do I, love? And do I look like a Hangman's Child?'

'They let you go?'

The irony made him chuckle, as he had not done since they arrested him. He laughed more loudly, at Warder Lupus, Orator Hawkins, Bully Bragg, Flash Fowler, judge, jury and hangman.

'Oh, yes,' he said at last, 'they let me go, in a way of speaking. They must'a known I'd a job to finish for you, and Pandy, and his Maggie. When I was cold in Newgate, I kept thinking how warm I always was with you.'

But there could be no such warmth that night. No chance of safety until Jack Rann held the keys to Pandy's fortune. So long as they hunted him, he was still the hangman's child.

11

Rann had first surveyed the chambers of Masters' Court with Pandy Quinn eight months before. The lawns and gravel paths of the Inner Temple had been busy with law students, nursemaids and children beneath September trees. Now he came to rob the man with whom he once planned to strike a bargain.

'Barrister' Saward's practice had never been more than an occasional brief for the defence in assault or receiving stolen goods. Even that dwindled among rumours of suspect dealings in probate and bank-bills. But Saward had known the law for thirty years and there was no conviction against him. At sixty, he lived in his Inner Temple chambers, among a coterie of clerks, coachmen and whores.

Pandy Quinn had known more than any policeman about The Barrister. It cost only a few sovereigns to coax the 'vixen' of an introducing house, a procuress of young girls for the old man's bed. From this, Pandy knew that document-forms for bank bills, which only a licensed attorney might buy from a law stationer without questions asked, were Saward's weapons. If a pile of these were now missed from his desk or deed-box, Jem the Penman must suffer quietly rather than draw the attention of the police to his loss.

The beauty of such bills, as Pandy had said, was that they might be written as easily as cheques and traded as safely as bank-notes.

As Rann entered Middle Temple Lane from Fleet Street, Miss Jolly on his arm, St Brides struck midnight. The golden-skinned figure of the Chinese Shades was covered by a high-waisted walking-gown in green silk with a matching bonnet.

'I got to do what I must and get clear,' he had said firmly. 'I ain't got weeks, let alone months.'

They passed the barred windows of the bailiffs' office, where debtors were first confined after arrest. Between a patent office and a wine cellar, frequented by runners and managing clerks, stood a gateway to Masters' Green.

There were lights at a few chambers' windows, but the paved alleys and courtyards were deserted. The quarters from the Temple Church rang clear and cold. At the far end of the path, Rann passed under a dilapidated arch into the cul-de-sac of Masters' Yard. There was no grass at the centre of this small paved quadrangle. Its buildings shut out sun and moon alike. The column of a broken pump stood on one side, a solitary iron post with a bubble gas-lamp on the other.

The outer door to each staircase and its chambers was approached by steps between area railings, open day and night, the names of tenants painted in a column on the stone facing of the entrance. They passed a little barber's shop, a display of dirty-white legal wigs in a paned window. The topmost name on the next doorpost announced 'James Townshend Saward, Esquire, M.A., Barrister-at-Law'. Rann glanced up and saw that the outer room was in darkness.

'Nothing to fear,' he said gently, tightening his hold on her arm. 'I'll do what's needful. He's got far more cause to be frightened of us.'

'So you say!' But she made no attempt to pull back.

'Wait in the shadows of the pump. I'll signal from that middle window, if I have to. It's where his office is. So long as I see you, I'll know I'm safe. No police, no one coming in. If there's police or a sign of trouble, start a row, so's I shall hear. I'll be out 'cross the roof faster than they could run up the stairs.'

'How long?'

Rann shrugged.

'Half an hour, near as a toucher. If you ain't here then, I'll follow home.'

Faltering gaslight glinted in Miss Jolly's dark vigilant eyes as she turned to him.

'And that's the worst of it, Jack? The worst of Pandy's plan?'

He lied easily.

'Much the worst. With a clever girl like you, the rest is good as done.'

He studied the gold of her complexion, the seductive slant of her eyes, the dark hair combed back from the slope of her forehead. Not many in his profession would have brought her, for fear of making her a hostage or from a belief in bad luck. But Rann knew that his last and best robbery was impossible without her. He kissed the odalisque profile, her cheek cooler than the warm night air, and turned away.

Crossing the courtyard like a shadow, he thought of Soapy Samuel and Bully Bragg, who dismissed Miss Jolly as a shop-mouse, a funeral-mute in childhood, sleeping among half-finished coffins, then a slop-shop needle-girl, later an attendant with down-cast eyes waiting meekly on customers at the Conduit Street *Artiste-en-Modes*. It was as well that they should continue to think so.

Beyond the doorway with its painted names, wooden stairs led up four sides of a dingy whitewashed vestibule, a single gas-lamp like a distant star high above the drop. At the top he stopped by a brown unpainted door. The keyhole showed that the outer office was still unlit. A rim of reflected light placed Saward in the inner room. There was an uneven murmur of conversation. Rann tried the door and found it fastened.

A three-slider domestic lock. The panelled oak of the door was shabby but almost impregnable, resplendent with dull brass furnishings. The lock was a few minutes' work. He took a small tin from his pocket and a slender metal rod, thinner than a pencil. The tin held yellowish wax which smelt of cobblers' shops.

Rann smeared the little rod and stood with the gaslight on the keyhole. He used the rod like the barrel of a key, revolved it and withdrew it. Looking at the marks on the wax, he saw the crude three-slider he had predicted.

From a roll of soft leather he took three steel probes, the length of sewing-needles. Frowning at the lock's shoddiness, he tried one in the keyway. A lever of the mechanism yielded and lifted. Holding the first probe in place by the heel of his left palm, he tested the lock with a second. When two were in place, it was easy to lift the third slider and turn the handle.

Rann knew better than to open a creaking door. He took a small tin oil-can, a flat round container with a long spout, moistened the hinges, then wiped them so that no trace should be found. Then he pushed gently. The heavy door opened silently. He entered the darkened room and closed the door behind him.

Voices came more clearly from the inner room, light showing round the door, but he paid them no attention yet. When they took their leave, Saward would show them out by candle or oil-lamp rather than bothering to put up the gas in the office. Rann struck a 'silent' light, a match whose scraping made no sound. The brief flare of it showed two armchairs set before a plain desk, where The Barrister received clients. A small mirror hung on a wall-nail. Several black iron deed-boxes with names painted in white were stacked by the uncurtained and cobwebbed windows. The turkey carpet was worn almost to its canvas backing.

He moved to the broad desk, one foot where the other had been to cut the risk of a creaking board. The desk was scattered with papers tied in red ribbon. Bills, cross-bills, injunctions, pleadings, indictments, petitions. He lit a second match and saw that none bore a recent date. They were the theatrical props of Saward's imposture. Two large office candles stood in tin holders. The air tasted of hot tallow from their snuffing. Tall bookcases were lined by volumes in yellow calf or plum morocco, titles incomprehensible to him, *Impey's Practice*, *Fearn on Remainders*, *Coke's Reports* and *Foster's Crown Cases*. Beyond the desk was a tray with a plate of stale biscuits, a decanter long empty, and a dead hawk-moth.

Through the door, a boule clock chimed with the expensive sound of a hand stirring dainty teaspoons in a drawer. A man said, 'Well, old chums, shall we say a bank of a hundred sovs for My Lord tomorrow night to make the wheel go round easy? And Joanne-on-the Sly taking his mind off his losings by showing him something too pretty for sitting on?'

Rann knew the voice as Saward's, whose own gaming debts had led him to forgery. There was a mutter of laughter from other men, two of them, Rann thought. The game was over and their dupe had left.

'Ain't I right?' Saward continued. 'He's a gentleman, not half! And even when a gentleman thinks he sees huggery-muggery, he looks away rather than have a beastly row. Gentlemen don't care to quarrel at cards, God bless 'em. Not when there's a young lady present.'

There was laughter, a clink of heavy glass against light glass. They were pouring. No one would come out for the next ten minutes.

'The beauty is, Jem,' said a man's voice at a higher pitch, 'I lost my piece of plum to you, and you was so obligin' as to lose it all to Nipper. It takes suspicion off you, and if you nor me don't complain at losin', why should His Lordship? Eh?'

'If he comes back or not, he's left gold and paper tonight,' a third man said. 'I don't risk a sport busting up and not paying his ticks. But Pretty Jo shall get him back, I think.'

A hand fell appreciatively on bare rounded flesh. Rann thought with shock and then amusement that she might be partly or wholly naked in the room with them.

'Smooth as ivory velveteen, if there was such, ain't it, Pretty Sly?' Saward asked wistfully and the sound came again.

Rann struck another light. Desk or deed-boxes? There was nowhere else in the fly-spotted office to keep such documents. He stepped behind the desk. It was a mere table with two drawers under the ledge. Neither was locked. Bank bills would not be left in unlocked drawers. He opened them softly and felt that they were empty. The deed-boxes, then. There were four of them under the window.

To provide for a quick response, he tested the sash-window, eased the catch back and opened it an inch at the bottom. From Masters' Yard, he had mapped the way with his eyes. The ground was thirty feet below with area railings that would spear the body of a falling man. A little to one side of the stone window-ledge, however, was a drainpipe with a gutter ten feet above it. Behind the Georgian balustrade of the roof, outside the attic windows, there would be leads about two feet wide. He would be over the roof and down a pipe on the far side of the building while his pursuers were still thundering down the wooden stairs.

Folk who bought tin deed-boxes imagined them impregnable, each with a lock opened by a unique key. Rann knew that most manufacturers were content with half a dozen different locks for all their boxes. A man with a dozen keys might open half the boxes in England. Safes were for valuables, deed-boxes for privacy.

From the folded leather, he took a little key with adjustable teeth. In his apprenticeship to Pandy Quinn, they had bought second-hand tin boxes for practice – and once or twice an old safe. With a skeleton key, he had worked until he could open a deed-box almost by touch and instinct.

The profile of a deed-box key was a series of steps, the longest being the furthest in. It was a simple matter of screwing on steps of varying lengths on the steel shank until they met all four levers in the lock and moved the bolts aside. He could tell from the lock's resistance on his fingers what the lengths were likely to be. It had seldom taken longer than a minute to open such a box.

He tried the first lock and frowned. The whole box shifted as he twisted the key. It was empty, or nearly so. Slowly he tilted it, listening for the movement of papers or packages. He tilted further and turned it upside down. Nothing. It was empty. So were the other three. The Barrister's tin boxes were merely for show, like the legal documents cluttering the desk.

There was nowhere else in the outer room for the bill-forms. Yet they were somewhere to be found. To believe Jem Saward honest with other men's bank bills was easier than trusting the old Penman at cards.

Some men and women consigned valuables to unpredictable hiding-places, the frame of a picture, the cavity under the treble strings at the back of a piano, within the bottom of a bird-cage. He had known all these. Now he must see the interior of the inner room. Sooner or later, the card-players would leave. Jem and the girl would retire to an attic bedroom. But he must see the inner room first. He lifted the sash-window a little more and listened to their talk.

'I shan't half be in a wax if My Lord don't play tomorrow,' said the man with a boyish voice, 'I signed a debtor's note for fifty sovs two months ago, from a money-changer by Temple Bar. They never give fifty nor nothing like, but it was fifty at three months and must be paid. Seeing I put another fellow's name to it!'

There was a round of good-natured laughter. Rann sat on the inner sill and eased his shoulders into the night, testing the ledge with his weight. Holding the coarse smoke-roughened ashlar either side, he straightened up and with one hand slowly pushed the window down. Tiny fragments of stone broke from the edge of the sill under his feet and, after a long pause, rattled on the area paving far below him.

He paused, then with the drop and the spear-like railings at his back, reached for the drainpipe. Beyond it, was the sill of the inner room.

The pipe was strong and firmly attached. He crooked a leg round it, then one arm, and let it take his weight. A metal collar, where two sections of the pipe were joined, gave a tenuous foothold. Holding tight with his arms, he slid his other foot on to the further sill. Again the stone fragments rattled down, but at last he stood outside the curtained window of the inner room.

The gap between the drawn curtains was wider than he had expected. Blue-grey cigar smoke funnelled into the lamplight. Curtains and window were open a little in the humid night.

A chair scraped and he saw a rubicund man standing up, carrying a fur-cuffed coachman's cape and a fur cap with side-straps that buckled under the chin. The high-pitched voice had come from a man the size of a boy, in dark clothes and white cravat. An ink-stained cuff marked him as a copying-clerk. A young woman leant back on a Regency sofa that had been covered in banded silk. There were handsome upright chairs of Hepplewhite design, a mahogany gloss of sideboard, sofa-table, and an inlaid walnut bureau. The green velvet of the walls was hung with formal silhouettes, minia-tures, and oil portraits in gilt surrounds.

The young woman was holding an ivory hand-screen, as if it were a fan, to keep the heat of the fire from her face. Her dark hair was unpinned. It lay aslant features that showed a certain provoca-tive crudeness, perfectly matched to the clients of an introducing house. Her easy appeal had first lured 'His Lordship' and then distracted him from the game. If Joanne-on-the-Sly still wore her waist-length corset, it was only because a lady's maid would have been needed to dress her again. Corset and stockings were all that covered a pale and rather meagre figure. Rann knew he had seen her before, a bunter from the French House off Drury Lane, where Bragg was part-owner. It did not surprise him that Bragg should hire her to an amenable lawyer like Jem Saward.

She yawned and spoke to someone who now moved into Rann's view, his voice warmed by food and drink. Saward was tall and sunken-cheeked, with a stoop, his dark hair long and lank. In black coat and white tie, he looked like a consumptive butler drinking himself to death on his master's port. Two gold watch-seals shone on his shirt-front and a large seal-ring gleamed on his little finger. Rann doubted that the ornaments to Saward's evening dress had been paid for. Nor was he surprised that the companions for an evening with His Lordship should have been the old barrister's coachman, copying-clerk, and whore.

Sensing that their master was now encumbered by their presence, the coachman and the clerk left. Saward removed his eyeglasses rimmed with gold and folded them in a red leather case. He looked at the disorder of the room. Then the old penman turned the gas down to a glimmer and took the girl by the hand. Without speaking, he twirled her up like a dancer while the sleek dark hair spilt about her head. He followed her appreciatively up the attic stairs, leaving the gas-lamp low, his eyes watching her movements with calm appraisal.

Rann heard the boards and springs as they entered the attic room and stretched upon the bed. He raised the window of the room and slid inside. He guessed the hiding-place. Deed-boxes and desks were the first place a search-party might think of, but even Scotland Yard would hesitate to drive an axe through the delicate furniture of Inner Temple chambers.

The gas bubbled softly as he turned it higher. Despite the gap in the curtains, the air was thick and hot. Two packs of cards lay scattered on the baize of a gaming-table, its walnut surround polished to a gloss of liquid honey. There was a litter of empty glasses and piled cigar bowls, scraps of paper on which reckonings had been made, a handful of IOUs. On a table to one side were the remains of cold goose-liver pie and plum pudding, one empty bottle of hock, another almost finished in an ice-bucket, and a flask of seltzer beside it.

He crossed to the bureau, an elegant Chippendale design. Drawers and upper flap were unlocked. That was to be expected. The invitation of an unlocked bureau suggested that no one need use violence to search such an inconsequential piece. Rann tapped and felt, sliding a hand under the ledges of the drawer-openings, trailing his fingers along graceful beading, in search of secrets.

A bureau was for love-letters and indiscretions, not to defeat a professional cracksman. A thief with an eye soon measured the places in the structure which no other drawer or cubby-hole occupied. Then it was only a matter of tapping the wood to find a tell-tale hollow sound. A common housebreaker would carve his way with a chisel. Rann preferred the skill of searching for a hidden spring.

His fingertips struck a hollowness beneath the polished surface. He had the flap of the bureau down on its supports and was facing the drawers and pigeon-holes inside. Between two sets of drawers there was an inlaid panel, four inches across and about eight inches tall. He tapped it and heard the hollowness once more.

There was no sign of a catch, no place where a catch might be concealed. He opened the drawers on either side of the panel, drew them from their recesses and searched in the wooden frame. He found a thin strip of springy metal and thumbed it back. Abruptly, the entire section of the drawers and the panel came free so that he drew it out like an open box, four inches by eight and a foot deep.

Under it, in the wood that formed the flat surface of the bureau, was a box-like cavity that might have held a jewel-case or a couple of quarto volumes. But he touched paper whose first sheet was thin and crisp and blue. He drew out the topmost bundle of oblong forms for bills of exchange, printed in the usual copperplate, blanks for the names of parties and the sum of money, the date and stamp of endorsement. But they were of no more use than unsigned IOUs.

He searched under the blank exchange forms and found a printed bank-bill the size of a large currency note. It was issued by the Bank of Baltimore, on cream paper with a sepia design of a mythological figure by a castle wall. The sum and payee had been filled in. But the date for payment had passed. Why had it not been cashed? Rann examined the script in which it had been completed and guessed that this was the work of an apprentice forger with a blank bill. He put it back and knew that he had yet to find Pandy's treasure.

There was pink bank-paper, which a French attorney might buy from a law stationer. The luckless apprentice-forger had written on it a name that all the world recognized too well. 'N.N. Rothschild and Sons, Paris'. None of this was Pandy's scheme. Rann might as well have offered the bank his death warrant.

Underneath these papers was a third package, larger than the other two. His heart quickening with hope, he examined the brown paper in which it had been wrapped. The package had been through the post, the stamps black with cancelling ink. It bore the address of Waterlows Printers. The blood beat in his temples with triumph as he stared at its contents.

Oblivious to the movements of passion above him, he held the printed bills in his hands. There were fifty or sixty forms, none filled in, headed by printed names: The London and Westminster Bank; Baring Brothers; Union Bank; Drummonds, Pall Mall; Brune & Co, Marseille; Suse and Sibbeth; Schroeder & Co; Mitchell, Yeames & Co; Brown, Shipley & Co; The International Bank of Hamburg and London; The Russian Bank of Foreign Trade; The Bank of Montreal . . . .

Pandy Quinn had heard how the ghostly Jem the Penman had intercepted 'samples' returned from the banks to the printers after approval for final casting off. Somewhere there had been bribery of a clerk to conceal an exchange. In the printer's furnace, the bills were spared and a package of political pamphlets or religious tracts went to the fire. Some knew the story but had no idea that Saward might be Jem the Penman. Others guessed the Penman's identity but knew nothing of the story. Pandy Quinn had heard and believed both.

Every bill was good for three months. Rann's eyes followed the printed wording: *Pay value received without further advice to the account* . . . . Without further notice might give a thief three months to get clear. He looked back at the Bank of Baltimore: *Pay value received and charge to the account of* . . . . The holder of the account need know nothing until the bill had been traded like a banknote for three months more and came to be redeemed. When a printed bill; stamped and completed, was presented to a bank, the bank could no more refuse the money to the holder than it could refuse twenty shillings silver for a golden sovereign.

Of course, the banks would smell a forgery as soon as it was passed over the counter. Even Saward had been unable yet to make use of these blanks because the old penman had no genuine bill with names, dates and endorsements to copy. The least fault of penmanship, the slightest error in placing the bank's acceptance stamp, the smallest mistake in a serial number, any failure to match serial number, names, previous endorsements, sums paid, would lead to disaster.

But as he talked about the impossibility of passing off such a forgery, Pandy had chuckled like a happy child.

'They know it can't be done, Jacko. And that's the very reason that it will be.'

Impossibility was the centrepiece of his plan. With an eye for a lock and the bundle of blank bills that Saward had stolen from the printer, Pandy swore that a man might pull off a robbery whose proceeds would buy the crown and sceptre.

Rann looked about him, picked up a discarded newspaper, wrapped it in the brown paper and returned it to the bottom of the secret drawer. On top of it, he laid the other two packages. It was enough to deceive casual inspection.

Listening again, he heard the bed shifting, Saward gasping and the girl mumbling, as though he might be turning Pretty Jo. Rann pressed the little drawers and panels into place, closed the flap, and turned from the bureau. In the outer room, he slid the window-catch across, leaving it as Saward had last seen it. Taking the key to the heavy door from its hook, he let himself out on to the landing and went down the wooden stairs. But first he drew the little steel picks from the roll of soft leather and eased the three-slider lock until it snapped shut behind him. When Saward discovered his loss, he would first suspect Bragg's cronies.

His penny-dancer stood in shadow by the broken pump. Rann gazed at the piled dark hair, the profile and the eyes that would have graced a Nefertiti, the delicate ears and neck. His memory held the images of a slim straight back, and trim thighs, hips coppery pale by contrast with her warm brown waist. With a pang of longing for her, he swore to himself that, in comparison, even the treasure of fifty crisp sheets of bank paper was dust and ashes.

12

Above the plumes of horse-chestnuts and lime trees, the sky over Battersea was smoke-grey with a threat of summer thunder. A metallic smell of rain hung in the air of Cremorne's riverside pleasure garden. Its Oriental Circus had given way to an encampment of fairground booths, the promise of an afternoon's entertainment. Children too young to assist, slept on straw under the shade of the carts. Donkeys and thin horses grazed hungrily upon the turf.

Samuel, walking beside Jack Rann, wore the only professional costume that he had taken in his flight from Bragg, a well-tailored suit of clerical black, white tie and silk hat. In this he had worked the front-doors of Chelsea and Kensington as The Reverend Amos Prout, Secretary to the Archbishop of York's Overseas Mission. The mention of an Archbishop silenced all questions, and York was far enough from London to make enquiries difficult. Samuel's pathetic sincerity and copies of printed testimonials from converted heathen had proved, as he said, 'a choker' for his middle-class victims. He glanced at Jack Rann.

'Why here? I was safe where I was.'

'Safer here,' Rann said coolly. 'They'll come down that sewer one day. Where you won't find Bragg nor police is a kiddies show. We got to talk about Pandy.'

They walked slowly past brightly streamered tents and booths. On the grassy spaces, men in silken vests and plumed hats appeared as jugglers or acrobats. A shrill uncertain note flared from the trumpet of the Punch and Judy Show.

'Pandy was in a house last summer,' Rann said quietly, 'Lord Mancart in Lowndes Square. A roof job as usual. In through the attic window and doing the top floors while them and their servants was at dinner below. That's when it all began.'

Samuel turned a smooth elegant profile for the luxury of feeling the sun upon it.

'Take much, did he?'

'An impression.'

'Took what?'

Nursemaids in green and blue silks with feathered bonnets were hanging on the arms of impoverished swells. It was the furthest place in London from the men who wanted to take him back to Newgate and hang him.

'Pandy did a safe in a wall, Sam. A little toy. Behind a picture where anyone'd look. He was going to take an item or two. Then he saw a key lying there.'

'What use is a key, when the safe's open?'

'Walk up!' bawled a showman, sharp enough to make Samuel jump. 'See The Dominion of Fancy, or Punch's Opera. Now, gents, look up your 'aypence! Who's for a farden or a 'aypenny?'

Rann turned away.

'This key had a label, Sam. Property of safe deposit vaults. Lord Mancart's key to his private deposit. In those vaults, they have a whole wall of safe deposits a man can hire.'

Samuel gave a short laugh.

'Behind a door thicker than the hull of a battleship. Supposing, Jack, you could get that far in the first place.'

'Just listen, Sammy,' said Rann patiently. 'Pandy might have took a trinket or two, but he left them. He made an impression of the key in a tin of wax he always had in his pocket, when he went on business. No one knew he'd ever been there. Think what a man might do, if he had keys to all the deposits in a set of vaults!'

'Get any more keys, did he?'

'He took it slow, Sammy. Opposite the vaults is premises where Mag Fashion found a corner, her also giving a ride to the owner from time to time. From there, Pandy could see who came and went at the vaults. Me and him followed forty or fifty of them last summer. We got it down to about fifteen or sixteen. Who they were and where they lived.'

Samuel nodded with a grudging smile. He saw it now.

'And that's why you wanted those houses in Portman Square visited and mapped out?'

'More than those, Sammy. You gave us the way into the houses, where we couldn't get it otherwise. But Pandy pulled a stroke or two, cool as iced lemon. One we couldn't break. Big one in Belgrave Square, though it was empty for the summer except for the butler and housekeeper. House of the Honourable Fitzroy, who must know half the ladies' bosoms and backsides in Westminster.'

He chuckled at the memory of it.

'Mag Fashion drives up ladylike with me as servant. I ring the bell and ask the butler to come and have an urgent word with her, her having a tale of her sister of fourteen pregnant by the Honourable Fitzroy. The butler goes out fast to stop a shindy in the square. Sticks his head in the cab to hear what she says. In that time, Pandy was up the steps, in the door, and up the stairs. He skates through them empty rooms like a ghost on ice, opens a bureau and lets himself out over a back window sill twenty minutes later with no more fuss than a shadow.'

'With another impression?'

Rann shook his head.

'No, Sammy. We never found all fifteen or sixteen keys. Nothing like. Though with houses being empty for the summer, we once spent half the night looking in one of 'em. But five impressions we got and five duplicate beauties Pandy made.'

A broad-shouldered, bearded man in a sailor-suit, one leg replaced by a wooden furniture stump, stepped in their path.

'Happy Family Exhibitor!' he said hopefully. 'See an assemblage of animals of diverse habits living friendly in one cage. Birds o' prey, with pigeons, starlings, cats, dogs, rats, and mice! Thirty-six hours at Cambridge without food – and not a animal ate by another . . . .'

Samuel looked at the gently moving chestnut trees.

'So even if you got into the vaults, there's only five deposits you could open. You might come up with nothing but a handful of shine-rag.'

Rann looked over his shoulder, then turned to his companion.

'Sammy, Pandy swore that two of them keys were like twins. If anyone knew the truth of it, he would, having been a locksmith's boy. Even Pandy never saw how big this could be until he twigged that.'

'Meaning?'

'We reckoned they must have a hundred or two safe deposits with the same make of key. These are little keys, Sammy. There ain't no way you can vary a little key like that two hundred ways. Consequentially, two hundred locks might only have twenty or thirty different patterns of keys. Each key of those five might open half a dozen deposits. See?'

'No,' said Samuel scornfully, 'they wouldn't have that.'

'They must, Sam. After all, a man that hires a key won't know which of the other deposits it fits, even if he knows it fits any. And when he goes to his deposit, there's always a bank supervisor goes with him to open the main steel door and watch from a distance. There's no chance he could get near any but his own.'

Beyond the tight-rope dancers and the stilt-vaulters stood the largest canvas enclosure with its banner and a flag flying the Stars and Stripes. 'Mrs Jarley's Waxworks'. The little band outside, which had been playing 'All Among the Barley', struck up an American polka to signal the start of the show.

'You still got copies of the five keys?'

'Tomnoddy has, Sam. He never asked what they were but he kept them all the time I was away. That's why he gets his share.'

'And you say you could open a dozen or two of them deposits?'

'Yes, Sammy. Bragg and his mob got wind of something like a house done but nothing stolen. That's why Pandy was taken. And that's why, even when they was hurting him, he'd never have told them the truth. It's what all this is about.'

'Gold and sparklers,' Samuel said, scepticism softening in hopeful laughter.

Rann shook his head.

'No, Sammy. Gold and sparklers has to be fenced. I daren't do it. The minute I try, I'll have Bragg or the law on me. I don't want jewels nor gold, Sam. They're no good to me now.'

Samuel stared at the horse-chestnuts again, perplexed.

'Then what's in it, Jack?'

'A fortune,' Rann said. 'We'll talk about it in here. This place is safer than anywhere you've been for months past.'

He dropped two sixpences into the hand of the money-taker by the canvas flap of Mrs Jarley's Waxworks and led the way inside.

13

The benches on the grass were half filled, the red curtains at the far end just opening. Mrs Jarley, in black dress and bonnet, commanded a liveried attendant to wind the mechanism. A waxwork monster, the Feejee Mermaid, appeared as a girl with a glossy and impassive face, concealed to the waist by long fair hair, a tail of green cambric from the waist down. The life-sized creature, looking-glass in hand, began to comb her hair in a series of awkward jerks. A piano sounded wave-like chords, as Rann led Samuel to the unoccupied rear bench.

'Right, Sam,' he said gently, 'you know more about faking than anyone, seeing you served time for it. Take these and tell me what they are. Brought your glass?'

Samuel nodded.

'Two bank-bills here, thanks to young missy's penning. Which is a ringer?'

Samuel took the oblongs of sky-blue bank-paper, crisp and thin. He held them under a horn-framed map-reading glass.

Each appeared identical. Lines of printed copperplate script promised to pay the bearer a stated sum on presentation to the issuing bank, Messrs B.W. Blydenstein, Great St Helens, City of London, up to three months from the date of issue. The sum to be paid had been lately filled in, its figuring black and thick, like the first word of a lease on an indenture. Samuel turned the bill over. It was blank on the back, except where two holders had endorsed it as it passed from hand to hand. The endorsements were in red, signatures in blue, next to the bank's acceptance stamp.

Samuel examined each bill, white hair slicked back from his smooth rodent face, an air of genial plausibility restored.

'One's fake, seeing's both got the same serial number written in. Perhaps both. You might as well ask your little wriggler to copy your death-warrant, Jack Rann.'

He offered the paper back but Rann made no attempt to take it.

'How's that, then, Sam?'

Samuel looked at him, the map-reading glass held aside.

'What I can see in two minutes, banks would see in two seconds. You wouldn't get past the greenest counting-house clerk with these bits of paper.'

'They're real bills, ain't they?'

'Until they was interfered with.' Samuel's voice dropped as he scanned the blue paper again through his glass. 'Someone's took the original ink off. Written in new names and figures.'

'Show me,' Rann said.

Samuel held each sheet to his nostrils and breathed deeply.

'Chlorine,' he said sadly. 'Smelling bad paper ain't a figure of speech, Jack. Every faker thinks a quill-pen full of chlorine will take off ink, so that bank paper can be written over. It'll take off ink, but not without a smell that lasts six months.'

'Only supposing you put it to your nose,' Rann said.

'They smell it before it crosses the counter. And once they see your Miss Jolly's writing, they'd sniff good and strong. What's the ink that was on here first?'

'No notion, Sam. What might it be?'

'Office ink made with gallnut and iron, as a rule, if not with logwood. Chlorine's the only thing that takes off both.'

He studied the paper again and shook his head.

'You ain't used to blue paper, Jack. There's a reason why banks prefer it to white. Whatever takes ink off blue paper decomposes the dye. Where the writing was on blue, once you take it off, it leaves the paper yellow. When you come to overwrite, seeing you want different names or figures, you leave what they call yellow-spot round the edges of the new script. A yellow rim round the new writing. You mayn't see it but a bank clerk can twig it in a second.'

'What about the beauty of the penning?' Rann asked.

Samuel looked up again from the paper.

'Copying script is a child's game, Jack. You think because your young piece has a neat hand to copy, your bills will pass? There's hundreds in the penal colonies for the rest of their lives thought just the same as you. Except the rest of your life wouldn't be that long, would it, Handsome Rann?'

'Anything else amiss with that paper, Sam?'

Samuel gave a sigh, looking through the glass once more.

'How much more d'you want? Slum goods like this will hang you, Jack. All the care in the world won't alter the truth that chlorine turns blue paper yellow and smells a mile off. Apart from the printing that was on the bill to begin with, there's nothing genuine here but the bank's acceptance stamp.'

Rann relaxed and said very quietly, 'The stamp's fake, Sam. It wasn't the writing I wanted to hear about. Pandy knew about chlorine and yellow spot. The bills I use will be blank to start with. The stamp is what I had to be sure of. If that passes, the job's good as done.'

Samuel looked up, the scorn swept from his face.

'Now there's a thing,' he said. 'How's that bank stamp done?'

'Slate,' Rann said. 'Thin slate. We worked on it before I was fitted for killing Pandy. Young Jolly started with a pair o' school compasses, just to draw the circle of the stamp exact, and a steel sewing-needle fitted like lead into a pencil. We wet the ink impression of the bank stamp on a cancelled bill. With that we made an exact print on a hard dry potato cut in two. We strengthened that

108

print and reversed it, then stamped it in white on slate. The compasses scratched the circle of the design. The rest she picked out with the steel needle.'

Samuel looked at the stamp, then frowned at Cleopatra on the stage, touching the asp to her breast, lifting a pearl to her mouth until the clockwork ran down.

'Simple idea,' Rann said, 'not simple to do. Took her a month and more before there was a stamp fit to use. Even then, slate splits after a dozen pressings. Still, before Pandy was coopered, we'd got a boxful – and we got 'em still. You think that stamp's genuine, Sammy? Then I got genuine acceptance stamps for half the banks in London and more than they'd care to know about in Paris and Hamburg. That's how it started.'

'And you're the putter-up?' Samuel asked thoughtfully. 'A job that size?'

Rann scowled. 'Everyone who gets a sniff wants to know who's the putter-up! Orator Hawkins wants to know, because Mr Bragg wants to know, because Flash Charley Fowler wants to know. All looking for a king of the Swell Mob. But I'm the putter-up, Sam. Me and Pandy and our girls worked on this job half a year. We got it sweet as honey and smooth as butter. Then a whisper comes to Bragg, so Bragg and Strap and Catskin come asking Pandy. And Pandy's dead, but they're no wiser.'

'Stamp or no stamp, it can't be done,' Samuel said firmly. 'Even with new forms, you won't know what numbers to put on 'em. And you won't have the right signatures – not knowing the names of the holders that have traded 'em on.'

'I'll know, Sammy. And if they're genuine, a bank can't no more refuse you fifty pounds on a fifty-pound bill of exchange than it can refuse you twenty silver shillings for a gold sovereign. Better still, there's men that hold what they call bank post-bills for payment. They're only good for two weeks, but payable to anyone, same as money once they're signed.'

'They know a dud.'

'The banks won't see a dud,' Rann said softly and Samuel looked sharply away at the stage vampire, which pointed alternately to the moon and to its hungry mouth. 'Ask yourself, Sammy. A man signs over a bill of exchange to you. Or you buy a bill from the bank to cash for whatever the sum endorsed, or sell it on. You'd look at it close through a reading-glass?'

'Not if it was a bank, perhaps,' Samuel said, 'otherwise, yes. I'm too long in the game to be a duffer.'

'Once you'd looked and seen it right, you'd lock it in a safe or a deed-box, p'raps?'

Samuel nodded.

'And what then?'

Samuel fingered his white clerical tie, still doubting the point of the question.

'Leave it till it was cashed.' He shifted, as if something monstrous was forming in his mind. 'What else should I do?'

'Suppose it was a thousand pounds. Two thousand guineas. Where'd you keep it then?'

Samuel waved aside the mere suggestion.

'All right, then. Deposit. Bank or vault. A bill that big.'

Rann nodded again.

'And you wouldn't keep going to look at it?'

''Course I bloody wouldn't,' Samuel replied in a whisper. 'Not till I wanted cash. Why should I?'

'And seeing as you found it genuine when you bought it, you wouldn't keep smelling it and looking through a glass to see if the paper had gone yellow. You'd have done that at the start, wouldn't you?'

'You got the Devil's own nerve, Jack Rann!' Samuel said suddenly, with a laugh of pure delight.

'Exactly, Sammy. When this job is done, the bills I send to the bank for cashing will be genuine as the roast beef of old England. What's lying in vaults and deed-boxes will be the copies I leave there. They're the ones that'll have to explain to the banks.'

Samuel chuckled at the neatness of it. Rann lowered his voice.

'There's some can copy a hand, like Miss Jolly, or fake a bill. When they've done it, yellow spot or the smell of chlorine trips them. But there's not a bank or crib in London I can't open, with the hangman behind me. And if genuine bills are taken and copies left, it gives a new look to the whole business. Don't it? I got more than fifty blank bills, that was Saward's. Those I'll leave behind, with Jolly's hand on 'em, and come out with others taken in their place. Every one would pass the Scrutiny Committee of the Bank of England, just because they're genuine.'

Samuel looked at him, wanting to believe. Rann pressed on.

'True as sterling silver or twenty-four carat gold. As many as possible payable to bearer and can't be refused cash when presented. That's what me and Pandy meant to have. Enough to keep a man for life. And that's what I must have now.'

Samuel glanced at the waxwork Robin Hood and then away again.

'Trouble is, Jack, the minute you've stole those bills, someone might take one of your fakes to change it. But you won't know. Every time you try to change a bill, you might be second in the race. You come in second, there's an end of you.'

Rann smiled.

'I'm not going near a bank, Sammy.'

'And you think I am?'

'Sam, neither of us goes near a bank once this is over. And only you before the job's done. And you won't ask the bank for money, so there's no crime. At the first bank, you're old Canon Wilberforce that's taking a share in a joint-stock company. At the second, you're a silver-haired bishop from New Zealand that's dad of Miss Mag Fashion and must raise the wind for a marriage settlement. Third, you're attorney and guardian to rich Orphan Jolly and must consolidate funds in a wardship suit. That's all. In each case you arrange to send bills to be cashed into Bank of England bonds, that can be taken elsewhere and changed for coin. And you're never seen again. Messengers take them to the bank for you. Easy as buying a pound of cheese.'

'What when it's the same bill a second time and there's a stink?'

'Pandy and me thought of that. If there's a stink, you won't be there to smell it, nor shall I. Any case, bills run three months and we'll have those with longest to go. The duds'll be traded on between holders for weeks or months, not cashed.'

Samuel's eyes were on the waxwork figures, as if something else was worrying him.

'How'll you live till this comes off, Jack?'

'The girl's room. Off Haymarket. Bragg thinks she's lodging in Shoreditch with Mag Fashion in a two-pair back. On'y he don't know quite where!'

Samuel smiled. Then he asked, 'Exactly where's the vault, Jack?' Rann shook his head.

'The fewer that know, Sammy, the fewer can tell.'

'If I don't know what I'm in for, Jack, I'm out of this.'

Rann sighed and looked round carefully at the other benches.

'In Cornhill, Sam.'

It took a moment for Samuel to respond. 'Cornhill? Walker's Vaults, opposite Trent's Mourning?'

'That's it,' said Rann quietly.

'You seen the steel vault-door you'll have to bust before you set eyes on the safe deposits? You seen the building you'll have to get into before you even see that steel door?'

'I seen all that, Sam. A dozen times. And if I ain't the man to get in, how am I sitting here, not lying in a shroud six feet down in quicklime by Newgate wall?'

But Samuel shifted with dismay on the wooden bench.

'Anyone walking down Cornhill can see that vault door day and night, Jack. Two spy-holes through the steel shutters and gas always burning. Policeman looks in every twenty minutes. It's why Walkers say they're safer than the Bank of England.'

'They do, Sammy. They do say that.'

'You'd be on show every second, Jack. Vault door with mirrors all round to show anyone near it. You'd need hours at a lock like that. Even you can't make yourself invisible.'

'Not all the time, Sammy. But I think I could be invisible if I had to be. For a little while. Same as no one saw me leave them death-wards. Mag Fashion got word from a jack that's stiff for her. They still don't know how I got out. Think Lupus or Jessup forgot to lock the cell door. Reckon I got out through the chapel gallery, disguised as a woman with clothes that Hawkins or Sue Berry left hid there on a Sunday.'

'Cornhill Vaults could hang you yet,' said Samuel glumly. 'First off, you'll have to crack them twice. Until you do it first, you won't have genuine bank-bills for your little shop-mouse to copy the details on your blanks. You'd have to wait for her to do the penning. Then you must take the copies back and leave them. It's not on, Jack. You might crack a crib, but even you can't do Walker's Vaults twice before it's noticed. No one could. This ain't a china pig, it's iron and steel. They'd tumble to it first time. If you have to snoop for a second chance, you'll be seen, took back to Newgate and stretched before you know it.'

Rann whispered to him, 'I'm going in once, Sam. They'll be copied in there. In the vault. No other way.'

Samuel shook his head.

'Not you, Jack Rann. You're not a faker! Hardly sign your own name.'

'No, Sam, but Jolly is. Me and Pandy decided it was the only way. When I crack that vault, she's coming with me.'

Samuel stared at the mechanical waxworks, as if trying to calculate whether this made the scheme better or worse.

'And as for a shop-mouse,' Rann continued bitterly, 'when she was a child in the slop-trade, she must get every stitch and seam neat and exact. Starved and whipped when not so. But them that treated her so cruel gave her the best training for nimble fingers to fake a bill or a name. See it on those papers. Neat and true as fancy lace.'

Soapy Samuel fingered his clergyman's tie again and gestured at the stage with his other hand. He said in a whisper, 'Suffering God, Jack! They're bloody real, not waxworks. Seen the eyes blink. Seen 'em breathe! They're watching us!'

'What if they are?' said Rann irritably. 'They come from America. They got no cause to be interested in us.'

Samuel got to his feet.

'I don't care. I ain't going to be watched. I'm off.'

'They'll remember you all the better running off with a face like a poisoned cat!'

As Samuel came to the end of the bench, his way was blocked by a well-dressed woman, two curly-headed girls clutching at her skirts. She had just come in and was putting her purse away. Samuel inclined his head and raised his hat, his face a smiling moon. The woman smiled back. Samuel ruffled the curly heads. Rann heard the unctuous clerical tone. 'Little angels of the Lord . . . . So pretty ... so blessed . . . . Would that all little children, all little heavenly lambs might be . . . .' He had found a card in his notecase and was pressing it into her hand.

Rann looked away, exasperated, until Samuel and the woman parted. Then he got up and walked outside. The clerical impostor was staring thirstily into his palm.

'Two sovs and a chinker,' he said, more cheerfully than he had said anything that afternoon. 'But the best of it is, Jack, she feels happier this minute than we shall ever know. Warm inside and good as gold. She don't miss a quid or two. Folks like her never give what they'd really miss. So where's the harm in all that, Handsome Rann? Eh?'

THREE

PLAIN DUTIES

14

'God knows,' Verity said glumly, 'I couldn't a-made a worse mess. I may choke to say it, Mr Stringfellow, but Mr Croaker give me what I deserved. And that brute Fowler, I can't help seeing he's right. About the smuggling at least. That's what riles me most. I must've wiped out months of work. How could I be so stoopid?'

Julius Stringfellow, cabman of Sovereign Street, Paddington Green, shook his head, picking at a gap in his teeth with his forefinger. The suction applied to a scrap of ham and egg seemed a comment on his son-in-law's imprudence.

'Your trouble, me old sojer, is taking no account of superior numbers. Superior numbers has all the time in the world to lay a snare. And that's what they did. Good and proper.'

Stringfellow was dressed in an old green coat, brown breeches, and billicock hat. As usual after supper, he sat among the remains of broiled bones, ham, and eggs at the kitchen table, his glass of porter half-finished. He was poking at the crevices of a harness brass with a well-used handkerchief. An odour of hot straw and horse-hide ebbed and flowed about the latch of the kitchen door.

Verity looked up from the toecap of a new boot, whose pimples he was smoothing with a hot iron, so that it might be polished to the brilliance of black glass.

'Bragg and his lot watched me all that night. Fowler too. Watched until they saw a chance with that young person. If old

Tollis, the lighterman, hadn't been on his barge and sung in tune, I'd be in Horsemonger Lane Gaol now for attempted ravishing of Lambeth Sue, let alone grievous bodily on two of Bragg's prizemen.'

Stringfellow got to his feet, supported on one side by the wooden leg which had served him since the loss of his own at the siege of Bhurtpore almost thirty years earlier. Verity frowned, the tip of the iron close to the stitching. To touch the cobbler's thread would burn it through and cause the entire toecap to fall off.

'Well, you ain't in Horsemonger Lane Lock-Up,' said Stringfellow bracingly. 'Reduced to plain duties you may be, but you got no cause to blub until you're hurt worse than this. A man's been with the Rifle Brigade at Inkerman and the Redan knows better – or should do. Never call retreat – ain't that what they say?'

'Yes,' said Verity sadly, 'I 'spect they do.'

The old cabman lifted the door latch.

'On warm nights like this,' said Verity quietly, 'it wouldn't come amiss if you was to stand the old horse a bit further off.'

The atmosphere in the mews cottage in Sovereign Street was depressed. Stringfellow ambled off to attend to Lightning, the elderly cab-horse with its bony flanks and patient manner. He could be heard whistling softly to it as he plied the sponge and bucket.

Verity picked up the second boot and studied it. He put it down as the latch at the bottom of the staircase clinked and the cottage door opened. Bella Verity, daughter of Cabman Stringfellow, slipped past her husband, sat down in the low nursing-chair and picked up her small blue work-basket. Despite her plumpness and fair curls, she seemed a diminutive partner, her prettiness illuminated by her habit of smiling to herself while she worked, as if at some secret happiness.

'Care killed a cat, Mr Verity,' she said presently.

'So it might, Mrs Verity,' – he studied the next toe-cap again – 'but Mr Inspector Croaker is more likely to be the death o' me!'

She looked up at him, her face drawn in a parody of anxiety.

'But it don't matter, Mr Verity! Even if you got to spend the rest o' your life on sentry-go outside the houses of quality, keeping nuisance away. Think what we got! We got little Billy and Vicky; we got food on the table; clothes to our backs. There's poor souls'd think us rich! You got Paddington Chapel on Sundays. They think the world of you down there.'

'Wait till this gets out,' he said bleakly. 'No one's going to think the world of me then.'

'But I will,' she said quietly, 'and I know Pa will. I will, Mr Verity, always and always.'

She came behind his chair and put her arms round him.

'Never say die,' she said gently. 'If Mr Fowler done wrong and Mr Bragg's a brute, they'll answer for it soon enough.'

'I hope so, Mrs Verity – Bella.'

'You was brought up to know it's true!' she said reprovingly. 'You was taught it every Sunday.'

Verity sighed and patted the hand that lay on his lapel. He nodded.

'And I mean to go on. I'll find them houses where Soapy Samuel went. I'll see what happened there. Mr Croaker can't stop me doing that. I'll see about that knife Flash Fowler says he found down Saffron Hill. But I'll be doing it alone.'

'No you won't!' she said with another little flare of anger. "Course you won't! Don't you think you will! There's people out there'd be proud of you, if they knew. Thousands of 'em. And they'd help you, if they could. And they will. Not nasty Mr Inspector Croaker but people that's brave and true. You'll see.'

Verity stared at the door to the stable, where Stringfellow was whistling his unmelodious tune to the horse. He wondered if Bella might be right. Later they lay in the ancient bed to which Julius Stringfellow had brought his bride, the late Mrs Stringfellow of a cholera epidemic, quarter of a century before. The London sky was starlit beyond the window with its curtains drawn back in the summer warmth. At the foot of the bed, two cradles were occupied by Billy and Vicky, each showing the round red face and black hair of Verity himself.

Above them, in the attic, he heard Stringfellow's fruity chuckle and a few muttered words. He sat up in bed.

'Your old father got someone up there with him!'

'No,' said Bella innocently, 'I asked about that. Pa says he seems to have took to talk in his sleep of a night. That's all.'

The chuckle was repeated and the attic bedsprings shifted. Before Verity could ask the next question, Bella's foot touched his and she turned towards him.

'Oh, William Clarence Verity,' she said happily, 'even if we hadn't food on the table, nor clothes to our backs, I'd still be no end proud of you . . . .'

15

Verity stood at ease by the red oval of an iron pillar-box, the morning sunlight still cool. In tall hat, frock coat and dark trousers, he was dressed for duty. The first point on his beat was outside a cream-painted portico and steps leading to the double-door of Lord Tregarva's town-house in Portman Square.

A morning stillness in the pale sky cast its silence over the cypress and beech trees of the central lawn. Against dark London brick, Lord Tregarva's area railings and his iron-canopied veranda lined by urns of gilly-flowers shone with a gloss of fresh black paint. Oblong bas-reliefs on blank upper walls, cream swags on a ground of pale Wedgwood blue, marked Portman Square. Its elegant terraces seemed as secure from criminal conspiracies as anywhere in England. Verity's fault was to think otherwise. If Baptist Babb read Orator Hawkins' lips correctly, Lord Tregarva's house and three of the five others visited by Soapy Samuel last summer were near neighbours.

A clock towards Marylebone began to strike ten, entitling the officer on duty to stretch his legs. He drew the regulation tin watch from his fob-pocket, checked it, and paced slowly along the balconied houses. Crossing old Tyburn Road, he studied the façades of Park Street. Lady Lisle's villa stood apart from the others. He frowned and wondered how that entry had been planned. The chestnut trees of Park Lane ahead of him, he passed the fine gilt-tipped railings of Sir Isaac Thorne's mansion in Upper Brook Street. Once again, it stood detached from its neighbours. Portman Square was Rann's preferred territory with its stretches of connected roofs.

He turned and walked back. At the first corner of Portman Square, several passers-by were looking in horror at a pathetic human sight. A blubberish young man of twenty-five or thirty, hatless and dishevelled, sat against a house wall. A tin bowl with a few coppers lay before him. His sleeves were pulled up, trousers hoisted above his knees. The exposed limbs were ulcerated, festering to a point where amputation of all four seemed the kindest remedy. Pus ran down his forearms and shins. The little group of benefactors stared with revulsion and pity. His voice was a thin, yet penetrating wail.

'Good and kind Christians! Help a poor sailor scalded in the engine-room of HMS *Ulysses* on the bursting of a boiler. Help a poor unfortunate what served his country ten years but has no pillow at night save the 'ard stones of the pavey! A poor Jack Tar of the China War what hasn't a crumb in his mouth the last four days. Help a fellow being, reduced to eat the very scraps of bread thrown in the street to feed the sparrows . . . .'

From time to time he flexed a pus-laden limb, causing the women to draw back their skirts, the men to avert their gaze. Verity stepped softly to the front of the little group. He went up to the injured man and aimed a sharp kick, intended as a sideways blow to the seat of the ragged trousers.

'Get up, Infant!' he said sternly. 'Get up, you miserable, idle, thieving little tyke!'

There was a gasp from the group of witnesses. An elderly woman said reprovingly, 'My good man!'

Verity turned to them. ''s all right,' he said confidently, 'there's nothing wrong with him. He's Infant. Otherwise known as The Scaldrum Dodge.' He kicked the cripple with a little more energy.

'Get up, you worthless young cadger!'

'Infant' put his hands on the wall behind him and appeared to pull himself up with great difficulty. His eyes turned in mute appeal to the onlookers as his protectors. He hung a moment against the stonework. Then, for fear that the crowd might scatter, he began to utter wordless howls of despair.

'That's right,' said Verity with patient scorn, looking confidentially at the bystanders, 'you cry away, my lad. You'll find as how it exercises the lungs, cleanses the features, rinses the eyes, and softens the temper.'

Infant looked up dry-eyed.

'Fucking jack!' he said bitterly. His sympathizers caught their breaths and went abruptly on their way.

Verity took the offender by the lobe of an ear, leading him back towards Lord Tregarva's residence. At the approach of another pedestrian, Infant would howl like a broken spirit, the rest of the time he came quietly. At the area railings by the little gate that led down to the kitchens, a middle-aged woman in a white apron and cap watched their approach.

'You never come down for your tea, Mr Verity,' she said anxiously. 'Oh, my lord, look at him!'

'Don't pay any notice to him, Mrs Baker. He's Infant. Lives off the scaldrum dodge. Likewise cadging and scavenging.'

'But his poor legs! And his arms!' She covered her mouth with her hands in a pantomime of dismay.

'With them same legs, Mrs Baker, he done a runner a dozen times from Mr Samson and me. And we almost never caught him. We find he understands reason best when his ear's hurting.'

He led his prisoner down the area steps. At the bottom, Mrs Baker turned with hands under her apron as though she might weep into it on Infant's behalf.

'But the poor, poor soul! He looks hurt so awful, Mr Verity!'

'Yes, he do, don't he? You got the scullery pump handy a minute, Mrs B?'

She led the way to the scullery with its iron-handled pump on a long suction-shaft and a stone water-trough under the spout.

'Right, Infant,' said Verity, 'get them arms under that spout. Sharp's the word, an' quick's the motion!'

There was a clang of the iron handle, the suction of a piston, and a gush of water over Infant's reluctantly extended arms.

'Why,' said Mrs Baker softly, 'it's washing off!'

''Course it is.' Verity directed Infant's right leg under the spout with his boot. 'Soap and vinegar. Soap the arm, spot the vinegar on top, leave it a minute and the lather comes up like running sores. Infant never done an honest day's work in the 'ole of his miserable life. Brave Jack Tar scalded when a boiler burst! Nearest he's ever been to sea is the tap-room of Paddy's Goose down Limehouse docks.'

'Why's he Infant at his age?' she asked cautiously. 'Hasn't he got a proper name?'

'If he has, he never said. Foundling orphan, sent down Mrs Rouncewell's, Elephant and Castle, among them fallen creatures and their out-of-wedlocks. Whenever anyone called him, him having no name that he knew, he was naturally called Infant. He been Infant ever since.'

He let the pump-handle drop and turned to the offender.

'Right, my son. The only reason you ain't down Bridewell already waiting for the birch to soak is you might be of use.'

'I ain't useful,' sobbed the fat young man defensively.

'Shut that noise!' Verity glowered at him. 'I'll decide what you'll be.' He led Infant back to the kitchen among stoves and hot closets, scrubbed pine tables and rows of copper pans. The housekeeper set an extra chair for the young man. Then she went to the oak corner-cupboard, returning with a dark bottle of wine cordial, three glasses, a jug of hot water and sugar lumps in a blue china bowl.

Verity looked at the wine cordial and the sugar.

'It's a consideration he don't deserve, Mrs B.'

He took a first sip of sugared wine-and-water, savouring it.

'Right, Infant. You got one chance: I find you're playing me up, and it's justices' sessions for you. Charges of impersonation, obstruction, threatening behaviour to ladies. That's six months of eating slum-gullion down the House of Correction. And the birch for threatening. See if you ain't got something to sing about then!'

Infant looked at him helplessly, like a fat child.

'I never threatened! Never!'

'I was there, my son. At this moment I got a distinct recollection of threatening. If I was to lose that, it'd only be from the shock of you telling the truth. See?'

The prisoner mumbled an ungracious surrender.

'Right, then. I get the truth or you'll have more grief than a month o' funerals.'

Infant sipped hungrily at his sugared cordial.

'What you want, Mr Verity?'

Verity looked at him, the round moustached face flushed with resolve.

'I'll tell you what, you idle monkey. You spent your life being unfortunate at street corners and poking down drains for coins. You ever been down Clerkenwell?'

'Sometimes,' said the young man cautiously.

'Oh dear, oh dear, Infant! You got a taste for slum-gullion and birch, ain't yer? 'Course you been down there! You been twice before the Clerkenwell bench, prosecuted by the society that suppresses mendacity. Don't play me up!'

'I said, didn't I?' Infant wailed. 'I been there sometimes.'

'Right. You ever find anything by poking about? With your head down a drain?'

'Sometimes.'

'Don't go on saying sometimes! Have you or haven't you?'

'Yes.'

'That's better,' said Verity encouragingly. 'Now. You ever found anything down the drains off Saffron Hill? Had the gratings off when no one was about?'

'In a manner o' speaking.'

'So you got a fair idea how those drains lie? Which way they run? You'd know where's the best place to look for coins that fell down them from the street?'

''Course!' Infant's pride was hurt by the suggestion that he might not know something so simple.

'And when you was lucky, you might toast your luck in a tap-room like the Golden Anchor up the hill in Hatton Wall?'

'More 'n likely.'

'Just suppose,' Verity suggested gently, 'you was unfortunate enough to drop a coin – or a silver spoon – down the grating by the Golden Anchor tap-room. You know where I mean?'

'I suppose I might,' Infant said, his eyes evasive.

'How long before it might fetch up at the grating down the slope in Saffron Hill?'

Infant stared with a half-smile, suspecting a trick, yet relieved that the question was no worse.

'It wouldn't,' he said at last. Verity felt his heart quicken for the first time since his humiliation by Lambeth Sue.

'How d'you know it wouldn't? It's downhill, ain't it?'

'I live off drains, when there's nothing better,' Infant said hopefully, 'so I pay attention to 'em, don't I? You got no cause to. Nor people that lives like toffs. But not a week go by I don't find something, if only a linen snotter what fell down a grating when someone did his nose. But I don't fish where I won't catch. Nothing comes to Saffron Hill from the Golden Anchor. It can't.'

Verity's dark eyes narrowed in suspicion.

'Why can't it? It's down the hill, ain't it? It's where anything'd be washed down in time from above?'

'That's what you'd think,' said Infant contemptuously. 'What anyone'd think that don't live by finding. But nothing comes down to Saffron Hill from Hatton Wall. It goes the other way, through to Hatton Garden – not down Saffron Hill. Golden Anchor and Saffron Hill are separate drains. They both run separate into a main drain that connects with Farringdon Road. They don't run into each other.'

Verity clenched his fists under the table.

'So if you was unfortunate to drop a silver spoon down the grating outside the Golden Anchor, it'd never fetch up at Saffron Hill? It'd go into Hatton Garden?'

'Supposing it went anywhere.' There was hope on Infant's face for the first time in their encounter. 'When they laid the drain for Hatton Wall, there wasn't one down Saffron Hill. Consequential, it went level into Hatton Garden.'

Verity stared at the blubbery young man, as if seeing something far beyond him.

'You know what, Infant? You are neat as a new tin soldier.'

They finished their sugared cordial. At the top of the area steps, Infant turned pathetically.

'What's going to happen to me, Mr Verity, sir?'

'My advice to you, my son, is hook it! Hop the wag! Off my beat! I catch you being unfortunate round here again, my recollection will come back like greased lightning. See?'

Infant gave a slight self-conscious grin. As Verity stamped his feet astride, taking up sentry-go with a soldier's timing, The Scaldrum Dodge sidled away down the pavement. On the verge of earshot, he permitted himself a small triumph.

'Fucking jack!' he called back contemptuously.

That evening, Verity, in shirt-sleeves, folded his plump arms on the kitchen table. Stringfellow whittled at a twig to test a newly sharpened blade.

'You ain't going to let it rest?' he said apprehensively, at the end of his son-in-law's account.

'No, Mr Stringfellow. Not when there's a villain like Flash Fowler making up evidence to see an innocent man hanged.'

'A dodger like Infant could be telling you tales.'

'No, Mr Stringfellow. I been to Clerkenwell tonight. When the sluices was open and drains running. I took slips of pink paper and dropped 'em in by the Golden Anchor. Must a-bin bloody simple-minded not to do it before. You know what?'

'No,' said the old cabman patiently. 'How should I?'

'I walked smart to Hatton Garden, and saw them pink slips go under the grating there. I tried some more and walked smart to Saffron Hill. Not one. Infant was right: Golden Anchor can't run into Saffron Hill, though it's down a slope.'

'Flash Charley ain't stupid enough to put a knife where it couldn't be.'

Verity sighed.

'You think he'd know? Like you or me, he saw two gratings on a hill and thought the drain must run down from one to the other, which it don't. As it happens.'

'You can't be sure he don't know.'

Verity looked at the old man, the dark eyes glittering.

'Mr Stringfellow, you lived twenty years in Sovereign Street. Flash Fowler been down 'H' Division eighteen months and Saffron Hill ain't even on his patch. You tell me which way the drains runs under Sovereign Street, 'cos I don't know.'

Stringfellow stared at him in silence. Presently he said, 'It ain't proof he didn't know. Not proof as such.'

'All right,' said Verity reasonably. 'Tell me where drains go anywhere on your routes this last twenty years. Not Paddington Green, then. Try Ludgate Hill, Blackfriars, Whitehall, Waterloo Road – where do any of them go?'

'Who cares? Down to the river, I should think.'

'You may think so, Mr Stringfellow! But you don't know, do you? No more does Flash Fowler, by the look of it. You don't know which grating is a main drain or a side drain. Do yer? Not after twenty years? That's how he made his mistake.'

'Could be any knife he found. Don't mean it was put there.'

'It's the stiletto Fowler swears killed Quinn. Not any knife. How many Italian knives get found down drains like that?'

'Could be Bragg or Catskin Nash put it there for him to find.

And him innocent.' Stringfellow hoisted himself to his feet.

'No, Mr Stringfellow. He does them favours, not the other way round. And I asked Mr Samson. That poor dab Sloppy Dick had the knife pointed out to him down the drain by someone who told him to go to 'H' Division for a reward. Saffron Hill ain't in 'H' Division. But Flash Fowler had his hat on ready. So Sloppy Dick's a witness who found the knife and watched the grating took up. And Mr Fowler says he only went into another Division, being called urgent, seeing the knife might be washed away. Huh!'

'What's Dick's reward?'

Verity's mouth tightened.

'Sloppy Dick been hired every day down the yard. Took on by a calling-clerk that owes his place to Bully Bragg.'

Stringfellow paused with one hand on the stable-latch.

'Don't prove nothing, though, do it? Could all be just as they say. If it was you been called, you'd have gone. And you wouldn't have waited, in case that knife was washed away.'

Oil-light gleamed on Verity's black hair and moustaches.

'If there's proof, Mr Stringfellow, I'll find it. I got two more duties outside Lord Tregarva's before rest day. I mean to see inside. See if that don't tell a tale!'

16

In Lord Tregarva's kitchen, Verity drained his mid-morning wine cordial.

'Seems funny, Mrs B, Mr Fowler called all this way, him being 'H' Division.'

A look of concern clouded the housekeeper's face. She turned to the butler's pantry as its occupant came to the doorway. Kingdom's springy hair, long face and high collar gave him a naturally startled look.

'On account of the calling-card, Mr Verity. The fellow we took for a reverend gentlemen left it. Miss Henrietta received the gent, she being one for good causes. Much taken with the house, the reverend was. Most knowledgeable about the ornaments. He never wanted money, only a patron for his mission in the docks. Lord Tregarva, being down Shadwell on business, thought to call on the mission. What it come to, Mr Verity, the address on the card was a public house!'

'His lordship went to the police office down Shadwell, not Scotland Yard?'

'If there was trickery, Shadwell was the heart. So Mr Fowler came enquiring. He found a dozen houses where this reverend person called. A joke, perhaps. No money asked. We never heard more.'

Verity stared into his empty glass.

'The fact nothing was taken, Mr Kingdom, don't mean you was

never burgled after. His Lordship must have a lot that's under lock and key.'

'And must remain so, Mr Verity,' said Kingdom firmly.

Verity beamed at him.

'All I'd like, is you to do a little dusting, Mr Kingdom. I know dusting ain't a job for a superior servant . . . .'

'Dusting what?'

'Locks, Mr Kingdom, where items of value or confidence might be. Nothing you need to blush at, if you was to tell His Lordship. What gets dusted anyway.'

'But Mr Fowler been here.'

'Great respects to him, Mr Kingdom, but haven't you thought that some mischief could have happened here since Mr Fowler's visit?'

'Just dusting?' Kingdom asked cautiously.

'Nothing more, Mr Kingdom. And only upper floors, at that.'

The butler sat down opposite Verity at the pine table, the pale enamel of the hot-closets gleaming beyond his shoulder.

'If Lord Tregarva's been burgled, Mr Kingdom, I'd lay my pension on how it was done. Even if nothing was took, why does a thief take nothing? Because he means to come back!'

'I can't tell Lord Tregarva that, sir! Where's the evidence?'

Verity polished his hat-brim on his sleeve.

'Dust them locks and we'll see evidence, Mr Kingdom. If I'm wrong, you'll prove it in five minutes. Dust them locks!'

Kingdom and Verity, with Mrs Baker in attendance, went up the broad stairway. To one side of the main gallery was an elegantly furnished sitting-room with curved chairs and sofas. Against the far wall stood a French walnut bureau. While Verity watched, Kingdom stooped and gently dusted the brass furniture of the lock. He turned and showed the dusting-cloth.

'Nothing,' he said with relief. 'How should there be?'

Verity took his notebook and tore a thin spill from the edge of a page.

'Just try this in the lock, Mr Kingdom.'

Kingdom inserted the paper and twisted it. He drew it out.

'That ain't been smoked,' Verity said thoughtfully.

The next bureau was Miss Henrietta's, in a light and airy writing-room.

'Nor that,' Verity said as Kingdom handed back another spill.

A masculine dressing-room on the floor above was furnished with a small table of leather stud-boxes and ebony-backed brushes, the curve of a Carlton House desk under the window. Despite the summer warmth, a fire was laid to air the room.

'It's as far as I go, Mr Verity,' Kingdom said, 'without Lord Tregarva and your superintendent. There's a safe and money-box that I wouldn't show nor touch.'

Verity crossed to the Carlton House desk. He tore another spill. The long drawer was locked, its keyhole at one side, a more sophisticated mechanism. He slipped the spill into the keyhole and turned the paper slowly, testing the interior of the lock. He drew the paper out and looked at it. His plump face creased in a frown.

'I'd say you was burgled, Mr Kingdom. Not long ago. This got carbon all over. Smell it! Someone smoked that lock. They've had the drawer open, I'll swear. A lock like this wouldn't stop them.'

'Smoked?' Mrs Baker looked at the sergeant uncertainly.

'Smoked the lock, Mrs B. They hold a steel probe in a flame till it's black with carbon. They ease it in, and turn it. Sounds easy but takes practice. They turn the probe so it passes the wards of the lock. They turn it, pull it out and the marks in the carbon shows where the levers are. Then they work two picks in a lock of that kind. Or screw metal steps on a key-shank to meet the levers, raise 'em, and free the bolt. They close it the same way. There's cracksmen could have this desk open in less time than it took me to tell you how it's done.'

'Nothing was missed, however,' Kingdom insisted. 'No papers.'

Verity looked at him,

'Mr Kingdom, I know them. A man they called Pandy Quinn

that's been dead a few months. Worked with Jack Rann and Soapy Samuel. But Rann would never leave carbon behind to tell a tale. Pandy Quinn wasn't as clean, but he'd have a lock like this open. And he could climb.'

'Climb?'

'Oh, yes, Mr Kingdom. You was probably burgled through the roof. While His Lordship was at dinner and you and the others was busy downstairs.'

Kingdom sat down on a narrow Egyptian settee, opposite the dressing-mirror.

'What am I to tell Lord Tregarva?'

'The full story, Mr Kingdom. There'd be a way to the roof, I suppose?'

'Mr Fowler went out on there,' Kingdom said, leading the way up the attic stairs.

'Find anything, did he?'

'He said not.'

The window of a lumber room opened with a little difficulty. Verity eased himself out and stood in a narrow gully. Beyond the parapet stretched London rooftops and chimney-pots from Marylebone to the river. The towers of Westminster stood tall across distant billows of green in the royal parks.

Where Lord Tregarva's property ended, the gully was blocked by a low wall and a circle of sharpened metal spokes, rising six feet and curving out over the drop to the pavement below. Neither Jack Rann nor Pandy Quinn would attempt it, not out of respect for spiked metal, but rather for fear that the rusting device might crumble under a man's weight and throw him forty feet to the pavement.

'Closed off between each house,' Kingdom said firmly, 'just because of burglars.'

'What ain't closed off, Mr Kingdom, is up there. The ridge of the roof. They come along there easy as crossing a street. You got a roof-ladder?'

Kingdom handed out a short ladder, used to distribute the

weight of a man and protect the slates. The incline was long but shallow, the climb to the ridge easy.

'Watch them slates, Mr Verity!'

''s all right, Mr Kingdom. This is the way they come.'

He climbed the wooden rungs until his fingers touched the rougher ridge tiles. He pulled himself slowly above the roof-line. The fresh spring breeze at this height smacked into his face. He let go with one hand to snatch at his hat, which he had unwisely kept on to have both hands free. But he was too late. In dismay, Verity watched it lift and sail down over Portman Square towards old Tyburn Road.

'My hat will be the death of me . . . .'

He recalled a story of attic thieves. The robbery was over and they were making their way back along the crest of the roof to an empty house which had given them access. In such areas, they were smartly dressed to avoid attracting notice. The wind caught a silk hat. It was found in a roof gully, identified by the hatter's number, and four men went to penal servitude for fourteen years. Perhaps Pandy had heard it too. 'My hat will be the death of me . . . .'

Verity sat astride the crest. There was nothing to prevent a man at this height from working his way along, clambering between the pots of the chimney stacks, from one end of Portman Square to the other. The darkness of a night in October or November would have given complete concealment.

'Mr Fowler was up there, Mr Verity. Nothing to see!'

Verity edged forward. There was debris galore on London rooftops, blown there, discarded, left to rot. The north of Portman Square had only long attic gullies on either side, easily kept clear. To the rear, across the mews of Portman Place were flat parapeted roofs fifteen feet lower. A natural trap for airborne litter. The rooftop wind caught in them and eddied, swirling paper, scraps of cloth, the broken form of a child's kite, skeletons of at least two hats, in a city where the loss of headgear on a windy day ran into hundreds of hats and bonnets. These two were not to be recovered.

They could only be seen by looking down from fifteen feet above, over a gap of twenty feet. Verity came level as close as he could.

One was a silk hat, not Pandy Quinn's, unless borrowed from Soapy Samuel's wardrobe. In any case, sun and rain had turned the black silk to a lichen-green, a lidless cylinder and a warped brim.

The other was cheaper but tougher, a tall hat in fur and Saxony wool. Its fabric had weathered weeks of exposure better than silk would ever do, its animal fibres stiffened and waterproofed by a varnish of shellac. As usual, it was the crown that had cracked open. He could see that the interior lining had been repaired, from a small square label pasted inside. But the weather had rinsed and seared the letters or figures. Even the repairer's name had gone.

Verity straightened up, easing his neck and eyes. He moved back level with Kingdom who was still below him in the gully.

'Mr Kingdom! Miss Henrietta likes a good tune, I daresay. I'd be no end obliged if you was just to fetch me a pair of opera glasses for a minute.'

He pondered the summer blue above the chimney-pots until the butler's return. Kingdom moved up the ladder, stretching to hand over the glasses.

'Shan't be half a minute, Mr K.'

Lowering himself on the far slope, he slithered into the opposite gully. The hat lay across the mews in the bundled litter of the flat roof below him. He tried the glasses. Even now, the repair label was blank. He made out only three consecutive letters of the maker's name on the lining of the broken crown.

'L ... L ... E ... .' He worked his way back up the slope. A slate cracked under his bulk. Treading back down the ladder, he stepped into Lord Tregarva's gully and brushed himself down with his hands. He returned the opera glasses.

'Well, Mr Verity?'

'I'd say you was burgled, Mr Kingdom. Pandy Quinn and Jack Rann. It got their trademark. Still Pandy's dead and Rann's intended to be hung. So I daresay you won't hear from him again.'

'But why the glasses, Mr Verity?'

'Hat, Mr Kingdom, on the other roof. Not much to be seen of it.'

'Mr Fowler never said about a hat. Blown there afterwards?'

Verity assumed what he hoped was an expression of innocence.

'Afterwards, Mr Kingdom. That's how it must have been.'

17

Verity and Samson turned into St Paul's Churchyard, the old low-beamed shops of print-sellers and tailors marked by dark shadow and white sun. Facing the shops, the monumental flank of the cathedral with its green burial lawn closed the view. In dark frock-coats and trousers, tall hats and woollen gloves, the two sergeants marched instinctively in step.

'Ask yerself, Mr Samson. Suppose you was to buy a hat.'

'I've bought a hat. Lots of hats.'

'Suppose the lining or something was to go. What'd you do?'

'Have it mended, of course. Unless it went too bad.'

'Yes,' said Verity reasonably, arms swinging. 'Who'd mend it?'

Samson looked puzzled, suspecting a trick.

'Who I bought it off, I suppose. I'd 'spect him to put it right. Seeing as he sold it.'

Verity's plump face glowed in appreciation.

'Exactly, Mr Samson.'

'All right,' said Samson cautiously. 'Why Keller?'

'L-L-E, Mr Samson. 's all I could read. Now, a hatter that has his name put in the crown of the lining like that isn't small fry. There's a livery company of hatmakers in the City of London. I been through the list. James Keller of St Paul's Churchyard. I couldn't read the repair label. But ten-to-one it's him, if he sold it.'

Samson paused, anxious with self-interest behind the mutton-chop whiskers.

'Oh, yes,' he said with heavy irony, 'clever story to tell Mr Croaker, I'm sure. That hat could belong to anybody.'

'One way to find out, Mr Samson.'

They strode past the buildings of Tudor and Queen Anne brick in the rhythm of the soldiers they had once been. Samson spoke without looking aside at his companion.

'You got any idea, have you, of the precious kick-up and row coming your way if you go and hand this to old Croaker? You mean to tell him how him and the Division got it wrong? How the red judges and jury got it wrong? And all this when that bugger Jack Rann hauls hisself out of Newgate and vanishes?'

Verity's flushed forehead creased a little in perplexity. He seemed about to reply and then thought better of it. They skirted a purveyor of lemonade and sherbet, wheeling a huge block of ice surrounded by lemons, a man with a basket of lobsters, crying, 'Champions a bob!'

The great cathedral dome spun above them in a rush of wind-blown cloud. A shop-bell on its spring rattled faintly as Verity pushed open the door of James Keller, Country and Travelling Hats. The window displayed several hats on polished wooden blocks, accompanied by umbrellas, fur cuffs, gauntlets, and livery capes. The dim interior was like an old-fashioned parlour, except for a counter to one side. A polished oak-table with several long-backed dining-chairs occupied the centre of the space. The mahogany tall-boy was stacked with the unmistakable shapes of brown hat-boxes, open shelves lined with plaster heads decked in silk top hats, velvet hunting hats, servants' livery hats, bridesmaids' hats, and ladies' hats for the promenade or the carriage.

At the table, adjusting a round wooden band by which the heads of clients were measured, was a small stooping man in a waistcoat. He looked up, found his spectacles, and put them on his nose.

'Mr Keller?' Verity asked hopefully.

'Mr Keller ain't exactly here just now.'

'Likely to be back?'

'Not really.'

'Why's that, then?'

'Gentleman passed away two days since. I'm Mr Manuel.'

Samson stared, as if not believing. Verity intervened.

'You got no idea, Mr Manuel, how sorry I am to hear.'

'You come about a hat?'

'To enquire about a hat, Mr Manuel, bought and repaired here.'

The stooping man put down the wooden measuring band.

'You police?'

'Verity and Samson, Mr Manuel. 'A' Division.'

'And what's the hat?'

'A beaver, as they say, sir. Bought here and fetched back here, it seems, for repair. Property of the late William Arthur Quinn, also known as Pandy Quinn.'

The stooping man pulled his jacket on over his waistcoat, as if he now felt cold.

'What about it?'

'Might you have repaired it, Mr Manuel?'

Manuel drew a thumb over the corner of his mouth, perhaps feeling a stray crumb.

'You know I did, don't you?'

'How could I know that, Mr Manuel?'

'Mr Keller told you. Not you, but one of you. The boy was sent to ask me.'

'But Mr Keller's—'

'Dead,' said Manuel with a small satisfaction. 'He sent the boy down to the basement, saying police wanted to know. There's just me and the boy. The boy boils the fur and does the varnish. I do the shaping and trimming.'

'Who was the policeman?'

Mr Manuel attempted a little laugh.

'How should I know? The boy come and asked. I looked in the

repair ledger. There's names and numbers. The ledger number matches the ticket in the hat.'

Verity looked at Mr Manuel with something like affection.

'And where might the ledger be, Mr Manuel?'

'Gone,' said the stooping man.

Affection turned to consternation.

'You haven't got it?'

Manuel stopped just short of a smile.

'If it's gone, how can I have it? We keep ledgers for repairs, to see which numbers match which name. Repair done, we don't need to match it in the ledger. Quarter Day, we finishes the old ledger and starts the new. We keep the previous quarter, just for the overlap of hats coming in and going out mended. See? You got any idea how many repairs go through here? We'd have ledgers to sink an iron-clad!'

'Perhaps,' said Verity coldly, 'you'd have the goodness to show last quarter's ledger.'

Manuel shrugged and fetched it. It was tall and narrow, bound in leather. It cracked as Verity opened it flat on the table. He ran his finger down the names.

'He was in the ledger before that,' said Manuel helpfully, 'and the jack that came before you was a bit cleverer. He had the number of the repair. That's how we found the name.'

'Quinn?'

'If that's what it was. If that's who was wanted.'

'And you'd remember all this?' Samson asked sceptically.

Mr Manuel looked at him, unimpressed.

'I'd remember one of our customers being asked for by police, wouldn't I? First and last time it's happened.'

Verity closed the ledger as reverently as a hymn-book.

'You would remember, Mr Samuel. Of course you would. And we shan't bother you further. Sorry you was troubled twice. And if you was to pass our condolences to Mrs Keller and the family, we'd be no end obliged.'

Manuel emitted a high squittering laugh.

'You'd need to be obliged, sir. He lived and died in the arms of ladies that's hired by distance, like hansom cabs. There's no Mrs Keller I ever heard of, only that strapping trollop Noreen that does tidy work in the big shop down Holborn. She's suited again already.'

Verity turned with dignity to the door. Manuel called him.

'One thing! There ain't a reward in all this, I daresay?'

Samson smiled. 'If there is, Mr Manuel, you shall be the first to hear of it.'

Outside, as the May sunlight fell on the twisted timbers of ancient fronts, Samson turned to Verity.

''appy now? Got everything you want?'

Verity made a grimace of intellectual concentration.

'Mr Samson, suppose you'd gone there and found that repair, what'd you have done?'

'Clapped the cuffs on Pandy Quinn.'

'But Flash Fowler never did.'

'No,' said Samson humorously, 'but then I don't suppose Flash Charley thought a dead body was likely to run off very far.'

'Mr Samson, you know anything about quarter days, do you? If Flash Fowler saw that entry in the ledger for the quarter before last, he must'a gone there before they changed at Christmas. Pandy Quinn wasn't coopered for another month!'

'Not much odds,' Samson said with a sulky shrug.

'It makes odds that, all those weeks, Pandy was never so much as asked a question about Lord Tregarva's roof. Quinn and Rann could have done the house inside out in that time!'

Samson's scorn deepened.

'Talk sense! Flash Charley would have passed it on to Mr Croaker and 'A' Division, Portman Square being their manor.'

Verity's plump scowl relaxed, as if he suddenly saw the solution to a difficulty.

'Yes,' he said brightly, more pleased than Samson had seen him all afternoon. 'Of course, Mr Samson. That's just how it would have been. Wouldn't it? I should'a seen it from the start. I'd say that just about does it!'

18

Henry Croaker wagged Verity's memorandum in his fingers. A gleam in his narrowed porcine eyes might equally have been anger or triumph. From the oak swivel chair at his desk, he looked up at the hatless sergeant paraded before him. Verity stood at attention, chest out, chin up, facing his commander.

Croaker wagged the paper again. The dry withered tones of the chief inspector's voice were finely adapted to the flights of official irony in which he lashed his subordinates.

'Be assured, Sergeant,' he said quietly, 'the man that would box clever with me shall drink a bitter broth!'

A slight frown of incomprehension clouded Verity's features.

'Yessir,' he said uncertainly.

'You would make fools of us all? You would make us a laughing stock in every other division?'

'Not sure what you mean, sir. With respect, sir.'

He did not need to look directly at the chief inspector. Henry Croaker, frock-coat buttoned up military-style to his leather stock, his face the colour of a fallen leaf, dark whiskers finely trimmed, was an enduring image in his mind.

'Have no fear, Sergeant, you shall understand full well before I have done with you. Or it will be no fault of mine!'

In his jubilation, Croaker seemed to sing the words to his victim. Verity waited. Above and behind the chief inspector's head, the panes of the window looked across the river below Westminster Bridge, busy little steamers with crowded decks and trails of smoke from thin stacks, barges with rust-brown sails. Verity took the continuing pause as an invitation to justify himself.

'With respect, sir—'

'Silence!' sang Croaker. 'I will have you at attention until you take root in my carpet, if I choose!'

He sat back, savouring the moment.

'Misemployment of police time, while on foot duty in Portman Square. Such misappropriation of time for which a man is paid is tantamount to the misappropriation of the money paid to him for his services. Eh?'

'Yessir.' Verity again strove to sound humble.

'Pray, explain your search of the property of Lord Tregarva without a warrant or authority, in His Lordship's absence!'

Verity felt his face grow warm.

'Not like that, sir. With respect, sir.'

'Was it not, Sergeant? Tell me, then, what was it like?'

'Only went with Mr Kingdom, sir, His Lordship's butler, to check the entrance from the roof as secure against intruders.'

'And tried the locks on a bureau, cabinets and Carlton House table belonging to Lord Tregarva and Lady Henrietta?'

Verity stared at him, astonished.

'Nothing like that, sir. Mr Kingdom happened to do dusting on the way. When he touched a cloth to the brasswork on that table, it come away black. Natural enough, I remarked it was carbon. It being black, I mentioned thieves smoking a lock.'

'And it did not occur to you, Sergeant, that the black was a simple deposit of soot, no doubt collected there through the slovenliness and dishonesty of servants in failing to clean their master's property?'

'Not how it looked, sir. With respect, sir.'

'To me,' said Croaker crisply, 'it looks like slovenliness and dishonesty. It looks so because Lord Tregarva's residence was visited by a detective officer after the suspicion of a theft and no such dust was found.'

'Yessir,' said Verity, humble again, 'matter o' regret, sir.'

'And it is also a matter of regret that you then passed yourself off as an investigating officer, upon your rest day, to question without authority an employee of the late James Keller, Esquire, Master-Hatter of St Paul's Churchyard? Are you not aware that, when not upon constabulary duty, your authority to visit and question is no greater than that of any other citizen?'

'No, sir. With respect, sir.'

In the late morning a faint digestive moan sounded from Chief Inspector Croaker's martyred entrails.

'It is a nice point of law, Sergeant, whether your unauthorized visit to Mr Keller's, off duty, may not be charged as impersonation, contrary to the Police Act and triable as felony! I shall submit the decision to Superintendent Gowry.'

Verity stood his ground.

'Matter of the hat, sir, belonging to the late William Arthur Quinn . . . .'

He looked at Croaker's face and stopped.

'A broken hat upon a roof, Sergeant. Blown from God knows where, like a thousand other hats in this city! I know nothing of hats! I will hear nothing of hats! The man Quinn is dead. What can it matter?'

'Yessir,' said Verity contritely. 'Just so, sir.'

Croaker paused again, saving the best mouthful until the last.

'Therefore, pending consideration of disciplinary proceedings, I shall recommend to Mr Gowry forfeiture of three days' money, in respect of improper use of paid hours in Portman Square.'

'Yessir. Very good, sir.'

Croaker looked up at him.

'And now,' he said, 'dismiss! Get out!'

Verity pulled himself up, stamped about, and strode to the door, arms swinging. He opened the door, went out, and closed it behind him. The sky was blue through the glass above the broad staircase. In his excitement, he quite forgot about the loss of three days' pay.

That evening, Cabman Stringfellow spat aggressively on a harness brass.

'Superior numbers, me old sojer. Them brutes lays a snare and you walks right into it. You don't never learn, do yer?'

Verity stared at him across the littered supper table.

'Don't I, Mr Stringfellow? When the Rifle Brigade was before Sebastopol, I seen snares laid by just one or two men. And I seen half a regiment cut to pieces in consequence.'

'Still, this ain't Sebastopol, Verity, and you ain't the Rifle Brigade.'

'No, Mr Stringfellow. But yesterday I laid a snare for superior numbers, and this morning Mr Croaker marched them slap-bang into the middle of it. Him being nothing but an artillery lieutenant!'

Stringfellow picked a tooth with his useful nail.

'How's that, then?'

'I thought a lot before I wrote that memorandum to Mr Croaker. I knew what he'd do the minute he was told what I found at Portman Square and at Mr Keller's. Having finished with Pandy Quinn, he'd go on something dreadful about there being nothing more to it. That's the meanness of his nature.'

'And what if he did?'

'Mr Stringfellow, when a man goes on something dreadful, he's apt to let slip words that he never meant to say.'

'Such as?'

'Remarking that the hat I'd seen on the roof at Portman Square didn't mean nothing about that lock being smoked. Mr Stringfellow, how can that hat have nothing to do with carbon in the lock, if it shows Quinn was up on Lord Tregarva's roof with Jack Rann? What's Mr Croaker think they were there for?'

'But that's not to say there was murder, is it, Verity?'

'Consequence enough for Flash Fowler to go asking round the hatmakers.'

146

'But it don't prove nothing!' Stringfellow patted the table to add emphasis.

'It proves, Mr Stringfellow, that Flash Fowler asked Mr Keller. And he must have done it while Pandy was still alive. His repair was only in last year's ledger. So Policeman Fowler saw it before Christmas was out. Pandy never died until a month after.'

'And Flash Charley never did nor said nothing all that time?'

Verity shook his head.

'Mr Croaker thinks the hat's not important. Now, Mr Croaker may be a brute and a tyrant, but the only reason he can think that Pandy Quinn's hat ain't important, is that he never knew of it. He said to me in his very words this morning that he knows nothing about hats and doesn't care about 'em! But he doesn't know because Flash Fowler never told him of Quinn's hat on Lord Tregarva's roof and Quinn being in that house. Fowler never told anyone, excepting Bully Bragg and his friends.'

Stringfellow shifted on the hard straw seat of his kitchen chair.

'P'raps Fowler never thought it that important to mention to Mr Croaker.'

Verity's dark eyes narrowed.

'At the inquest, Fowler didn't say it wasn't important; he said he didn't know about it! Twice! Never heard of this hat – what in truth he'd been asking about!'

'How d'you know? Inquests ain't written down. You wasn't there.'

'But Jack Rann was there, in handcuffs. Baptist Babb saw him repeat Fowler word-for-word, to Orator Hawkins in Newgate.'

'What you saying exactly, sojer?'

'Mr Stringfellow, Pandy Quinn's dying words were that his hat would be the death of him. As if them that killed him for his secret were talking to him about his hat. That's how they knew he and Rann was on Lord Tregarva's roof.'

'Policeman Fowler never cut him?'

'Fowler was the only one to know that hat was on the roof. But when Mr Kingdom, the butler, asked if he'd found anything, Fowler said there was nothing up there. And then he went off smart to the hat-shop and found the hat was Pandy Quinn's. At Keller's, they knew they'd repaired the hat but never knew why Fowler asked. And Fowler never told Mr Croaker nor anyone in the Division. "My hat'll be the death of me", Pandy said. And it was, poor devil.'

'Was it?' Stringfellow asked doubtfully.

'Mr Stringfellow, Mr Babb saw Rann repeat Pandy's words about his hat. If Bragg and Catskin Nash knew about it when they cut Pandy, the only person who could'a put them on to Pandy and the hat was Flash Fowler.'

'And if Bragg nor Catskin was never told, then who cut Pandy?' Stringfellow's tongue ran expectantly on his lips.

'If it happened that way,' Verity said simply, 'Fowler used the knife to make Pandy tell a tale. To get the knavery for himself and Bragg. When the knife slipped, there was perjured witnesses enough to get Rann hanged for killing Quinn. Perjured so as not to face the trial themselves! Either way, Flash Fowler thought he was so clever! But I got the brute, Mr Stringfellow! The inquest never knew he'd seen that hat at Portman Square nor gone asking Keller. How should they? And newspapers don't give two lines to the likes of Rann or Quinn. Mr Croaker couldn't know of the hat, without Fowler told him, which he never did.'

'You going back to Mr Croaker?'

Verity stared at the stable-door with a plump frown.

'Mr Stringfellow, there's a man gone to the gallows by now on Fowler's evidence, but for climbing out of Newgate. First off, I mean to see that right, if I can.'

148

19

The plate-glass display windows of Trent's Mourning Fashions were dressed with swags of mauve and curtains of black velvet. Strong sunlight over the roofs of Cornhill was scarcely reflected in the dim theatre of funeral costumes. Samuel, smoothly shaven and clerically dressed, dismissed the attention of a shop-walker with a tired wave of his hand. At every enquiry, the pretext of Miss Jolly as a daughter on a fruitless search for a becoming funeral costume was easily acted out by Samuel as a grieving husband, Rann the sympathetic son-in-law.

They took cover beyond a velvet board whose mourning jewellery showed how a curl from the head of the deceased might be encased in a black and silver brooch, bracelet or locket, even in a gold ear-ring, stud or cuff-link. Rann looked about to ensure that there was no one within earshot. He stood with Samuel by the display windows that looked across to the Cornhill Vaults.

'Mr Trent got a private office over there – and rooms for a love-nest. Two floors above the vaults. There's mornings Mag can't hardly walk down all them stairs.'

He looked about him again.

'That's our way in.' He shrugged at the simplicity of it. 'Trent can't hardly wait with Miss Mag. He'll only hurt himself, though, going at it like that.'

Samuel wanted to laugh but recalled that this was a temple of grief. He extinguished a smile in his grey cambric handkerchief and blew his nose.

At this time of the evening, Cornhill was growing quiet. The banks and the vaults had closed, only the drapers and a few of the jewellers' shops were still open. It was Samuel's first view of the vaults in Rann's company. The building was a solid commercial block at the Leadenhall end of Cornhill, finished in white stucco. To its left was the arch of Sun Court and a glimpse of Tudor brickwork. The Cornhill Vaults occupied most of the ground floor in the main block. The floor above it and the ground floor to one side contained a tailor's workshop. These and the uppermost rooms were leased by Mr Trent.

Leaving Miss Jolly in the fitting-room of the drapers, Rann and Samuel crossed between hansoms and twopenny buses. The windows of the strong-room that opened on Cornhill were protected by shutters of inch-thick steel, lowered when the firm closed for the day's business. But the shutter on Cornhill was pierced by two pairs of eye-holes. Day and night, the gas burnt inside. Far from hiding Milner's steel door to the vault, it was displayed to the world. Each policeman on the beat had orders to check at twenty-minute intervals that all was well. The eye-holes showed the interior of the strong-room with a large mirror on the rear wall.

The glass framed a reflection of a flat steel door with a double keyhole and a wheel for retracting the bolts of the lock. The door was set in iron-plate running the length of the room. The main walls were also lined by iron-plate whose studs were plainly seen, regular as embroidery. Sheet-iron formed the floor.

The pavement was empty now. Rann directed his comments quietly to Samuel.

'Iron lining on the wall and steel door on the vault. Double Treasury lock. Other walls lined with plate-iron after Acutt's warehouse was burgled by breaking in from the next store. Iron plate on the floor. Can't say about the ceiling. P'raps they can't iron it because of the weight. So they put in the mirror. Anyone that dropped down is caught in the glass. You might run fast if you could get back through the walls or the floor, but you couldn't run off up through the ceiling. That's what Milner's must have told them.'

'You never mean to spider down through the ceiling?'

'No, Sammy. Even if it ain't iron-plated – and I'd swear it ain't – there'd be such damage. When I've done this job, it must look as if it never happened. At least for as long as it takes to cash the bills. Couple of weeks, any rate.'

'You can't bust through iron plate.'

'I never said I could, Sammy. I know I can't.'

'Nor you can't bust up through an iron floor.'

'I know that likewise, Sam.'

'And you can't come down through the ceiling because, even if it ain't iron-plated, they'd see the damage.'

'I know that too, Sam.'

'Drains? Chimneys?'

'They'd have stops on the drains, Sammy. And flues in these places have iron plates that only open from inside. I been a sweep's boy, ain't I? I should know.'

'Suffering God, Jack Rann,' said Samuel mournfully, 'even if you hadn't got to carry that little wriggler Jolly, this isn't a runner. Not even much of a starter!'

'Oh, don't you worry about that, old Samuel Wilberforce. I'll do it all right. I got no option now. And them thinking it can't be done is no end useful. Look there! See how they put that steel vault-door and its locks on display. Look at the lock plate. A fool can read it from here. Milner's Double Treasury.'

'How's that help you?'

'Because, Samuel, if there's an article in this world Pandy knew a thing or two about, it's a Milner Double Treasury. Thanks to Pandy, I know what its inside looks like. Five levers must be lifted. But the key don't move a bolt, as you'd expect. Instead, it connects

151

with a set of cog-wheels, which lift a steel arm and take pressure off the main bolt. You have to do it twice. Two keyholes. Different keys. Even then, the bolt don't move until you turn that wheel on the door beside the keyholes. It's connected to five other bolts that all draw back together, top to bottom of the door. No one can't jemmy a door with six bolts. See? It's a clever lock, is a Double Treasury.'

'Is it?' asked Sammy hopefully.

'Too clever,' Rann said quietly. 'So as to stop a man making a key to fit, they use keys that can be altered every day by changing the metal steps on the key's shank.'

'But how's that help you?'

'Sammy! Using a key-shank! Fitting steps to it until they'll lift the levers and open a lock! Ain't that my trade, Sam? Ain't it the very thing I was brought into the world to do?'

For the first time, Samuel's sleek aquiline face began to reflect optimism.

'Sammy! It's as if they tried to think of a lock to please Pandy Quinn and Jack Rann. And they went and made it – just for us. Now do you see, Sam? That's why Pandy chose the Cornhill Vaults. That's why it got to be here and nowhere else!'

Samuel looked at his shoes and began to laugh downwards, so that the world should not see him chuckling in his black mourning suit. He shook his head and crowed a little with happy admiration.

'Handsome Rann!' he murmured happily. 'Oh, Pandy Quinn and Handsome Rann!'

Several days later, Canon Wilberforce spent an agreeable half-hour in conversation with Colonel Maidment, manager of Drummonds Bank in Pall Mall East. Accustomed only to the quietude of the cathedral close at St Asaph, the elderly clergyman's London visit concerned the financing of a joint stock company, which the canon's brother was promoting.

By the end of the discussion, it had been arranged that Canon

Wilberforce's secretary would bring a number of bills to be discounted, as soon as the canon had time to return to the close and bring the paper back to London. Bank of England bonds would be issued in their place, in the canon's name.

Colonel Maidment hinted only the least doubt at the wisdom of the investment and the unique legal obligations assumed by investors in joint stock enterprises. That, however, was a matter for Canon Wilberforce. The manager contented himself with suggesting that advice might be sought from the family solicitor. The bank would, of course, charge its usual commission for the proposed transaction. Indeed, Canon Wilberforce, with the unworldly honesty of his cloth, mentioned this consideration himself before the manager could raise the matter.

On the following day, the London and Westminster Bank in The Strand welcomed the auxiliary Bishop of Wellington during his furlough. He was shortly to return to New Zealand for the marriage of his daughter to the son of the provincial governor. The matter of exchanging individual bills for more generally negotiable bonds, to facilitate the marriage settlement, was almost lost in the manager's frank admiration of the animal attractions of the fair-haired young woman who accompanied her father. The manager might, indeed, have overlooked the question of the bank's fee, had not the moral rigour of the bishop raised it first.

On the following day, a scattering of banks in the city and the suburbs arranged facilities by which a frail old guardian would encash bills to be replaced by Bank of England bonds. It was a matter of wardship. Those who saw the almond-eyed and golden-skinned young ward, could not help wishing that they might have had such a loving duty to discharge. They accepted the old man's instructions in a daydream of being part loving guardian and part guardian lover to such a provoking little creature.

FOUR

THE CLIMBING-BOY

20

Samuel watched from the bow-fronted little shops of the station arcade as Arthur Trent walked the length of the platform at London Bridge with the young woman on his arm. Trent's grey suiting was clean cut, his dark Mephistophelean whiskers freshly trimmed. The lines of carriages making up the evening departures were overarched by a vault of sooty glass. Italianate pillars of yellow brick at either side of the tracks enclosed the station offices like the side chapels of a vast cathedral. Maggie walked beside her admirer, blonde chignon stirring sensuously in a black silk bow. With quiet pride, Mr Trent led his prize to a dragon-green first-class carriage at the front of the train. The railway guard tolled a handbell, his five-minute warning of the train's departure.

To an onlooker, it might seem that Samuel was relishing the self-confident swagger of Maggie Fashion's sturdy hips. But at a little distance from the carriage both her pale-grey gloves fell to the platform, a few feet apart, apparently unnoticed. A porter picked them up and hurried after Mr Trent, to be rewarded by a coin and a dark smile. Samuel turned away.

He looked round once at the train. The doors of its green carriage were shut. A whistle split the air and the double-humped engine emitted a snort of steam and a tolling bell-note. Beyond the station canopy, low sunlight picked out the rusty sails of East India merchantmen on the river below and threw long shadows over the

157

engine-sheds of the Greenwich Railway Company, across the dust heaps and market gardens of Bermondsey.

Twenty minutes later, Samuel's cab was in the slow-moving traffic behind Nicholson's Wharf. Miss Jolly sat in the far corner, in a costume suited to breaking and entering. The dark hair was piled under a fur shako. She wore a short blue tunic and cherry-coloured riding-pants, tight enough to suggest the uniform of a stage drummer-boy at a Cremorne Gardens masquerade.

At the Marquis of Granby, Jack Rann was there before them, in a high-walled booth of the saloon-bar. The Granby stood where the streets of banking houses and the coster markets converged. Porters sat at tables in a sawdust tap-room, their beer in pewter tankards, waiting for a night-call from sailing barques that came up to Tower Quay.

Samuel pushed open the mullion-windowed door, staring through tobacco-fogged air. His clerical dress was covered by the old coat and long muffler of an ancient dock-office clerk. One or two drinkers glanced at Miss Jolly, in her ambiguous costume of cherry pants and drummer-jacket, the profile of a golden Nefertiti, a stray tendril of dark hair uncovered by the shako at her nape. But the old men returned to their conversation. Whether she was dressed for a caper or a fancy lech was nothing to them.

Rann spoke softly as they slid into the booth on the far side of its narrow table.

'Foreman from the tailor's last to leave. Twenty minutes ago. Building's empty.'

'Trent's gone till Monday.' A smile tweaked Samuel's smooth face. 'Mag dropped both gloves. So she managed to leave the attic window unfastened as well.'

'Good. Then we got all we need.'

Samuel looked at him without expression.

'We agreed, Jack: what I didn't know, I couldn't tell. No matter how bad they hurt us. That's over. I want to know the rest.'

Rann shrugged and looked at the other drinkers.

'I'll get to the roof and through his attic, Sam. Trent got two keys on his fob. One opens his rooms and one opens the cutting-room on the floor below. Both open the street door. Mag pleasured him so hard but never could get her hands on those keys to press 'em in wax. Then, he leaves the cutting-room key by accident in the mourning warehouse opposite. She sees him go to a safe in his rooms and take a spare set. See?'

'You mean to bust his safe as well,' Samuel said uneasily.

'I mean to have his keys, not waste time on a skeleton. I'll come down the stairs and open his door in Sun Court. It's dark and no one to see. You'll have missy here and the bag of tricks. When you hear me, walk smart under the arch and in.'

A waiter in white apron over a black waistcoat took their orders. Rann paused and resumed.

'Trent's private stairs go up past his cutting-room to his door at the top of the building. Walker's Vaults got a separate door on Sun Court. Brigade of Guards wouldn't break through that. Down through Trent's cutting-room it's to be.'

He paused again as the waiter set down glasses and jug.

'On Monday, Sam, there mustn't be a whisker out of place in the vaults. Supervisors look the place over first thing. If this blows up while we're still changing the bills, we're done for.'

'You still taking young missy in with you, Jack?'

'Only way, Sam. You wait in Trent's rooms. Watch the street. Policeman on his beat every twenty minutes. You'll have a bell, like a school bell. If you see anyone, ring it hard in the fireplace. It'll sound through the building that way but not outside. When it's clear again, ring single notes.'

'And if there's trouble? Like someone coming for Trent?'

Rann's heart sank at the worry in the smoothly barbered face. He smiled.

'Any of that, Sam – take what you got and hook it. Down the stairs. Out the street door. It's a Yale lock, lets you out but not in. If you can, ring the doorbell on the vaults hard as you go by. But it won't come to that. Not now.'

Samuel tried to speak but his throat was too tight. He cleared it. 'Right, Jacko.'

'Me and missy go through the tailor's cutting-room below Trent's door. Runs the length of the building above the vaults. At the far end, it comes down to street-level next to the vaults. Just a room for shop trade that's shuttered after dark. Pandy went there, pretending to be measured for an Aldershot coat. That's where Jolly stays and I bring the bills out to her to be copied on our blanks. She'll have the blank bill-forms, the inks and dips from the carpet-bag. I'll have the tools. Shutters are closed now so she can work there till Monday, if she has to.'

'And you?' Samuel's smile was of doubt rather than triumph.

'Floorboards under the tailor's fitting-room carpet should come up easy. Pandy saw them. There's a partition wall in the foundations between the tailor and the vaults. Under the floor is too shallow for a cellar, that's why they keeps the coal out the back. Any case, Walker don't want coal under the floor, seeing he'd need a coal chute and someone might get in that way.'

'Yes,' said Samuel scornfully, 'but when you break through that foundation wall, you can't never make it good. Even if you put it back, they'll see the stones were moved.'

'They don't go down there, Sammy. It's not used. They don't go down more than they go down the drains or up the chimney. They couldn't tell you if the stones in that wall has been loose or tight, damaged or not, for ten years past.'

Samuel was not reassured.

'Once you're under the floorboards, you still ain't in their vault, Jack Rann. And seeing the floor above you'll be lined with sheet-iron, you may never be.'

Miss Jolly's eyes caught the tawny light of the dark-panelled bar as she looked from one to the other. Rann closed his hand over hers and stared at Samuel.

'The office behind the strong-room ain't an iron floor,' he said quietly, 'just boards. I'll have them off the joists easy as winking.'

'And the carpet?' Samuel asked.

'It'll come up with the force of the boards in the corner.'

'How d'you know?'

'Six months ago, Sammy, I was there with a broken gold chain to mend. Only eight-carat but if a man's fool enough to pay for mending trumpery, what's it to them? I stood in that office, while they looked the chain over in the workshop. Dropped a sovereign in the corner and had to pick it up. It's nailed boards under that carpet. And they can't nail boards through sheet-iron. I know where the carpet ends, where the desk and chairs is. And though I was never in the strong-room, I stood long enough in sight of the door of that room to get a good view of the lock. It's nothing, Sammy. A five-pin Yale. They'd rather trust the vault-door beyond it and the deposit boxes. And the mirror and the spy-holes from the street.'

Samuel looked round at the other booths, to make sure no one was listening. He turned back.

'What I'm saying, Jack, is you might get in as you say but how can you get out without a trace to show you been there? Ain't it plain?'

'No, Sammy, it ain't.'

'There's no way you can leave the place as it was! Not the carpet! Not the floor! Not the partition wall! And if you don't, the game's up, soon as they open the door on Monday morning! You can't get back under the floor and then nail the boards and the carpet back after you. They'll see it first thing. And then they'll be down the foundations and they'll see the damage to the wall.'

'I ain't going back that way, Sammy,' Rann said simply.

'You'll stay there?'

Rann shook his head.

'There's no other way in, Sam, but there's another way out.'

'Where?'

'Chimney in the back workshop. The furnace for gold and silverwork. Not as big as a foundry, but I spent half my life in chimneys like this. It's big enough. Old brick, about fourteen inches across at the base. Say twelve at the top.'

'Twelve inches!'

'I was a climbing-boy, Sam, younger than you first went to school. Do it on the slant. I could do ten inches on the slant, let alone twelve. And I knew chimneys in banks and vaults before I was eight years old. There's a grille to let smoke up but stops a man getting down. Set deep in the brick with iron bolts. Has to unbolt from below to let sweeps and brushes through. Then falls back and locks under its own weight. You'd never get in that way – if you did you'd be covered in soot. But that's how I mean to get out and it's why they'll never know I was there.'

'You'll still be caught in the flue, Jack.'

'It's a main flue up the building, Sam. Stand in Sun Court and you see it. Starts at the furnace. Goes up past the tailor's. No grille at the top. I been there with Pandy and let a line down. I can get up and out on the roof.'

A gummy corner of Samuel's mouth twitched. But there was no smile.

'Sammy,' said Rann, in a kindly whisper, 'if I thought I wasn't coming out, I wouldn't be going in, would I?'

21

Jack Rann hung by his fingers in the thin starlight, a gaunt spider. Sun Court was a black pit below, a shaft of Tudor brick which the glare of London sky and the stars failed to penetrate. But Mag Fashion had dropped her gloves at London Bridge. On Monday, if Mr Trent guessed his rooms had been entered, it was not likely that he would care to discuss his weekend absence with the police. A clock chimed the half-hour from St Michael's, across Cornhill and Lombard Street.

Rann's bony fingers were hooked over the parapet by the attic windows. Against his back lay the short steel head-bar and hammer. He extended a leg for a firmer lodgement. Light and lean-boned, he pressed against soot-crusted London brick. To cut a deeper toe-hold in the flaking mortar with a steel file might betray him.

He had climbed the wall as if on the face of a mountain. A fool would try the drainpipes and might find a lethal smearing of tree-grease at attic height. On the parapet, his fingers were alert for a barricade of sharpened glass. But there was none. Mr Trent's attics, two floors above the Cornhill Vaults, were a private world of pleasure.

In black moleskin trousers, dark vest, and canvas shoes, he scaled the remaining height, unobtrusive as a ghost. Slithering over the ledge, to hide his silhouette in the starlight, he used the edge of a file to test each attic window. The second window opened, as if on oiled hinges. Hunched on the sill, he slid his legs into the room and looked about him.

His heart gave a thump of alarm at the thought that these might be the wrong rooms. But there were no others. Reason returned. All the same, he first took the attic for a child's nursery, starlight on a wooden piebald rocking-horse fitted with toy harness. Pandy had hinted at the ordeals of Maggie Fashion in trapping Mr Trent. The proprietor of the mourning showroom would scarcely want a servant, let alone the police, to enter a room where such curious devices lay on the table by the toy horse.

Three times, Rann and Quinn had lain concealed on the opposite roof to be sure that only Mr Trent and a young woman came or went from the building between Saturday evening and Monday morning. Now he went down the stairs and surveyed the rooms below, then closed the dark green velvet of the curtains. A blade of light, when the tenant was thought to be away, would cause less suspicion than shaded lights moving behind plain glass.

He turned on the gas of a wall-bracket and set a match to the mantel. The light flared, settled, and showed him a bachelor's rooms. Sporting prints, leather or velvet chairs, plain tables. Beyond the dining-room was a narrow larder, at its end a tall square surface covered with cheese-cloth. Trent hoped that a burglar would take it for a game cabinet or a cold cupboard. Rann raised the cloth needing only to confirm the manufacturer's name on the safe hidden beneath.

It was a Tappin Steel that looked solid as a cannon. Trent must think it so. But its makers rarely used hardened steel frames when cheaper metal would do. Few purchasers examined the thin upright corner-bars holding the impressive-looking flanks. A man with a mallet might open it. Rann had something more decisive.

He began with a steel wedge in the crevice between door and upright, two inches above the lock. Wrapping his hammer in lint, he drove the tapered steel in. Then he knocked the wedge askew until it fell out. Next the head-bar, a bolt of steel two feet long with a tip that was both tapered and slightly curved.

The wedge had jarred the door narrowly from the upright, opening the crevice and giving the head-bar purchase. He struck the head-bar several blows with the hammer and then, like a man pushing a grinding-wheel, used all his strength on the head-bar to force the door and the bolt clear of the frame.

Not enough. He tapped in a larger steel wedge, then drove it with powerful blows of the hammer. At last the bolt jarred away from the weakened upright. By testing with a pick in the keyhole, he felt the bolt itself was loose. With a grimace of scorn for such shoddy workmanship, he unwrapped the lint from a 'Jack-in-the Box', a steel lever on a brass stock that would wind into a damaged lock with a pressure of half a ton. Useless against a bank vault, the Jack-in-the Box was a killer of such domestic safes as this.

He felt the last of the levers give way and moved it with a long steel blade. Inside the safe was a money-box, a jewel case, and several packets of papers. The money-box was not even locked. On its green leather lay a pair of keys.

Something else caught his eye: an envelope of yellow-edged photographs, processed in collodion that had been worked to exhaustion. They were sold in back rooms of the dusty little shops along Holywell Street. The pretext for these was Andromeda chained naked at the mercy of an erect male Gorgon.

Rann stared at the lean figure of the naked girl, the slant of dark hair across bold features, the heavy mouth, scorn and self-satisfaction improbably shown in the captive's eyes. Turning to embrace the rock as a refuge, the dark hair swept her back as her monster took a whip from his belt. With her back to the rock she endured his thrusts. Rann knew her. Sly Joanne had been with Jem Saward and his friends in the 'Barrister's' rooms. In the Gorgon, he recognized through wig and whiskers Bully Bragg's man, Hardwicke, happy with his scourge, and the subject before him.

165

'Well, there's a thing,' he said softly, using his picks to work the damaged lock until the bolt closed as best it would.

It was a bonus he had half-expected. The girl had broken some rule of her employment by Bragg. Faced by loss of her work in the introducing-house, or a mark that would ensure she never worked again, Pretty Jo preferred to act the heroine of a brothel melodrama for paying admirers.

When Arthur Trent returned, let him find his safe broken open, his keys and valuables in place, but his photographs of Andromeda's violation and flogging gone. If he suspected any man, it would surely be Bragg or those who ran the girl.

The two keys in the safe were servant keys, rather than a master. Each would open the street door. Only one would open the cutting-room and the other Trent's rooms. He tested the lock of Trent's rooms, went down the darkened stairs and opened the street door.

Samuel slipped out of the shadowed archway, the courtyard dark around him. A clergyman carrying a carpet-bag was a common sight between one terminus and another. A policeman on his beat would more likely salute such a figure than suspect him.

A second figure scurried from the archway on Cornhill, Miss Jolly in her pink fleshings and shako, like a ballet-girl by starlight. She had shed her blue tunic in the warm night. A coster's white shirt was tucked into her waist. Rann followed her upstairs, so unexpectedly caught by a twinge of desire for her, the movements of her trim thighs and tautly rounded hips in the suggestive tightness of cherry hussar-pants, that he felt more amusement than passion.

In the room, Rann indicated the photographs on the table.

'We'll take these. He'll see his safe's been open and nothing else missing. He'll hardly go to the police to complain these been taken. If not, he can't go at all.'

'Bragg's girl – Pretty Jo!' Samuel said.

'But it mightn't come amiss, Sam, if Mr Trent should be too

anxious for his honour to go looking for Mag or enquire as to what don't concern him. If a jack should ask what happened in the vaults tonight, he might be last to say.'

He buckled the carpet-bag and slung it on his back. Now that the job had begun, it was a cold equation of skill. He might be caught, but unless he pulled a stroke of this sort soon, they would catch him anyway. There was less danger to him in robbing the Cornhill Vaults than in stealing an apple where the world might see.

He handed Samuel a bell from the carpet-bag, an iron shell with a clapper and handle to ring children to school.

'Ring it in the fireplace, Sammy. Ring long if you see someone. Ring short when they've gone.'

Samuel nodded apprehensively and Rann continued, 'Any trouble, get straight into Sun Court. But, as you go by, ring the street bell of the vaults good and hard. We'll know there's a screw loose then.'

'Right,' Samuel said huskily and then cleared his throat. 'Right.'

'We're going down now,' Rann said. 'We'll bring the bills up from time to time.'

'How long?'

'Hard to say, Sam. There's the vault door. I know a way to open it but you could be having breakfast before I'm in.'

There was a quiver in Samuel's face, quickly checked.

As he led the way down the stairs, a chill cramp gripped Jack Rann's entrails. There was fear, after all; the fear of being alone. It was his first time without Pandy Quinn. Pandy, who worked without expression at a lock, in triumph or adversity, had been like an elder brother. When a lever would not budge or a bolt held fast, Pandy would tease it in some new way. Rann knew that it was not he who could crack any safe in London but Pandy Quinn. And Pandy had bled to death on a tap-room floor in Clerkenwell, so many months ago.

He glanced at Miss Jolly. She said nothing and showed little, as they came to the door of the cutting-room. But the tight-lidded almond eyes moved quickly and unpredictably, as if she could not help it. She was frightened, how should she not be? Perhaps he had better have gone without her. Suppose her nerve broke in tears, hysterics, unable to copy the endorsements on the bills . . . .

'This is easy,' he said quietly. 'Just the tailor's door.'

He tried the servant-key and let out a long breath. Then he kissed the cool gold of her cheek.

'See?' he said quickly. 'Nothing to it. And this is your way out, whenever the time comes.'

She took his hand, pressing it to her face for reassurance.

'And you, Jack?'

'I'd be up the chimney before they could get through the street door.'

He struck a match, lit the dark lantern from the carpet-bag, saw the flame settle, and opened the shutter. Before them stretched the length of the cutting-room, half-a-dozen heavy tables set at intervals, several high-backed chairs at each. Above the centre of each table was a double-branched gas-lamp, low on a long brass pipe from the ceiling. The green conical shades had been painted white on the underside, increasing the glare and heat of the mantel. Cheap coats in various stages of completion lay chalked and pinned, Brighton coats, Oxonians, and Chesterfields. Three men and women would work on a coat, each man as a rule cutting out and sewing the right or left of the main body, the woman stitching the arms and sleeves. Rolls of cloth and boxes of thread lay on the carpeted floor beside each chair. At each place were cotton reels, scissors and baskets of pins.

With shutters closed, the workroom was still hot and unventilated after the day's tailoring, an acid smell of new cloth from bales stacked by the far wall. Rann put down the lantern, went to the first table and set a match to the two mantels in their coolie-hat shades. By the wall-clock with its Roman numerals, it was twenty minutes past midnight. He checked a shabby silver-plated watch in

168

his pocket, its pearl face set with six cheap stones.

'They must a-known we'd need light to copy by!' he said cheerfully.

She looked at him and he remembered her childhood in such rooms, the heat and glare which brought blindness to many of their inmates, the rule of a reformatory master or mistress, starving or whipping for work not neatly done.

There was an unlocked door at the far end, leading to the lower room where the cheap coats and cloaks were sold, a show-shop which dispensed garments directly to the public. A circular iron staircase led down to the darkened shop at street level. Here, too, the windows were shuttered against thieves.

Rann said a prayer for Pandy Quinn, who had come this far and reconnoitred the shop. At the rear was a row of fitting-rooms. Rann doubted if anyone had taken up the dusty hessian or seen the boards beneath for ten years past. He worked at the corner of a fitting-room by the back wall. Hessian came up easily, bringing the tacks with it.

'When you leave,' he said, as she stood over him, 'lay the carpet on the boards and knock the tacks in their holes. No one won't look close then whatever happens.'

He drew the hessian back. Beneath it were six-inch boards, eight of them forming the width of the fitting-room floor, running forward under its wall into the shop.

'They'll have to be cut,' he said, 'two of 'em. Cut a couple of feet from the wall, where the first joist must be.'

'What if they see it's done?'

He screwed a hacksaw blade into its frame.

'They ain't looked under this carpet for years. They won't look for years more. Even if they do, they won't know what the boards are supposed to look like nor why they might have been cut. I can dirty them in ten seconds.'

When the hacksaw had started the cut, he chose a heavier blade. The board was loose on the joist. He levered out the nails that held it by the wall. A brief struggle freed it, opening a dark drop beneath the fitting-room floor. The second board was easier. There was room to lower himself. He handed Miss Jolly a small leather writing-box from the carpet-bag with the pens, inks, and enlarging-glass.

'All you do is wait,' he said, hugging her with one arm. 'I'll come back as soon as I get the first bills. Anything wrong, you go straight up to Sammy, or out through the street door. And there'll be a necessary closet back of the workroom.'

He kissed her cheek, feeling moisture. Perspiration in the closed room, or a tear of fright? Then he lowered himself and his feet touched uneven rubble.

Five feet down, too shallow for a cellar. Lowering the carpet-bag, he shone his lantern at the wall dividing the tailor's shop from the Cornhill Vaults. As he started towards it, there was a shriek and a scuttling. A rat the size of a young rabbit sprang past, making for safety in the far corner of the rubble-strewn space.

Jack Rann put down the carpet-bag by the roughened wall. It was not load-bearing but a stone partition several courses high, no thicker than a single block. The damage must be done on this side. There was not a chance that Mr Trent would investigate his foundations. If he did, his enthusiasm for the perversities shown to Pretty Jo or Maggie Fashion might counsel silence.

With a wide-bladed cold-chisel and a muffled hammer, he began on the mortar between two stones at mid-height. It flaked and cracked. He choked twice with the dust. The blows of the hammer on a chisel, deadened by lint, would be inaudible in the street.

Even so, he listened for the bell, working round the perimeter of each block. With a smaller head-bar, he prised the stone towards him. It was more than he could lower or lift. But with the next stone free, the pair turned through forty-five degrees, he might open a gap a foot high and eighteen inches long.

In dust and dark, he was as far from the world as a drowned sailor in the depths of the sea. He thought it had taken twenty minutes to free and turn the blocks of stone. Perhaps more. He shone the dark lantern through the gap and saw another rubble-strewn expanse. Lifting the carpet-bag, he slid after it like a diver. It was the small hours of Sunday morning but at last he stood directly under the strong-room floor of Mr Walker's Cornhill Vaults.

22

Lantern light cut a path along boards and joints above him. Rann knocked with the head-bar at intervals. The dull resonance lightened abruptly, confirming where the plate-iron of the strong-room floor ended and the office began. Having sealed the strong-room with iron, Mr Walker saw no need to protect the rear office. Rann aimed for the far corner. Boards under a carpet and no furniture above. He prayed it might still be so.

Crouching in the cobwebbed corner, he found a short renewal board on only two joists with a longer one next to it. He tried them. The short board was nailed on the joists but free at the wall. With the tapered head-bar and hammer, he prised the steel between board and joist, then drove it home. He hung with all his weight. Nails groaned and squealed in wood. He felt them give as the short board sprang an inch from the joist. There was only carpet above.

He worked the board, moving it clear, sliding the head-bar under the carpet, and wrenched again. The carpet-edge came up, taking the tacks with it. Now he could fold it from the black-varnished border of the floor. His narrow lantern-beam shone into a darkened room above him.

The long board lay over several joists. With the head-bar, he freed it from two joists nearer the wall. It was held by a weight above. The corner of a desk perhaps. If need be he would cut it at the next joist with his hacksaw. But he made one more effort to lift it and slide through. It sprang an inch or so with a thump and a crash. But he could raise its nearer length. There was space enough.

Rann lifted the carpet-bag, pulled himself up, shone the lantern and saw office windows covered by cream shutters of stoutly panelled wood. The thump had been the overturning of a small table. The crash was the breakage of a Meissen candlestick with a pink rose design on a white ground.

He put the table upright and gathered the fragments of china. At the worst they would suspect that a clerk or a customer had broken it and hidden the damage.

He unbolted a rear door from the office to the brick extension. Galvanic batteries, used in electro-plating, gave its workshop a corrosive metallic air. A three-foot square furnace was set in the hearth and a fourteen-inch flue sloped back from it. To increase the draught, the flue would narrow near the top. Twelve inches, if he was lucky. It was tight – but to a climbing-boy of Rann's build and experience, it was enough.

He went back to the office and the opposite door to the strong-room. Beyond it were the constant gaslight and spy-holes from the street. He knocked firmly on a panel of the door. The resonance was deadened again by sheet-iron lining on its far side. To open it by any means except the lock would be impossible.

Bringing his cheap bracelet for repair, Rann had noted that the door was held by one of the new cylinder-locks with the stamp of Linus Yale upon it. It would have more than three thousand combinations for the keys that might raise its five pin-tumblers. Mr Walker thought it enough. Even a man who could open that door, would be on view to every passer-by and policeman through the spy-holes in the steel shutters.

In his mind Jack Rann saw the interior of Linus Yale's lock, plainly as a schoolroom map. Unlike a Chubb or a Bramah, where only the levers were moved, the entire cylinder of a Yale turned with the key. The keys were sheet metal, cut flat in an attempt to prevent a thief working a pick in the narrow keyway. Five steel pin-tumblers, each thick as a match and held by springs, dropped as the key was withdrawn. To turn the cylinder and draw back the bolt, the key was inserted upside down. Its contours lifted each steel pin level with the circumference of the cylinder. Only when each was lifted by a unique distance would the cylinder turn and the bolt draw back.

Pandy Quinn had bought several specimens of Yale's invention to work upon. And even Pandy had taken a month to perfect the opening of it. Rann, who watched his progress, had since dissected a dozen locks of this type with the care that a practised surgeon might have given to a choice cadaver.

Where damage did not matter, he would drill through the pins. A fine diamond-head in an American off-centre brace would enter the keyway and cut through the ends. Shorn of their length, the pins no longer held a cylinder in its locked position. But the damage would be discovered when there was no resistance to the key. Mr Walker's lock must remain in working order.

He unstrapped the bag and laid out a small brace with a wooden mushroom-grip and an off-centre steel shaft to add force to the drive. In its mouth, he fitted a diminutive diamond-head that a watchmaker might have coveted.

Pandy Quinn had calculated that to cut the pins one by one divided the possible combinations by five each time. By leaving the two innermost pins to exert pressure on the key and work the lock, he might reduce the combinations from more than three thousand to about thirty.

Thanks to Maggie's courtship of Arthur Trent and her tracing of the contours of the Yale for the rooms rented from Mr Walker, Pandy had gone further. As a locksmith's boy, he knew that a suite of Yales for such a building would differ in the outer pins but that the deepest pins would probably be the same in all of them.

His legacy included two dozen keys, which he had filed to oper-ate the two innermost pins of a Yale based on the pattern of Mr

Trent's. Better still, with such a key in place and two rear pins resting in its contours, there was just room to use a fine probe that might raise the next pin to a point where the cylinder of the lock would turn and free the bolt. With three or four pins left intact, it would feel to Mr Walker or his supervisor that the lock was working as usual.

Jack Rann knelt, hands and eyes level with the keyhole. The fine diamond-head entered the keyway, catching at first on the side. He frowned and adjusted it so that it cleared the mouth in the lock-plate by an invisible fraction of an inch. Then the veins in his narrow wrists swelled with exertion as he wound the shaft of the brace slowly but with all his weight and strength. Each pin was a pygmy in bulk but a full minute of metallic grinding passed before he felt the first one give.

He put down the brace and took a fine needle of steel to coax out the broken fragment. Now there was more space and the next pin would be easier.

He listened, touched the bit to the second pin and turned the brace. Then his heat beat in his throat as he heard the explosion of a bell-clapper that seemed close as the next room. Samuel's warning, carried by flues and hearths. Jack Rann waited until the man on his beat moved off and Samuel rang a single note several times.

The second pin sheered off under the drill. It seemed as far as he need to go. He studied the lock and saw the bit had cut straight and true. There was not a scratch on the edges of the metal lock-plate.

Patiently, he took the flat steel keys from their pouch and tried each in turn. After a dozen, the cylinder turned a fraction of an inch before jamming. Rann drew the arm of his shirt across his forehead. Despite the heat, he shivered and took the slender probe of hardened steel. It moved easily in the keyway, above the flat outer length of his steel shank. Then it was a matter of sense and touch, pressing the nearest pin upwards against the spring that held it in place, turning the key at the same time to raise the inner tumblers.

Nothing moved. He eased the steel needle a little, breathed

deeply, and shivered again with relief as he felt the cylinder turn, taking the bolt with it.

He put away his tools and pushed the door gently. Through its gap there was a white fire of gas shining steadily on squares of iron, studded and painted battleship-grey. The corrugated steel of the window-shutters with their two spy-holes were like blind eye-sockets or dark wounds. On the rear wall, which he could not yet see, was the mirror that reflected the strong-room to the street.

A policeman was the only probable passer-by in the small hours of Sunday morning. That gave him twenty minutes before he heard Samuel's bell again.

The flat steel vault-door, with its twelve-inch lock-plate, twin keyholes, and bolt-wheel, was set in the wall to his right. Its metal plate was embossed as Milner's Double Treasury with the maker's address in Finsbury Pavement. Rann took another breath and let it out slowly. Before entering the strong-room, he chose a small boxwood wedge and jammed it into the strike-plate of the Yale to keep the bolt open. Then, with heart pumping, he stepped into the white brilliance of unshaded gas. The silent spy-holes faced him from the street like gun muzzles whose triggers might be pulled at any moment.

He was safe enough, unless Samuel fell into a doze ... unless the bell sounded too faintly for him to hear ... unless Samuel was trapped .... Working on the Yale he had been absorbed and calm. Now he felt his hand shaking. But Jack Rann spoke softly to the soul of Pandy Quinn and swore to be true.

A year ago, with Pandy at his side, two country-dressed trippers had studied the vault-door through the spy-holes on quiet Sundays or Saturday evenings when the commercial length of Cornhill was deserted. Several times, he and Pandy had gone to an abandoned cotton warehouse in Shadwell. The safe once used by its owner was still there. It was not Milner's Double Treasury but worked on the same principle. The watchman had taken two sovereigns to leave them alone for an afternoon.

With force and unlimited time, a large steel 'alderman' head-bar would jemmy the best single-bolted safe or vault. But Milner's set of six steel bolts, holding the door top to bottom, was proof against jemmying of any kind. Mr Walker was safe in the knowledge that only the lock would open his vault.

In Rann's narrow skull lay a map of the Double Treasury Lock, as plain as the design of the Yale. The central bolt to which the five others were linked was round steel, thick as a broomhandle, held shut with a ton of pressure from a steel bit. The bit was secured by two steel arms on pivots. Each pivot was activated by a set of three cogwheels, each set controlled by a separate lock. The first cog of a set was moved by turning the key, until the others followed.

No one man would be trusted to open the Cornhill Vaults alone. The first key would move the cogs to lift the first lever. But only when the second key was turned and the second lever had been raised was the pressure of the steel bit on the central bolt removed. Still the door would not open until the wheel to one side of the keyholes was turned, drawing back simultaneously the six linked bolts.

Treasury locks were designed for keys whose steps could be varied constantly. A resetting of the first cogwheel's position in each lock would make a key which opened the door on one day useless on the next. Pandy Quinn's answer had been the micrometer, often spoken of but seldom seen.

When a lock was opened without a key, it was most often by a locksmith, called when the owner lost a key or the mechanism was faulty. Quinn had been the first to hear of James Sargent's new micrometer, designed to chart the interior of a closed lock. The American locksmith claimed that he had measured the position of pins and levers to a ten-thousandth of an inch, using a watch-face as his dial.

Quinn never saw Sargent's invention, whose prototype was kept on the premises of Sargent and Greenleaf, locksmiths of Rochester, New York, but its principle was clear to him. Rann unwrapped the lint from Quinn's copy. For this device, Orator Hawkins had offered him the run of Newgate and two more weeks of life; for this, Pandy Quinn had died.

Quinn's micrometer was simple by comparison with the American original, a single hand on a watch dial, instead of hands for hours, minutes and seconds which Sargent had devised. Yet to measure a sixtieth of an inch on Quinn's dial was straightforward and to measure a hundredth might be possible.

The copy consisted of a metal probe, slimmer than the shank of a key, with a single metal step at its end, large enough to encounter the levers but thin enough to pass the steel wards which sometimes guarded the keyway. The probe was connected to a two-inch corrugated strip of metal. On this hung a miniature weight that could be adjusted as if on the arm of a weighing machine. While the probe moved, its progress turned the wheel-mechanism of the watch, measuring the distance travelled, the watch-hand moving in time with it.

As the probe approached the first lever of the lock, the little weight was moved to maintain the tension and balance between the probe and the dial. At the first lever, the probe was turned on its side to clear the lever and the wards of the lock, then upright again until it encountered the second lever. At each of the five levers, the position could be read from the dial.

His ears alert for the rattle of Samuel's bell, Rann carried the micrometer out of the rear office, pulled shut the Yale door, and knelt at the double-lock of the vault. Five levers. He could be certain of that. With the dial supported on his palm, he eased the probe into the first keyway. The hand moved slowly through the minutes of the hour. One by one they made their map. Eight, nineteen, twenty-nine, thirty-five, forty-seven.

He tried again, to test for error. But months of practice had made him near-perfect. The second time, each reading was one minute earlier on the dial, but this confirmed that he had got the relative distances between them accurately. Then it was a matter of measuring the second lock. This time he did it only once. The figures were identical to the first lock, though those employees who held the keys would never be allowed to know it. Owners did not advertise that they often used identical keys and settings for the twin locks. Some did it for fear of losing one of the keys. Mr Walker, perhaps, was not prepared to pay good money to have the cogs of the locks constantly reset to different keys.

Rann looked round to make sure he had left nothing on view. With the micrometer wrapped again, he opened the door of the rear office and closed it after him. By the light of the lantern he began to fit the first shank of a skeleton key with five metal steps of the smallest size, spaced at the micrometer readings. The irony, it seemed to him, was that he was doing exactly what Milner's or Mr Walker would do in varying their settings.

The key to a variable Treasury Lock was itself a skeleton. The shank ended in two downward prongs, an inch apart with a steel screw connecting them. The steel steps were threaded on the screw and tightened in whatever order and contour the locksmith or his client chose and changed as often as required. Combined with the six steel bolts, it was the despair of the housebreaker and shop-burglar. But a technician like Pandy was entitled to believe that it must have been made for him.

Of the smallest key-steps, none was likely to make contact with the levers of the lock, even when set at the right distance. One size at a time, Jack Rann would work his way up until the first step touched a lever. He must then increase the height of the others until every step seemed ready to raise its lever and turn the first set of cog-wheels.

He finished the key and heard the clatter of Samuel's bell. A minute or two later the single bell-notes signalled that all was clear.

Back in the strong-room, his face ran with sweat under the flaring gas of the summer night. But he felt the calm that came from doing the thing he did best in the world. No mechanic, no lock-smith, could match what Pandy had taught him. His hand was steady as he screwed the first metal teeth tighter on the key-shank and tried it in the lock. As he expected, none of the smallest steps touched the levers. It might be hours before he could defeat the vault door.

Beside him were the steel key-steps in a watchmaker's pouch. He worked, kneeling by the vault until, at the fifth attempt, a lever grazed the outer step. He drew the shank out and saw a slight scratch on the polished metal. Then, in a long interval between the sounding of the alarm bell, he increased the other steps, little by little, until each of them met a lever, as squarely as the key created by Milner's themselves.

He held his breath and tried the key he had built. It passed the keyway and he felt the tip engage the talon or notch at the rear of the lock. The shank was held firm enough now for its steel steps to lift the levers. In the hermetic silence of the strong-room, he heard and felt the levers move, almost through ninety degrees. And then they jammed.

Jack Rann let out a gasp of frustration. He tried to ease the key back and draw it clear. But the far tip of the shank seemed trapped in the talon. Worse still, the talon and levers held his key-shank askew, so that it would turn neither way. He could not move it but dared not leave it in the lock for the first policeman at the spy-holes to see.

To pull the key out by force was more than his strength could match. Calmly, despite the cold sweat on his face, he tried to edge it deeper a fraction. Faintly, he felt that one of the metal steps had now cleared a minute obstruction. Turning the shank again, he heard a set of quiet cogwheels move. A steel arm rose in a slight eccentric movement from the powerful bit holding the central bolt.

Before he could try the other lock, the distant clamour of Samuel's bell sounded. Rann cursed, gathering the watchmaker's pouch of key-steps, scrambling past the Yale door. As he closed it, the bell rang single notes. A false alarm? A passer-by with no interest in the spy-holes? A policeman too late on his beat to pause?

In the strong-room again, he tried his key in the second lock. For some reason it engaged the talon but missed the levers. Yet he knew it must be right. He had worked it too far in or not far enough. By drawing back a little, still lodged in the talon, it turned its circle. As the second set of cogwheels moved, he felt the last pressure released from the main bolt of the steel door.

Now it was a matter of collecting the carpet-bag and slowly turning the bolt-wheel at one side of the lock-plate. He heard the hushing sound of six steel bolts drawn back in unison. The heavy wheel served as a handle by which the weight of the door could be pulled slowly open.

Jack Rann slid clear the shutter of the dark lantern, took his carpet-bag, and stepped into the darkness. Pulling the heavy door until it would appear closed behind him, he stared at the interior of the Cornhill Vaults.

23

Like caskets of the dead in a necropolis of the ancient world, rows of steel deposit boxes presented their blank silvered faces to the tawny flicker of the oil-lamp. There were more than he had imagined. They stood three tiers high on metal shelves, the lowest a couple of feet from the floor. Numbered in order, the ranks ranged down the longer walls to either side and across the shorter walls, as well as in two ranks back-to-back down the centre of the vault. The front of each was fifteen inches square and its depth about two feet. They were not designed for bulk but for confidential documents and small items of great value.

Jack Rann walked down the aisles and saw that the numbering ran to 364. With the five keys cut by Pandy Quinn from the wax impressions of the autumn burglaries, he might open as few as five boxes or as many as fifty. Pandy's chance discovery that two of the stolen keys were identical had made the larger number possible.

He walked slowly back along the ranks of steel, then stopped and listened. He was hidden from the spy-holes but might no longer hear Samuel's bell. At whatever moment he left the vault, there could be eyes at the spy holes. He and Pandy had seen no watchman at night. But if a watchman visited the premises, the unlocked doors would be found. The wheel would be turned, shooting six steel bolts across and trapping the thief in the vault. Samuel and even Miss Jolly might find a way out. It was a condition of his gamble that Rann would be beyond rescue.

As in most safe deposits, the steel boxes were fitted with key exchangeable locks. Both the client's and the banker's keys would close a lock but only the client's would open it. Rann tried the locks with the first of his five keys. It opened nothing at all. Either his own wax impression or Pandy Quinn's copy had not been true. But here and there, as he tried the second key, he felt the first levers of the little locks move, the shank turning through a quarter circle. This time, the cut was true.

A single key would fit several locks. This suggested almost a hundred varying patterns. At the first deposit box which his second key opened, he stared into a bare steel cavity. Neither he nor Pandy Quinn had considered that some of the safe deposits might be unused. The second proved as empty as the first.

The third box yielded a will, two mortgages, and two leather boxes set with wine-tinted stones. Going through the papers, he found one inland bill of exchange, drawn on Drummonds Bank, Pall Mall East, six weeks earlier for £250 at three months notice. The paper had been endorsed twice and had seven weeks to run. It was Rann's first trophy.

Some bills would be no use. He needed those drawn on banks for which Saward had stolen the blank forms. A number of these required the return of the bill to its bank for an acceptance stamp at each endorsement. For these, Miss Jolly's needle had carved a counterfeit stamp in slate. If a bill was genuine and unpaid, the previous endorsements registered, no bank need look closely at a stamp.

Rann knew that in the next hour he must have enough bills for his penny-dancer to start work. By the lantern-light, he moved down the ranks of steel, trying each of the five stubby keys in each lock. One after another they jammed at a quarter turn. Only at the end of the first row did another move through a half circle. With time at his heels, he drew the steel drawer open, turned the key back to free it, and hurried on.

Two locks opened in the next row and one in the third, completing the ranks that stood against the first long wall. He began on the centre ranks. Until then he had supposed the vault to be completely sealed from the light and air of the outside world. Only as he moved down the centre aisle did he notice a small square grating in the far corner of the ceiling and a watery flush of light from the early summer dawn. He looked at his silver-plated pocket-watch and saw that it was after four in the morning. Time had fled, like a malevolent genie stripping him of life. If Trent had chosen to return before Monday, the robbery might have been impossible.

He began to search the steel boxes already open. In one hand he held a list of Saward's blank bill-forms with their values and dates, the names of banks where those were entered. He had opened nine drawers so far. Four held nothing. One had half-a-dozen inland bills of the London and Westminster Bank on pink treasury paper. They matched Saward's blanks. Rann chose the largest sums. Three for £200 and one for £500. Six weeks to run on each. On his list he marked the number of the box.

He took two overseas bills from the next box, inscribed in copperplate on pale blue for the Bank of Montreal at £500 each, three bank post-bills written by hand, payable to bearer for £150. The post-bills had only two weeks to run but it was long enough.

After half an hour he had matched a dozen of Saward's blank forms with those in the opened boxes. Some were for no more than fifty pounds, one was for a thousand. Counting as he went, he thought the total had passed £4,000. But the copying must begin at once.

He and Pandy had known there was no way of concealing the robbery while it was in progress. Rann left the vault as it was, the steel boxes open. If he pushed the door of the vault a fraction of an inch to admit sound but not enough to show that it was open, he would hear Samuel's bell. A policeman might be staring through the spy-holes into the gaslight. But a policeman would not stand there long enough to risk being late at the points of his beat, where an inspector might be waiting. Rann decided to count to a hundred. If there was no sound of the bell, the policeman had either gone or not arrived.

He counted slowly and heard nothing. Then, keeping his face from the shutters, he pushed the heavy door, slipped past and closed it again. It was a dozen steps to the Yale door. With the dark lantern in one hand and a leather wallet of bank bills in the other, he stepped into the darkness of the rear office and pulled the door behind him. There was no movement, no sound of alarm. Then he jumped as a hand touched his shoulder and a voice behind him in the darkness said,

'Jack Rann!'

The shock of it winded him. He turned with the lamp before him and saw the oil-light glimmer on the questioning beauty of her almond eyes.

'What's wrong?' he gasped. 'What's gone wrong?'

'Nothing,' she said softly, 'not now. But you were so long, Jack. I came after you this far.'

He put the lantern down, wound his arms round her and said, 'Go back.'

Miss Jolly shook her head, short and hard.

'I'll do the copies here. Make it easier.'

'The pens and inks . . . .'

'Got them,' she cooed, teasing his doubt of her. 'There's gas in the workshop to see by.'

'We can't risk gas being seen from there.'

'Look at the shutter-crack,' she said patiently, 'it's morning outside.'

He stared at her and saw that the robbery might be easier, not more difficult, than he and Pandy Quinn had imagined. On a table in the jeweller's workshop, she had set out pens, inks, and enlarging glasses. Counterfeit dies, carved in slate, were arranged and marked like the tidy-work of a seamstress. Rann laid out the bills from the vault, chose the blanks from Saward's folder and watched her start on the first London and Westminster bill for £200.

Fifteen minutes later she had copied the sums and dates, adding the signature and the serial number of the bill. She worked in a hand that Rann could not have told from the original. More difficult were the endorsements on the back 'Pay to – or order', written by the clerk in red and signed in blue, accompanied by the bank's stamp. He could not swear that Miss Jolly's version of these signatures was a true one. But the beauty of it was that the possessor of the bill would no longer have an original of the endorsements to compare it with. Moreover, the stamp of the bank as acceptor had been brought to perfection by months of practice. With the originals before her, Miss Jolly could place the counterfeit stamps exactly where each individual clerk habitually marked his own. No mere forger could have guessed the stamping habits of every clerk. Jack Rann smiled with relief. He truly believed that Pandy Quinn's masterpiece would not fail.

'I'm going back,' he said presently. 'I'll be safe enough except when I come out again from the vault to the strong-room. An hour from now, stand at the door there. Open it a crack and bang on it once, about every minute, so long as you don't hear Sammy's bell and it's all clear. If I don't hear that bang, I shan't come out until I do. See?'

She nodded and looked down, impatient to get on with her copperplate and signed endorsements. Rann kissed her on the neck, turning to the Yale door with a lighter heart.

An hour was long enough to find eight more steel drawers that answered to four keys. Six yielded nothing. Of the others, one had a pair of Rothschild's bills on pink paper, the first for £250, the next for £600. Rann stared at the sums with a feeling of unreality. He still could not believe that mere paper could be transformed into heaps of gold coins. But Pandy Quinn had promised it was so, and Pandy had known the truth.

At the second drawer, the promise was redeemed: Rann found the treasure that he knew must be somewhere in the Cornhill

Vaults. It was the safe deposit of Lord Tregarva. Pandy had chosen with care the men whose houses were to be burgled and had sworn that Tregarva was the prize. There were more genuine bills of exchange than Jem Saward had ever possessed blanks. In a wooden box beside them lay rows of gold sovereigns, perhaps for payment of the men who melted and milled Tregarva's steel, some coins still in unbroken paper tubes, new-minted from the Bank of England.

Suppose he abandoned the bills of exchange and settled for the gold? Pandy Quinn, his good angel, would not let him do it. His share of the coins alone would let him run but never hide.

Rann waited his hour, then pushed the vault door a fraction. He listened and heard the distant knock of Miss Jolly's knuckles on the wood of the Yale door.

On the table in the workshop lay completed copies of bills from the London and Westminster Bank, the Bank of Montreal, and bank post-bills. As his dancer worked on, Rann checked them through. The dates, serial numbers, sums to be paid and endorsements matched the originals like the most perfect images.

The time had come to break off. Pandy had planned a robbery that would take a night and a day, perhaps a second night. Somewhen in the day, they would stop to eat and sleep. That interval was planned as carefully as the rest of the scheme.

The bank-bills now copied must first replace those taken from the vault. The vault door would then be closed but not locked, good enough when seen from the spy-holes. The Yale could now be locked and easily opened again. No policeman at the spy-holes would have cause for suspicion. The carpet and the boards must be replaced in the rear office, though not fastened down. The bills that had been copied and the carpet-bag would be taken out. To return to the vault, Rann needed only a picklock, a pocketful of keys, and a smaller head-bar. The alderman head-bar, hammer, drill, and micrometer had done their work.

Half-an-hour later, he followed Miss Jolly through the foundations and into the tailor's premises. Closing the cutting-room door, he led her to the stairs and up to Trent's rooms. Samuel waited, his smooth pale face drawn with anxiety but his voice chuckling with hope.

'How'd it go, Jack?'

Rann nodded and sat down in a Viennese armchair of fringed red velvet with a deep fan-shaped back. Samuel's amiable rodent face broke into a smile and he began a slow deep sound of merriment at the sight of the bills. But Jack Rann was already asleep.

24

When he opened his eyes, Samuel was watching Miss Jolly copy the last bank post-bill. Rann had fallen asleep in early afternoon. Now the light was full through the window over Sun Court. The bells of St Mary-le-Bow pealed for Evening Prayer.

'Almost six, Jack,' said Samuel quietly.

'It never is!' he yawned. 'We'll have to move, Sam.'

He sat up in the velvet chair and saw a jug of milk next to a plate of bread and butter. Samuel watched him drink from the jug and fold a slice of buttered bread.

'Move?'

'Mr Trent,' said Rann through bread and butter. 'Last night we knew he was in Ramsgate. Tonight he could come back.'

'Why, when he's gone two nights?'

Rann shrugged.

'Not having all he hoped. Bit of a turn-up with Miss Mag, p'raps. Who knows? All I say is, we got to be ready tonight as wasn't necessary yesterday.'

Samuel's eyes moved quickly. Rann stood up and put a hand on the bent shoulder.

'I'm only saying, Sammy, what might happen. That's all. If you see trouble while we're down below, take the bag and go straight down the next floor. If they're too close for you to get to the street door, the cutting-room ain't locked. Go in there. Wait for Trent to come up here, then go down.'

But Samuel's self-assurance of a few hours earlier had wilted.

'You never said . . . .'

'Sammy, we got to keep our eyes open, that's all. Goes without question, don't it?'

He folded the bank paper that had been copied, slipping it into a leather handkerchief-case and closing it in the carpet-bag.

'And don't forget the bell, Sam. So long as you play your tune on that we're safe.'

In his pocket were the keys and picks. His lantern waited in the tailor's fitting-room. For his exit from the vaults he took only the short steel head-bar. Holding Miss Jolly by the hand, he led her through the cutting-room, under the floor to the rear office of the vaults.

'We can't put up light once it's dark. There's just a crack in these shutters. They'd notice light if they was looking for it. We'd best finish before dark.'

He left her, went cautiously back to the vault and placed her latest copies of the bills of exchange where the originals had been.

Forty-four blank bills from Saward's bureau were now reduced to eight. The keys in his possession had opened seven more boxes. Three of them yielded nothing. The next held a dozen bills drawn on various banks in several denominations. Five were a match for Saward's blank drafts on Baring Brothers, Brown Shipley & Co., and the Union Bank Pall Mall. The sum of the first was £1,000, the second was for £150. The largest of the rest was for £3,000. All had been in the possession of Lord Mancart, himself a director of the provincial bankers Mitchell, Yeames & Co.

Rann hesitated at the size of the payments. But each was validly endorsed. There was no reason on earth for a clerk to question them. Lord Mancart, a banker, would have a hundred such bills through his hands for endorsement every month.

Best of all, Samuel, the clerical gentleman, had paved the way for a marriage settlement, the liquidation of funds in a wardship suit, and a partnership in a joint stock company. Two thousand pounds was not excessive. Several bills for trivial sums might draw more suspicion.

In any case, a bank scrutineer would not look twice at his own firm's bona fide bills before payment was made. Those drawn on Baring Brothers, Brown Shipley, or the Union Bank Pall Mall could be confirmed as genuine within the hour. The designs themselves would defeat a mere faker. The Union Bank's paper was printed with a Greek key design too intricate to forge. Baring Brothers included an oak tree with a labyrinth of leaves, impossible to imitate. The endorsements on both were genuine. It was Lord Mancart, presenting bills filled in by Miss Jolly, who must explain himself. Rann smiled at the neatness of Pandy's work.

He was almost at the last box. It was unlike the others, half-empty but containing envelopes addressed to several men. The envelopes were sealed and he knew that he dared not risk betraying the robbery by opening them. All the same, he went through the pile and, as he did so, found one whose flap had been tucked in but not stuck down. It had a wax seal to identify it. There was a thickness of paper inside. He drew the contents out and stared at a sixpenny pamphlet of eight pages, crudely printed with a gallows emblem and black-letter gothic on its cover.

> 'Be Sure Your Sins Shall Find You Out!'
> Being the Last Confession of James Patrick Rann,
> otherwise Handsome Jack, to be hanged at Newgate
> Gaol on the 21st of May for the Barbarous Murder
> of his friend Pandy Quinn in the Tap-room of the
> Golden Anchor, Hatton Wall, Clerkenwell.

Rann blinked at the crudely printed paper, wondering if he had gone mad and was seeing only what lay in his mind. He glanced round him, looked down and read it again. Even the robbery of so many thousands of pounds went from his mind. He had known there were such catchpenny pamphlets printed for his death but his heart went cold and his stomach tightened at the sight of it. The courage kept up in the last few hours, dispersed like smoke. He felt sick with the dread of a trap.

No sane man would waste room in a safe deposit to keep a hawker's pamphlet. It lay in the steel box because he was meant to find it. The secret that he shared with Pandy Quinn, the meticulous plan, had been no secret at all. He stood in the tawny oil-light and knew that he had been caught.

Not caught by the police. So how and by whom? He took the last bills to the vault door, listened for Miss Jolly's knock and brought them to her. He said nothing. If he and she had been found out, the snare was too well rigged for them to escape it now. He sat and watched her copy the bills. But he sat with fists clenched on his knees and the ghost of Pandy Quinn warning him to get clear while he could. Two bills for £100 were left. The chance was no longer worth it.

'That's enough,' he said abruptly. 'Leave them.'

'Leave them?' The eyelids blinked as she looked at him. 'Why leave them, Jack? Why?'

'We got to move,' he said firmly. 'Now.'

He took the finished copies and the bills she had not begun. For £200, for £2,000, for £20,000, he would not stay. When he had replaced the originals with her copies, he went to the last deposit-box to look again at the black-lettered pamphlet. He dared not take it. That was what his hunters intended. Unlocking the box, drawing it from its envelope, he stared at the obscene black print that celebrated his death. And then he saw that on this second occasion he had unlocked the same steel box with a different key. It would open with any key, then. But why?

Closing the box and locking it, he slipped from the vault into the strong-room for the last time. He turned the wheel on the front of the heavy door and felt the six bolts whisper into place. With the key that he had built to open the twin locks, he turned the cogs and felt the steel arms close with a ton of pressure behind them. But he worked like a man in a dream. Then he was gone from the view of the spy-holes, closing the Yale on the office door.

'What's the matter, then?' She looked at him, her voice rising in apprehension at the sight of his face. Rann put a finger to his lips. He took the pens and inks from the table, clearing everything that might betray their presence. He helped her down between the floorboards of the rear office and through the foundations of the vaults to those of the tailor.

They came to the corner where he had taken up carpet and boards in the tailor's fitting-room. Rann pulled his head and shoulders above the level of the floor. He stopped and listened. There was not a sound in the building. He drew himself clear and pulled Miss Jolly after him.

'Right,' he said softly, 'you know what to do. Take the bills, the bag of pens and inks, the lantern too. When I go back down, I'll pull the two boards in place. Lay the hessian back over 'em and knock the tacks into their holes. Heel of a shoe'll do it. Then go back to Sammy upstairs. Lock the cutting-room. Put that key and the key to Trent's rooms in his safe, as if they were never took. He'll think it was them photographs of Pretty Jo that Bragg or someone was after. You and Sammy wait in the room for me. But if there's a screw loose, take the carpet-bag and clear out. I'll look for you at the Marquis of Granby.'

'But you, Jack!' Her slim fingers covered his hand on the edge of the board as he stood again in the space below. Jack Rann drew his hand out and covered hers.

'I got to go back this way, my love. The other floor and carpet in the vaults got to look right. It can't look right if I come up with you. If they think someone's had that carpet up, they'll look at the boards underneath. If they think they've been took up, they'll have that Yale lock apart. Once they see it's been drilled, they'll have Milner's in like a flash and perhaps find scratches, in the vault lock or in the deposit-box locks. Me and Pandy worked it out. There ain't no way but this.'

As quietly as he could, he pulled the two boards into place above his head, packing dirt where his hacksaw blade had gone through the longer board. He heard Miss Jolly draw the hessian into place at the corner of the fitting-room. A dozen light taps assured him that the tacks were in their holes.

It was almost black in the foundations as he made his way over the rubble. Gaslight in the rear office of the vaults shone through the open floorboards and dimly showed the gap where he had levered back two stones in the partition wall. Going to the open boards in the office floor, he reached up for the short steel head-bar, the length of his forearm.

This time he had fitted it with a forked cleaver to grip the corner of each block of stone and turn it back through forty-five degrees. With his head down and his hands gripping the steel bar, like a man turning a mill again, he brought the blocks into line. It was not perfect but it was good enough. Almost all the marks of damage were on the far side in the tailor's foundations.

Lodging the head-bar on the floor above him, he pulled himself up, slid the boards into place, drove the nails into their holes and tacked down the carpet in the rear corner of the office. He knew there was no sign, except his own presence, that the Cornhill Vaults had been entered.

As he turned out the gaslight and went through the workshop, he saw that it was twilight outside. Two men were crossing Sun Court in conversation, too low for him to catch the words. That they should be visiting commercial premises on a Sunday evening was odd. Yet once he was out of the building, there was nothing to make Mr Walker or the police suspect a robbery had taken place.

The chimney from the workshop furnace was the one he had recognized and measured with his eye from outside. It was square, the inner dimensions of the flue starting at about fourteen inches where it sloped back from the furnace, narrowing to ten or twelve inches at the top.

A novice would have looked in despair at so narrow a space. But Rann was no novice. He knew from practice what others deduced by mathematics. Fourteen inches became twenty inches 'on the slant'. Even ten became fourteen. Mathematics proved that he could do it. But Mathematics knew nothing of fear. Its calculations left out the utter darkness, coffin-like confinement growing ever narrower, soot thickening the air to a point where each breath was an agony. For Jack Rann, at that moment, it was the sight of the sixpenny pamphlet printed for his death which infected the air about him.

Pandy Quinn had planned the escape for a Sunday, when the furnace flue would be cool after a day's rest. Standing by the brick opening, Rann dismantled the head-bar into three sections. He took a length of string from his trouser pocket. Then he stripped the vest off over his head and drew off the moleskin trousers. Wearing only canvas shoes, he turned the clothes inside out, rolled them tight round the metal lengths of the bar and tied them with the string.

Climbing-girls as well as climbing-boys in his childhood preferred to 'buff it'. From decency, they first locked the door of the room where the chimney began, then stripped off their clothes on the hearth. Masters and mistresses of houses preferred not to know of these 'promiscuous practices', as the missioners called them. Yet climbing children, trapped and suffocating in narrow domestic chimneys, had often been caught tight on the rough brick as clothes snagged and rucked where a hand could not reach. In a nine-inch flue, the arms were wedged in the position in which they entered. One hand, stretched high to climb and brush, could not be lowered. The other, palm out at hip-level to push from below, could not be brought up. Jack Rann had sworn to Pandy Quinn that he could still climb a flue of nine or ten inches but he dared not risk it in vest and trousers.

The furnace was lined and faced with brick, standing a foot off the floor. In the fading twilight, it was black, empty, and dead. He knelt at its opening and stretched forward. His left arm would go above him, holding the tight bundle of clothes wrapped round the sections of the metal bar. He lay forward, in line with the angle of the flue, as the brickwork sloped back from the furnace-hearth.

At first it would be easy. The opening behind the furnace was two feet across, narrowing to fourteen inches a body-length beyond. Then the shaft curved from sight as it straightened vertically in the darkness. He had known such chimneys all his life. In the dark flue, whose air began to scorch his throat, he felt the familiar sandy texture of firebricks, with which it would be lined for the first twenty feet.

As the way narrowed, he eased the soreness of soot in his throat by spitting out the dust from time to time. The corrosive breath of it in his lungs was worse than the grazing from it on his hands. At intervals, the movements of his left hand above him brought down little showers of acrid powder on his head and shoulders.

In a fourteen-inch flue, he told himself, he could climb on the slant easy as eating pie. But his arms must be in place for the sudden narrowing. He would have no warning in the darkness. Only here and there a faint splash of light fell on the encrusted brickwork of the shaft from a small ventilation grille or the 'foul-air' pipes that ran off the main chimney.

He crawled at an angle, as the flue curved up from the furnace, his shoulders in diagonally opposite corners. Before it began to narrow, he touched an iron ventilation grille designed to protect banks and vaults from attempts to enter them by their chimneys.

The tips of his fingers found a square of corroded metal perforated by small holes. There was a catch on the inside that would open the two halves against the wall, allowing sweeps' brushes upwards. When closed, there was no means of opening it from above. Rann touched the catch. It was stiff but he felt it move. The two halves folded back awkwardly against the brick shaft.

196

Blind in darkness and soot, he struggled through. Then his heart jumped as he heard a man's voice. Who or where he could not tell. Perhaps it was Samuel. Or Trent. Perhaps someone had entered the cutting-room or the vaults. Perhaps it came from outside, the two men in Sun Court, or passers-by in the street. The metal grille was level with his hips now, about twelve feet above the hearth.

He was naked in the narrow flue, one arm above that could not be lowered, the other trapped by his side, his shoulders drawn in, his breath shallower. He listened. Like a shriek of terror, a bell rang. It was not Samuel's iron clapper but a bell that rang on and on, operated by mechanism of some kind. The sound came from a door, a street door that led to the tailor's shop or the vaults themselves.

There was no light below him and he guessed that the man who had spoken could not be in the workshop. All the same, if the building was searched, they would test the metal grille in the flue. They must not find it open while he was still climbing. He pushed himself clear, guiding it with his feet, letting it fall back and lock with as little sound as possible.

Soon he was gasping at the smart as the narrowing flue scraped flesh from the bony joints of his bare shoulders and hips. He could do nothing to protect his hips but he tried to draw his shoulders in more narrowly. Even the brine-hardened skin on his lower elbow was bleeding. He looked up to measure his progress. The bundle in his raised hand blocked any glimpse of twilight or night sky at the top of the flue. The narrowing shaft began to crush him in a last embrace, until he could scarcely work his lower hand. That arm was trapped, twisted by pressure until he gasped at the pain of wrenched muscles. His shoulders were concave to a point where he drew only quick and shallow breaths.

For the first time, he cried out and heard in his voice the sound that had begun so many childhood deaths. Twice, Rann had heard a trapped climbing-boy die. The first cry of alarm. The screams. The final helpless sounds. Others lost consciousness or were heard

197

only after the lighting of fires which killed them. In six or seven hours, Walker's men would light the workshop furnace. The way back was locked against him by the grille. He must go on or die.

Rann was well above the point where the flue had turned from a slant to a straight ascent. He guessed that the width here was twelve inches. A bulge of chimney-mortar, a lump of hardened fire-clay the size of an egg, might trap him. Had he worn the clothes that were in his left hand above him, the rough surface would have held him now as securely as a pair of claws.

The great danger was panic. Climbing-boys and climbing-girls who were trapped would struggle against the walls that held them, and were held faster still. In their exertions they breathed the foul air more deeply. Jack Rann paused. He felt no draught from the opening of the chimney above him, nothing but stagnant air below. He coughed black phlegm from the soot in his lungs and knew that, unless he could get free, he would suffocate before the furnace could be lit.

Even his ribs were scoured now by the crusted soot. The points of his hips were raw to the bone. Then, for the first time, he felt air, perhaps from a grille but more likely from the open sky above. There was a spurt of fright as he touched the smooth surface of engineering brick with which the last part of the stack had been re-lined. It was unyielding as iron. No amount of twisting or slanting would get past it if the way was too narrow. But he moved his raised hand, in which his clothes were held, and found room above him.

Like so many buildings adapted to industrial use, this one had a stack which stood about eight feet above a stretch of flat roof on a rear extension. He was in that upper part now. If he could climb where he was, surely he could reach the top.

At last he felt that his left hand was clear of the stack. He drew up harder, gripping the chimney rim until his head was level with it. The bundle of clothes and the wrapped sections of the head-bar fell softly on the flat roof behind Sun Court. He twisted, hung and dropped. With exhilaration beyond belief, he swore to himself and the soul of Pandy Quinn that he had not come so far only to die.

His fingers trembled a little as he undid the string, unfolded his vest and trousers, turned them out and drew them on. At one side was a drop of fifteen feet to the beginning of the parapet and the line of attic windows. A pipe, installed to drain the flat roof, ran down the wall and connected with another that drained the attic level.

Rann knelt and stretched down as far as he could. There was no lethal band of grease on the pipe, no other defence at this height. If a man fell from here, perhaps the law might call the use of tree-grease murder. He lowered himself, holding the pipe between his knees and with his hands. After the nightmare of the narrow flue, he felt beyond danger. His foot touched the parapet and he steadied himself. The building was silent. Trent's attic window was still open.

He must either go in this way and trust that it was safe or climb down to Sun Court. But if Trent or Bragg or the police were waiting in Trent's rooms, they would surely be watching below him in Sun Court as well. And if all was clear, he could not leave Samuel and Miss Jolly waiting for him. Also, to complete the plan, he needed to close Trent's safe.

A flush of starlight threw his shadow on the attic casement. The room was dark but his moving shadow was answered by a voice.

'Jack!'

Starlight caught an ellipse of almond eyes. He lowered himself into the room and seized her, regardless of the soot and blood.

'It's done!' he said with fierce triumph. 'Sammy still here?'

'Yes,' she whispered. 'Downstairs. He's to keep watch!'

'The bell?' he asked suddenly.

'A woman in black with a veil,' she gasped. 'Rang the bell but went away again. One of Trent's women, p'raps.'

Rann started to laugh with the relief of safety, he and the girl with their arms round one another. Miss Jolly gave a soft lilting murmur of simulated surprise as he lifted her and carried her to the bed.

'Later on,' – he nodded at the jug and bowl – 'we'll wash and use the clothes that's in the carpet-bag. We'll go to the rooms Sammy took at the Granby. But not yet.'

He drew down her pink equestrienne cavalry pants, as he had longed to do since watching the purposeful little swagger with which she went up the stairs the night before. He slid his hands under the coppery-cheeked smoothness of Miss Jolly's bottom, and made sooty love to his accomplice on Arthur Trent's white sheets.

25

Lord Tomnoddy stood among Grecian pillars at the Tivoli Corner of the Bank of England. He seemed lost in admiration of the tall windows and balustrading of the London and Westminster Bank on the far side of Lothbury. Few passers-by spared him a glance. Samuel had chosen him a russet tweed to make Short-Armed Tom the figure of a countryman in town, marvelling at all he saw.

Tomnoddy was to be inconspicuous. Samuel, under the *nom-de-guerre* of Mr Wilberforce, Attorney-at-Law, had also recruited three private 'bank-messengers'. They were men of genteel bearing and uncertain health who advertised for light work in the weekly papers of Holborn and Clerkenwell. Their pleas had been unanswered for some time. When chosen by Samuel they had shown a spaniel-like gratitude.

Each advertiser, at a conversation with Mr Wilberforce in a lounge of the Great Eastern Hotel, Bishopsgate Street, found the work even lighter and better paid than he had hoped. The attorney was settling the estate of a deceased nobleman before returning to his old-established practice in Cambridge. He was able to offer employment for a month, at a senior clerk's wages of two guineas a week.

In return, each man carried sealed letters to banks, insurance companies, and brokers in the commercial streets nearby, as well as to the post office of the Eastern Counties Railway Station, adjoining the hotel. From the banks and brokers, the messenger would bring sealed replies. Most of these contained little more than leaflets or formal answers to a general enquiry from Samuel as to the weekly discount rate or the market price of short-dated government stock.

If a messenger had absconded with such an answer, scenting bank notes or currency, he could have been replaced next day by other genteel paupers from the deep well of London's surplus labour. However, Samuel had a sympathetic nose for an impostor. The messengers he chose were evidently men of probity.

Mr Wilberforce's importance was plain. Among papers posted by his messengers, from the Eastern Counties Railway Station, were envelopes bearing addresses of imaginary landowners and legal partnerships, stretching from Cambridge to Edinburgh. Weeks or months later, these envelopes with their folded sheets of newspaper to bulk them out, would reach the Dead-Letter Office. Yet in London or the provinces, Mr Wilberforce and his clerk, James Patrick, appeared to be in correspondence with men of wealth and with the great houses of finance. As Samuel's clerk, Rann thought his first two baptismal names a sufficient disguise.

Several times a day, unknown to the bearer, the sealed letters from Mr Wilberforce to the banks contained bills of exchange to be cashed for Bank of England bonds. Soapy Samuel, as colonial bishop, joint stock investor, guardian of a seductive ward in chancery, had arranged these transfers in the previous fortnight. Now, on such errands, the messenger was shadowed by Tomnoddy and either Miss Jolly or Maggie Fashion.

It had been necessary to use counterfeit acceptance-stamps, carved from slate, on a dozen of the bills. Every other endorsement was genuine, the bill unimpeachable, tallying with all records, the stamp placed just where that scrutineer always placed it. No clerk was likely to query Miss Jolly's immaculate design. At the worst, with a timely warning, Samuel and Jack Rann would have left the

Great Eastern Hotel or the Marquis of Granby before the first enquiries began. The messenger alone would be left to explain the fraud.

One messenger had been detained at a bank. At Tomnoddy's signal, Miss Jolly scurried to the Great Eastern to alert Samuel and Rann. The two men withdrew and watched from a distance for the messenger or the police. Ten minutes later, however, the messenger returned with a sealed packet of Bank of England bonds.

A greater risk was that the duffer, as Samuel was apt to call the messengers privately, might smell out the scheme and help himself to the contents of an envelope. Tomnoddy, otherwise unknown to the dupes, was to confront any man who varied from the direct route back to the Great Eastern Hotel.

On the second day, the messenger who emerged from the City Bank, at the corner of Bishopsgate and Threadneedle Street, turned towards the river, rather than to the hotel where Samuel waited. He had gone a dozen steps when Tomnoddy tapped his shoulder and asked if he had lost his way. The messenger blushed, murmured something of lung tonic from an apothecary, and was escorted to the hotel. Cautioned by threats of dismissal and losing his character, he was plainly to be trusted for the remaining days. He never saw Tomnoddy again, his visits to the banks shadowed by Maggie or Jack Rann.

Samuel chortled and rubbed his hands as the bonds were delivered. He swore there was 'no reason why it should ever end'. Each evening, Tomnoddy took the documents and added them to those already bundled under a board in the shabby upper tenement of Preedy's Rents. Before the end of the week there were twenty-seven bonds, representing more than £9,000. Jack Rann knew the loyalty of Short-Armed Tom. Moreover, Tomnoddy understood nothing of bills of exchange or bank bonds. Within his hidden world of Preedy's Rents and the tosher's hunting ground of sewers and outfalls, no policeman in London had heard of him. He was the safest custodian of all.

Bills of exchange accepted by the banks were taken each evening to the central Bank Clearing House near Lombard Street. In this raucous financial market-place, their value would be credited to a bank against its day's debits, which it incurred when bills of its own were accepted by other banks. No scrutineer queried the bank-bills presented on behalf of Mr Wilberforce. A week or two might pass before the first duplicates were presented and the hunt began.

Of the bills that Rann brought away from the vaults, seven were bank post-bills to the value of £950. These promised to pay any bearer of the note a sum of money and were as easily negotiable as bank notes. However, they were redeemable within a fortnight, during which the duplicates now lying in the Cornhill vaults would also be presented. To liquidate the stolen post-bills in London might alert the banks too quickly. If they were cashed in the provinces, there would be a further delay of several days before they could be suspect.

As James Patrick supervised the last of the messengers' errands, Mr Wilberforce travelled, as he said, 'To Brighton and Back for Three-and-Six'. High above a stretch of glass-green sea, he stepped into the sunlight from the freshly painted station with its temple pillars of cast-iron and its arched glass canopies. For the benefit of the Southern Counties Bank, he had chosen to be Mr Samuel, prospective resident of the Royal York Hotel. The Southern Counties was a large institution but, being peculiar to the area, would take longer than its competitors to suspect a fraud. At Richardson's Bank in Western Road, which took special care of Indian Army officers, he would be Major Wilberforce. From previous use of the alias, he had a useful range of small talk.

At Richardson's bank, Major Wilberforce was the prospective purchaser for himself and three sisters of a seaside mansion in Brunswick Square, Hove. He hesitated as he handed the head-cashier the bills.

'I really wonder, you know, whether I should take so much money.'

The cashier looked puzzled and Major Wilberforce admired his own master stroke. Whoever knew a trickster to decline the booty?

'I wonder whether it is wise, you understand, to be carrying such an amount . . . .'

The cashier had the answer, as Major Wilberforce knew he would.

'My clerk shall accompany you to Brunswick Town . . . .'

Major Wilberforce shook his head, such courtesy quite defeating him, gallant old soldier though he was.

'That is kind,' he smiled. 'Exceptionally kind.'

Brunswick Square was a ten-minute walk. Its fine white houses with their bow-fronted drawing-rooms promised evenings of waltz and quadrille. Morning sunshine danced on the waves where Brunswick Lawns lay open to the sea. The major turned to his escort.

'Thank you so much, my dear young fellow. I can manage now, these last few steps. So very civil of you . . . .'

He walked slowly on, glancing once to ensure that the young man had gone from sight round the corner. Then he turned his back on the white houses and the sparkling tide. Soapy Samuel, thin and sleek, sped for the railway station again, sharp-faced and white-haired, nose forward in his urgency, a hunting rodent.

Next afternoon, Mr Wilberforce and his clerk attended the Private Drawing Office of the Bank of England. Their visit concerned the settlement of their deceased client's estate. The Private Drawing Office was divided from the adjoining Bill Office and Public Drawing Office only by wooden partitions. It was a new banking-hall, tall windows recessed between pillars, where the bank's bonds and bills might be redeemed. Across its centre stood a polished wooden counter, attended by three clerks. A bank porter in red jacket, white breeches, top-boots and silk hat, was positioned at either end.

A porter led the client to the counter. Mr Wilberforce had consolidated the proceeds of the client's estate in Bank of England bonds, recognized by the clerk as having been issued at the bank two or three weeks before. They were now negotiable and Mr Wilberforce wished them exchanged for Bank of England notes in denominations of fifty pounds. The clerk might think it unusual for such a sum to be dispersed by bank notes to the beneficiaries. But provided an attorney discharged his duties to the estate, the precise method was his own affair.

In its pillared grandeur, the Private Drawing Office had the silence of a great cathedral. Jack Rann watched and supposed that a smartly dressed attorney's clerk was the last man in London to be arrested here as the fugitive of a murderous tap-room brawl in Clerkenwell. The bank clerk looked up at Samuel's white hair and noble smile. He glanced down again. The bonds had been recorded and bank notes were being counted.

Rann knew that Bank of England notes were registered on issue, the holder's name traceable. Such was the fear of counterfeiting. But after such care, these notes might be taken a few hundred yards to the Continental Bank in Lombard Street and changed for Bank of Scotland notes, which were neither recorded nor traceable. Scottish notes might then be changed at will for sovereigns, American gold eagles or currency or coin of any denomination. This could in turn be used to buy bonds or stocks in any name the purchaser cared to write upon them.

'Oh, Pandy Quinn, Pandy Quinn,' he said softly to himself. 'What a dodge it was – and what a man you were!'

In four days more it might be over. Then, as the banks were presented with identical bills of exchange, the trail of the money would be lost among anonymous notes and coins, bills and bonds, bought and sold – and bought and sold again. A little less than £11,000, Samuel had thought. Jack Rann was not disposed to trust Samuel in everything but in this he thought he might be relied upon.

There had been one disagreement.

'We whack the lot,' Rann had said. 'Pandy and me decided. Equal shares.'

Samuel made a querulous dissent. But Pandy knew how soon, once a job was done, the quarrelling began. And how easily quarrelling might turn to betrayal.

'Better whack the smash and be over the hills,' he had said philosophically. 'Better than snatch the lot and be informed on.'

In any case, Rann had argued with Samuel, how else were they to value Miss Jolly's penmanship against Samuel's impersonations? Lord Tomnoddy as custodian against Maggie Fashion's seduction of Arthur Trent? And Mag Fashion, being Pandy's girl, was prime for a share. Each would have enough to cross the world and live a lifetime. With Pandy gone there were five: Jack Rann, Samuel, Miss Jolly, Mag, Tomnoddy.

Rann looked up again and watched the clerk entering the numbers of Samuel's notes in the register. Whack the smash, as Pandy said. Enough for all.

In four days Rann himself would be gone. Several men of his acquaintance had found cover in the flood of pauper migration. But he swore now he would be no emigrant, drawn through the streets of Liverpool in a crowded cart, left among ragged starvelings at Waterloo Dock, poked for lice by a Yankee commissioner, chosen and herded aboard a wooden six-weeks transport.

A man might travel instead on a steamer, first-class cabin-passenger to New York or Philadelphia for twenty-five pounds, and never be troubled by a single question at departure or destination. Next week, before the first of Miss Jolly's forgeries was examined, he might be in another world.

Pandy Quinn had told him, 'Let what name you go by be written on a Bank of England bill or bond for five hundred pounds. A man needs no passport but that.'

Samuel turned from the counter, features composed and without expression. The sleek white hair clung thinly to his temples. Now he need only change the Bank of England notes to any coin or currency that was not recorded.

An hour later, Rann sat in an arched window of Garraway's

Coffee House, on the corner of Change Alley, a shabby cul-de-sac. He watched the Continental Bank across Lombard Street. The bulk of the funds was now purchasing bonds in the name of James Patrick and four others, beneficiaries of the estate which Mr Wilberforce was winding up. The rest of the money would be in Bank of Scotland notes, gold sovereigns and five-dollar eagles.

Rann stared past the menu boards with which Garraway's was placarded, watching the green-liveried bank messengers and the clerks in tall hats and frock-coats. Samuel had warned him that the counting or weighing of sovereigns might be a lengthy business. Rann was to watch the side door, by which a policeman and a bank official would enter if there was trouble. But though it might be uncommon for an attorney to buy bonds with bank notes rather than with cheques, it was not remotely illegal.

Ten minutes after the half-hour, Samuel reappeared, crossing the street with his scuttling furtiveness. He passed Garraway's window without a glance at Rann and turned into Baum & Son, at 58 Lombard Street, dealers in foreign currency. If a man changed £1,000 in Bank of England notes for United States gold eagle coins, it was not remarkable in a major house of this kind. Then Samuel reappeared, opened the glass door of the coffee-house and joined Rann at a table furthest removed from the other customers.

'The way you walk, you look like a blackguard,' Rann said cheerfully as the old man sat down. 'That's half your trouble.'

'What I look like, Handsome Jack, ain't neither here nor there. It's who I am that counts. Mr Wilberforce of Lavery, Stokes, and Froggart, attorneys-at-law, Regent Street, Cambridge.'

'Which never existed,' Rann said dismissively.

Samuel arched his eyebrows in surprise.

'Which does exist, Jack Rann. I looked 'em up. Asked about 'em. You won't find a more estimable firm.'

Rann looked incredulous.

'Then you might have sold us all!' he said furiously. 'Suppose someone from a bank had written to Cambridge?'

208

Samuel chuckled.

'You don't think, Jack Rann. Why should they write? The first banks dealt with a bishop, a joint stock partner, and a guardian in chancery. Never an attorney. To be in-and-out in a week was always our plan, and we done it. Suppose the big ones round here, that met Mr Wilberforce the last day or two, were to write now. What's it matter? We'll be gone in a few days. No time now for them to write and get an answer. And with bills of exchange, we never went back to a bank where we'd already been. That's important: never go back to be recognized. Even suppose the jig's up and they could follow the money this far. They'd waste a week in Cambridge, ferreting, while you and me and the rest is travelling further off with every hour. See?'

Jack Rann shrugged.

'Two more days,' Samuel went on. 'Three more post-bills to be changed for cash. Monday morning, I'm Dr Wilberforce colonial bishop again, staying in Oxford at the Golden Cross off the Cornmarket. I can do Oxford and back by the Paddington train. Wilson Scrimgeour's Commercial Bank. Used to handling coins by the ton. What you need to remember Jack, is that you and Pandy never had all the answers. Locks you may know; walls you may climb; but with banks, my son, you are green as a leek and soft as new cheese.'

Jack Rann looked about him, his mouth bitter and tight but his eyes uneasy.

'You ain't seen Oxford yet, Sammy. And who knows you never may?'

For reasons that Rann himself could never have imagined, he was about to be proved right.

FIVE

HANDSOME JACK

26

In the warm air of Saturday morning, Tomnoddy and Samuel paused to watch a street-circus. A temporary platform stood on waste ground near Wapping Pier. Its makeshift stage was enclosed at the back and the wings by a tall canvas triptych. Above this, the windows of tenements could be seen on one side and the tall masts of the docks on the other. The canvas was painted with scenes of Circassian horsemen and dancing maidens, jungle lions and rajahs on jewelled elephants.

The childish audience was silent before the magic of Abanazar in his turban and evening cloak, and the feats of Goliath the strong man. Both were assisted by Madame Cynthia, her flaxen hair worn on her shoulders and fringed in the style of a Saxon warrior-maiden.

The strings of a three-piece band played a gliding waltz as Goliath in a black leotard presented Madame Cynthia to the on-lookers.

'No more strength in him than you nor me,' Samuel said, 'only fat.'

Madame Cynthia, firm and aggressive, crossed the stage with a paperbound volume, two inches thick, her bust carried high in a tight bodice, showing the same self-assured swagger of her back-side in the black fleshings.

Goliath took the volume. Bowing over it, he breathed and

snarled a little. Then, as if it were gossamer, he tore it across, and across again.

'Same as you could do,' Samuel said, 'suppose it was baked in an oven first. That got no more body than burnt paper, though they don't let it bake black.'

Goliath was now engaged in bending an iron bar across his chest.

'Work it in a vice first,' Samuel remarked, 'until it's ready to snap.'

'You got all the tricks, ain't you, Sam?' Lord Tomnoddy said admiringly. 'You might go on the stage yourself.'

Samuel chortled at the absurdity of it.

'Not but what I wouldn't mind bending that Cynthia Smith over my chest, Tom. That's a trick for me. There again, you was never down Brighton with the Swell Mob for the races. That Jennifer Khan, the Asian Venus, in them tight trousers, riding the circus ring with her bum in the air.'

Tomnoddy was about to reply when there was a movement in the audience, adults and children pushing their way to the street and the docks.

'Found-drowned,' a woman said, impatient for the spectacle. 'Fancy girl from Ma Martileau's.'

Samuel followed Tomnoddy to the wooden steamboat pier beyond the quay.

'It's the outfall, Sammy. It got to be.'

A claw worked in Samuel's entrails. Mother Martileau's was Bragg's house. He told himself there was not a chance in ten thousand it could touch Rann or Pandy Quinn. But the claw dug tighter in his guts.

They walked out on the pier with a smaller crowd, looking diagonally over the shallows to a muddy foreshore. The flood was still running, waves jumping like a shoal of fish in the sunlight. The stone quay was lined with bystanders looking down at the uncovered flats. A dozen men on the sleek mud stood round a shape that might have been a bundle of cast-off clothes.

'It ain't Miss Jolly,' Tomnoddy said quietly, 'nor Mag Fashion.'

'No,' said Samuel quietly, 'but from Ma Martileau's House, in them clothes and that long dark hair worn loose, I know her. I swear I saw her Sunday evening. While I was waiting in Trent's rooms, a girl in black with a veil rang the bell. She got that long hair. I half thought I knew her then but couldn't place her. In a hat and veil but with her hair down, like that – like a doxy does that's showing for hire. Ma Martileau's house! That got to be Pretty Jo, as they call her. I should've twigged last Sunday, Trent having photographs of her in his safe. I thought he must've bought them down Holywell Street, not that he might know her.'

'And you never found out what she wanted?'

'No, Tom, and never will. If it's Ma Martileau's house, that's her. I'll bet on it.'

Two more men were bringing a shutter down the stairs from the quay. A boatman on the pier called out, 'Found this morning. Made away with herself, the doctor says.'

Lord Tomnoddy looked carefully at the men by the body.

'Policeman Fowler,' he said softly.

Samuel studied the group, picking out Fowler by his fawn suiting. The examination was over, the doctor and his assistant turning away. The men with the shutter were lifting the girl's body, wet black clothes huddled round her and her feet bare. Samuel watched them with growing dismay.

'Suffering God!' he said sharply. 'Look at him!'

'Who?'

Samuel took a step away, drawing back behind the crowd.

'Him, stood back from Fowler. Looking this way! See?'

Tomnoddy stared and saw the man, whose frock-coat and tall hat had not at first made him seem like a policeman.

'Private-clothes, Sam?'

Samuel nodded and swallowed, like a man confessing his sickness.

'Verity. I know him and he knows me. Whitehall Division. Talk

215

of Brighton, swell men like Sealskin Kite and Old Mole? He coopered the pair of 'em in Patcham railway tunnel. And he put that Jennifer Khan in a place where the turnkeys kept her dancing. Why the fuck's he here when he's Whitehall Division? You see how he looked straight this way? He knows something.'

'Just move slow, Sam,' Tomnoddy said quietly, 'as if we ain't seen him. There's nothing for him to know.'

'Infant – what they call The Scaldrum Dodge. He let slip Verity been nosing them houses that Jack and Pandy worked last autumn. If he's been bum-nosing that Joanne dollymop down here, he likely followed her to the Cornhill Vaults. He could have talked to Trent and Walker by now. If he's not nosing her, he wouldn't be here.'

Then a far worse thought struck him.

'Tom! He knows Jack's girl! Miss Jolly! Twice he's took her in! He'd only have to twig her at the Chinese Shades and follow her. She'd have led him straight to us. Handsome Rann would have that little wriggler of his in the game! God knows he was warned different!'

A penny steamer bumped the pier timbers, bound for Rotherhithe and West Kent Wharf. The paddle wheels went astern to bring the vessel to a halt, metal fins thrashing the river to a hissing froth. Tomnoddy took Samuel by the arm and pushed him into the line of waiting passengers. Smuts from a tall black funnel fell in a thin drizzle across the wooden planking. The old tosher handed two coins to a clerk at the pay-box. With Samuel, he stood alone in the bows, the wind cool in their faces as the boat cut across the flood tide. Samuel shivered in the breeze.

'So long as it was Fowler, even Bully Bragg, we were wise to them, Tom. But we never had cause to look for Verity – and we never did!'

Tomnoddy shook his head to dismiss the old man's fears.

'He came for a doxy found drowned. No reason to look for us. If he knew about us, you and Jack would have been nabbed at the vaults. He won't catch us now, Sam. There's only Oxford on

Monday, then it's done.'

Samuel stared at him, white hair ruffled by the wind.

'I'm going nowhere near another bank in Oxford nor anywhere else, Tom! I'll bury my head till it's all quiet again. If I have to, I'll go back down the outfall or under the cellars of the old King James till I can get right away.'

Tomnoddy's rubicund face went through a series of silent answers and rejected them.

'But the job's done, Sam. There's been no bother yet.'

Samuel looked at him helplessly.

'They can find Handsome Rann's shop-mouse in the Shades any night they want, Tom. If they've had their eyes on her, she must a-led them this far. I daresay it ain't the vaults concerns them most of all. So far, they might not know that part of it.'

Tomnoddy pulled a face at the steamer's bow-wave.

'What then?'

'What they know Miss Jolly will give 'em if they sniff after her long enough,' Samuel said bitterly. 'It's not the vaults they're after, it's the chance to take Jack Rann again – and hang him this time, good and proper.'

27

Rann closed the door of the shipping office and crossed Jamaica Road. In his note-case he carried a receipt to James Patrick for a passage in three days' time on the *Batavia*, bound from Rotterdam and London to New York. He knew the ship by sight, a three-masted iron-hulled Dutchman with two short black funnels. A foreign ship was best. He spoke no word of the language and would seem to his companions like any other Englishman.

By Bermondsey Wall, a purlman's skiff was scudding among tiers of collier-brigs, selling drink to the grimy and half-naked coal-whippers. No one paid him the least attention among clinking capstan-palls, the rumble of wagons and carts from Horselydown Lane and Maguire Street, the engine-throb of a steamer off Swan Pier, the shriek of a railway whistle among the high platforms of London Bridge.

At the station piazza, he took a cab for Farringdon. There was a debt to be paid, though the thought of it cramped his heart and entrails. But he promised himself that if he faced the dark memory and came away free, he was safe for ever.

As the cab trembled and shook on the cobbled approach to London Bridge, he took the receipt for his passage, folded it long and slim, and inserted it with five gold sovereigns into the open hem of a large linen handkerchief. The bonds, letters of credit, and bank notes in the name of James Patrick were in a large envelope in the shipping agent's safe. When he boarded the vessel they would be returned to him. He had gold enough for two more days. His other arrangements were made. Even the partnership with his penny-dancer was dissolved. While they were together, the chances of recognition and betrayal were doubled.

'I'll write and tell you where I am,' he had said to her gently, as they lay in the little Panton Street room together. 'You'll see. You won't be able to get there fast enough.'

But he did not believe it.

At Cheapside, he tapped the roof with his stick and ordered the cabman to drop him. Like a man reliving a dream, he walked over the crossing and into Newgate Street. Beyond the little shops, dusty in the strong summer light of afternoon sun, with their advertisements for Hildyard's Patent Dog Cake and The Metropolitan Boot Company, the walls of the prison were black and silent.

Short of the prison wall, the chimney of Tyler's Manufactory, its lettering painted vertically down the brickwork, rose from a flat roof. Next was the garment warehouse and the arch of a dark courtyard. He turned to make sure he was unobserved, then walked into the yard and up stone stairs to the attic tenement.

She might have moved on in the last few weeks. Even if she still lived here, she might have gone out. At the unpainted door he thought he heard the baby's cry. Rann knocked and a bolt was drawn back.

She stood as he remembered her on that other morning, the same grey woollen shawl and white apron, astonished at the sight of him, but no longer afraid. Jack Rann in his grey suit and polished boots, brown silk cravat at his throat, was a rare vision in the Newgate Street garrets. She seemed about to drop a curtsy.

'Don't you know me?' he said quickly. 'You helped me. I'd got nothing but the clothes I wore. Not shoes on my feet. But I told you one day I'd thank you, though I didn't know how.'

'You're my stranger!' she said, half-startled and half-laughing.

He stepped into the room. The tarnished mirror in which he had appeared as a bloody ghost still hung on its nail. The basket of laundry was on the floor and the baby in its wooden cradle was on the table. The rush chair in which he had sat was still at the same angle.

He took a leather folder from his pocket.

'What's here is yours. It ain't half enough. Paper tubes has ten sovs in each. Each note is five sovs. A bank or shops will change 'em, not the market.'

'No!' she said, recoiling from the money.

'Yes,' said Rann. 'Now, listen. If you got any worry about getting the money changed, go down the Ratcliff Highway. You'd know it? Beyond Aldgate Pump?'

'Yes,' she said cautiously.

'There's an opening on the right to Preedy's Rents. Remember that. Preedy's Rents.'

'Preedy's Rents,' she said uncertainly.

'Ask for the top floor and Lord Tomnoddy.'

'That's never you!' she smiled at him.

'No,' Rann said impatiently, 'Tomnoddy's a man that's honest and good. He'll know how to help you.'

She looked doubtful.

'And you?'

'I can't stay,' Rann said quietly. 'I got to go a long way off. And I got to go alone. But not without doing what I promised. No more said, then. I got to be moving.'

He looked at the room, the young woman with her reddened arms, the child in the cradle. Then he surprised himself by an involuntary pang of misery at his exile.

'You'll be all right,' he said firmly. 'If not, Tomnoddy will see you are.'

He turned with his unexpected sense of wretchedness and isolation that she seemed instinctively to guess. The young woman seized him and held him briefly in her gratitude and understanding.

'God bless you, my poor stranger,' she said again.

He turned and hurried down the stairs. Forlorn as he felt, he sensed danger to himself in the bare room with its scents of fresh linen.

He went back again as far as Cheapside, then walked on to the Marquis of Granby. They were used to James Patrick by now, a man who might come and go for hours or days. Sitting down in a booth of the saloon bar, he watched the waiter serving an order. Then he looked up as a man slid on to the bench facing him. This was an old man, tall and sunken-cheeked, stooping, dark hair long and lank. In black coat and white tie, he was still the figure of a consumptive butler drinking himself to death on his master's port.

'Hello, Handsome Rann,' said Barrister Saward pleasantly, 'I understand you got something that belongs to me.'

'James Patrick,' Rann said helplessly, sure that Saward had never seen him before. 'I'm James Patrick.'

Saward chuckled.

'So they say. Attorney's clerk? That you?'

There was no way back. Rann nodded. Saward pointed towards the waiter.

'What's Coke-upon-Littleton?'

No way back. He felt himself forced another step on the path to his destruction.

'Stout taken with brandy.'

'Treatise,' said Saward jovially. 'Most famous treatise upon the law of real property. Attorney's clerk! James Patrick! You smell to me like Jack Rann. A snivelling little thief.'

Rann said nothing. Someone behind his shoulder echoed the conclusion.

'A snivelling little thief!'

He twisted and saw the four men standing behind him. Bragg, with his dark hair piled Pompadour-style, was looking down at him, the soft face with a mouth twisted by the humour of the situation. Moonbeam stood next, a leaden-eyed unmarked bruiser, the waistcoat under his jacket strained and creased by his size. Hardwicke and Atwell waited for their master's orders.

The waiter approached but Bragg turned to him good-naturedly.

'Not now, if you please, old fellow. The gentleman just remembered a bit of business to be talked over.'

He turned back to Rann. The upper lip above the teeth was a parody of a smile.

'Well, Handsome Jack. Seems you never learn. No sooner you get the chance but you must be thieving off respectable folk.'

'What's it to you?'

Bully Bragg considered his victim without expression, the eyes varying half an inch from Rann's direct gaze.

'It's a lot to Mr Saward. Still, what you got to ask yourself, Jack Rann, is simple. You want to leave here with us, nice and quiet and friendly? Or you want Mr Saward to give you in charge? You fancy leaving here in a police van with four officers that I can call at a snap of my fingers?'

'Flash Fowler!'

Bragg frowned, as if this truly puzzled him.

'Mr Inspector Fowler? He got nothing to do with this division. "H" Division. That's him. You'd know that if you was half-clever, Handsome Rann. But, then, if you was clever, you wouldn't be sitting here now. Would you? Do as you're told. You only got to give back what never belonged to you in the first place.'

This time there was no escape, nothing but the hope that Bragg would not hand him to the police but might let him live. The law was on Bragg's side. He had only to call a policeman and name James Patrick as the hangman's child.

Saward gave his own order to the waiter. Rann stood up and went with Bragg and his companions. They took him to a cab and then to a building off Drury Lane, which he knew as Mother Martileau's French Introducing-House. It had been a merchant's residence a century earlier, now far gone in decay. Its front formed part of a paved courtyard between two streets. One side of the building looked down on Drury Lane, the other on Crown Street.

The lower floors with their over-furnished mirrored rooms, softly padded chairs and sofas, revealed the house for what it was. A wide staircase followed the walls of the vestibule, under a dome of patterned glass. At the top, the oval arch of the stairway was closed by a wrought-iron wicket gate, locked and bolted. Such things were common in houses where children were confined to the nursery floor or where street-girls who rebelled against their keepers might be instructed.

Bragg unfastened the iron wicket-gate and Rann was pushed through. The attic passageway had several doors. Moonbeam unlocked one and opened it so that Rann and Samuel saw one another. Samuel drooped, his eyes pleading for forgiveness of stupidity and weakness.

''s all right, Sammy,' Rann said gently.

Moonbeam shut the door and locked it. He pointed at the next.

'Likewise, we got Mag Fashion in there. She'll be wishing otherwise in a while.'

'She knows nothing,' Rann said firmly.

'How most unfortunate for her, then!' Bragg turned, the comic pompadour hair wobbling, the face an expression of pure and delighted good humour. 'In there, Handsome Rann.'

Moonbeam opened a door on the opposite side of the passageway. Rann walked in but Bragg was not yet done with him.

'What I want, Jack Rann, is the dibs you thieved from the Cornhill Vaults – and which you couldn't have done if you hadn't also thieved Mr Saward's papers.'

'Cornhill Vaults?'

'It's over, Jack. We know it all, without asking Soapy Samuel or Mag Turnbull. We want it back, what Mr Saward lost. We mean to have it, with or without hurting. We got no interest in you after that. Go where you like. Do as you please.'

'I got nothing from any vaults,' Rann said indifferently.

Bragg shook his head.

'You never really thought you'd have it away? Police you might make fools of. Not old friends like us. You was down them fucking Cornhill Vaults on Sunday night! Year ago, you and Quinn were sniffing round them like greenhorns round a dollymop's skirt. You thought you was clever, waiting and following home the men that went to the deposits. But you was the one followed, Jack, you and that old fool Quinn. And them houses that were done last autumn with nothing took! The greenest stickman in the game'd know that was to get keys or papers! Eight houses, all with deposits in the Cornhill Vaults! Mr Saward found that.'

Rann stared at Bragg. The bully became waggish.

'I hope you enjoyed finding your gallows pamphlet in the safe deposit.'

Rann's heart missed a beat and Bragg chuckled.

'You got Mr Saward to thank for that, him having an arrangement there. Common box that don't belong to one client but the bank keeps oddments for whoever hands them in. Because any clerk might have to open it, it has to have a lock that any of the keys can fit. So if you was to get in, you'd be sure to open that one. Bit of a shake-up, was it?'

'I got no idea,' Rann said wearily. 'I never was there.'

Bragg sighed.

'Sunday night. Miss Joanne went there done up like a fourpenny hambone in black and veil. She'd need a bloody veil if she was caught freelancing on my board and lodging. She used to sneak there to give Mr Trent a romp before he got Mag Fashion. Last Sunday, Moonbeam was shadowing her. She never got an answer to Trent's bell but she hung around Cornhill, waiting for him perhaps. Moonbeam watched her, from down Leadenhall end. And you know what he saw, Handsome Rann? Later on a doxy comes out of Sun Court. Ain't Pretty Jo Phillips but remarkably like that randy little wriggler, Jolly, down the Shades, done up for arseyfarcey in tights and cloak. Then he sees Samuel. And you,

Handsome Rann. So don't bloody come it.'

'And you never thought your Moonbeam might be having you on?' Rann tried to sound as if he had not a care. 'You asked Miss Joanne, I s'pose.'

Bragg affected puzzlement.

'You know what, Jack? I never had a chance. She must've had a turn-up with her beau, Mr Trent. All events, her not getting an answer to the bell, she sort of despaired. Threw herself in the river. Body found. *Felo de se*, they reckon.'

'She wouldn't be the first of yours,' Rann said quietly.

Bragg lifted the corner of his lip from moist teeth in the same parody of a smile.

'You got hopes, Jack Rann! Not a mark on her! True, when she went freebooting with Trent those months back, she got a smacking. That's all.'

'Hardwicke thrashed her,' Rann said. He was watching carefully and saw that Bragg's eyes went still with a small shock.

'What you know about Hardwicke?'

'Hardwicke boasts to the world what goes on in this house, after a glass or two.' Rann spoke as if it was nothing to him. 'Hardwicke and Atwell. Drinking down the Three Tuns in Saffron Hill. Saying how photographs was taken and sold of him leathering Pretty Jo. Her being found dead now, p'raps it mightn't so easy be *felo de se*. Not if the inquest was to see the pictures of him doing it. Still, if that was for working away from home, why d'you kill her now? Not for going to Trent. I'd say she must have known something that could hang you. What was it?'

It was too late. Bragg had regained his balance, his eyes cold but no longer dead. Looking at Rann, he called Moonbeam.

'Get the things out of his pockets.'

Rann put them on the table. Bragg drew the banknotes from the note-case. He turned to Moonbeam.

'Take the rest. Give him his snotter back. He'll want it to wipe up his tears.' He looked at Rann. 'Fancy you're a smart boy,

Handsome Jack? Brave boy? Hurting won't make you give away your fortune? Still, we shan't start with you. First you'll listen to Samuel and Mag Fashion. You brave enough to hear them on and on – and say nothing? Are you, Jack? If you are, when they've said all they'll ever say, we'll come asking you. And if you won't say a word, and if we really think you won't, for a start you won't have much need for a tongue, will you?'

They went out. A key turned and the bolts slid across. The room had been a maid's bedroom. A mattress lay on the floor near a small wooden table with a hairbrush and a hand-mirror. A single window was bolted into place and covered by vertical iron bars no more than six inches apart. Even the high window-lights of Newgate's death cell had seemed easier. The creak of a board assured him that the corridor of this informal prison was guarded with equal care.

Rann stretched his hand between the bars and tapped the window. The glass rang thick as wood. Even if he could break the leg off the little table, it would never shatter such panes. There was no fireplace, no attic flue for him to work his way up. His cleverness had brought him back where he had begun. But now he had given Samuel and Maggie as hostages, whose first cries would break his silence. Beyond the guarded door and barred window remained only a dwindling hope that Bragg knew nothing of Preedy's Rents nor the whereabouts of Miss Jolly.

28

In private-clothes, Verity turned into The Strand at the end of a
blazing summer day. The wide pavements were afloat with crinolines, bonnets, muslin dresses, organdies and brilliantes. Young
men, hands in the pockets of peg-top trousers, lounged at the coun-
ters of cigar divans. Others watched the passing crowds from door-
ways whose signboards offered shaving and hair-cutting.

Across the river, tenements on the southern shore sprawled
along narrow streets. Authority had imposed a penny toll on
Waterloo Bridge to deter Southwark from infesting The Strand.
But the woman Verity wanted had crossed at dusk for thirty or
forty years. She would appear as the white lamps came on, high on
their swan's necks of cast-iron pillars, shining down the broad
boulevard in a chain of pearls. 'Old Stock' would be there every
night until she hid among the tenements to die.

The sky above Trafalgar Square turned from vermilion flame to
plum-coloured twilight. He looked for her beyond the 'aristoc-
racy' from clubs and night-houses, in silk hats and embroidered
waistcoats. She would be among girls who paraded their stretches
of pavement, twirling their parasols, holding up the train of skirts
from the foul moisture condensing on the pavement in the cooler
air of night.

Old Stock worked the little streets near the Adelphi, where the
homeless slept under riverside arches. It was an enclave of painted

cheeks and brandy-sparkling eyes, the stench of bad tobacco, raucous horse-laughs and shrieked obscenities.

"'ello, Ma!' he said at last. 'I hoped you might be waiting.'

Among the crinolines, she was conspicuous in a dirty cotton dress, her straw bonnet trimmed by faded ribbon. Grey hair and worn face, like the gin on her breath, marked her for what she was. Old Stock was employed to watch 'dress lodgers', girls dressed by their keepers to fetch high prices. She saw to it that her protegees did not run off to pawn the clothes or take men to rival houses.

'Mr Verity!' She gave him a faded smile. 'They give you Adelphi as a beat?'

'No, Mrs Stock, it's you I come to see. Hoping you might have something.'

The old woman grinned at him.

'I'm too cracky to have much for anyone now, sir. I watches that Miss Cat from the Wych Street house. She took three men back already. Almost caught a white choker that been psalm-singing at Exeter Hall, but he turned leery. Still, more 'n two pounds so far. Her being young, if a sour little bitch. I shall get a bit of it later. I don't do as well that way as I did. Still, I sweeps up too. They gives me grub for that. Very fair they is, to me.'

She was standing outside a gunsmith's shop, its small square panes displaying rifles with their grain polished to liquid perfection, brass and filigree, steel barrels sleek as satin.

'But you lost your best girl, Ma,' he said quietly. 'Your Joanne that worked with you a year back. Like a daughter she must have been after so long.'

The smile, and the energy, went from her face, like a player's mask. She nodded.

'They kept her indoors for special work lately. Now they say she wasn't right in the head. She never drowned herself, Mr Verity. I won't have it. Accident, p'raps. I'll go to the inquest down Shadwell Vestry. But what can I say and who'd listen? It's young Chaffey you want to see, that used to take Pretty Jo out a bit.'

'She had to do with Chaffey? Him that dresses for the surgeons down the Royal Free Hospital? I hoped as much.'

'He never had so much to do with her as he'd have liked, Mr Verity! She had to have five-shilling sweethearts. Chaffey's a larky young bloke, but often can't pay so much, 'cos he got no money. Never fortunate enough to pass his examinations to be a proper medical. But he helps at dressings and inquests.'

'Including Miss Joanne's?'

The old woman touched a handkerchief to the corner of her eye.

'I can't say it's square, sir. But the surgeon thinking otherwise, and Mr Fowler agreeing, I have to bite my tongue. But if Chaffey thinks it ain't square either, that's another thing. Suicide while the balance of her mind was disturbed? She wouldn't know the meaning.'

Verity's heart rose.

'P'raps, Mrs Stock, you'd do me the honour to take a glass o' summat hot and short with Chaffey, s'pose he was to be found. And supposing this little bit was for now.'

He drew a coin from his trouser-pocket and pressed it into her hand. At the pavement's edge, the brass lamps of a carriage cast tawny pools of oil-light on reddish tresses and the sharp line of Cat's young profile. Old Stock bared her gums in appreciation.

'I'll find you Mr Chaffey, sir, but I can't leave Cat. Thieving slut, and worse. She and Hoxton Liz had a barney last night. Nails and maulers. Consequence o' that, Miss Cat is going to wish she was wearing someone else's ears and backside when Ma Martileau reckons up the damage to Liz.'

She crossed the pavement and spoke to the girl. They set off, Verity and Old Stock together, Cat following several feet behind. In the streets by the river, an Irish fiddle in one bar competed for coppers with a mandolin across the alley.

The old woman looked round quickly and turned to a spacious public house near the steamer-landing of the Adelphi Stairs, its windows covered with white appliqué lettering for cigars, billiards, pyramid, and pool. Inside the Wine Promenade, the floor was carpeted. A bar of polished mahogany ran the full length of it, a stout woman and a tall man in a sailor's cap serving 'Mexico'. 'Crank', 'Sky Blue', and other combinations of gin. Old Stock spoke to the plump woman and led the way to a booth at the far end.

Chaffey sat at a drink-stained oak table, staring at the varnished pine of the partition in a distant reverie. He was a tall, pale young man with a dark love curl and black clothes. Old Stock looked about for the vixen-faced Cat, failed to see her, and said, 'Oh, bugger the slut!' She scratched herself, and sat down. Chaffey came out of his contemplation.

''ello, Ma! 'ello, Mr Verity!'

A waiter came to them.

'You'll take something, Mrs Stock?' Verity asked hastily. 'And Mr Chaffey?'

'Flare-Up, hot,' Ma Stock said firmly.

'Same as Ma,' Chaffey said. 'You come for me, Mr Verity?'

'Just information, Mr Chaffey. You got thoughts on the business of Miss Joanne?'

Chaffey looked quickly and reproachfully at Old Stock.

''s all right, sweetness,' the old woman said, 'I told Mr Verity my mind.'

Chaffey rubbed the side of his face as an aid to thought.

'I was her friend,' he said pathetically. 'They got no right to make her out a suicide, Mr Verity.'

Verity's face glowed encouragingly.

'I wouldn't argue 'gainst that, Mr Chaffey.'

Chaffey leant forward confidentially.

'What you want to know, Mr Verity?'

Verity watched the waiter set down gin and a jug of hot water.

'First off, Mr Chaffey, there was her boots.'

Chaffey stared at him over the steamy brim of a glass.

'What about her boots?'

'I was there soon after they found her, Mr Chaffey. She hadn't got her boots.'

Chaffey continued to stare at him with the apologetic look of one who has missed the point.

'Mr Chaffey,' said Verity generously, 'take a young gentleman of your considerable medical experience. You ever hear of a young person found drowned that had lost her boots?'

'They don't necessary wear boots, Mr V.'

Verity shook his head with a tolerant smile.

'I know that, Mr Chaffey. What I asked was, had you ever known an unfortunate found drowned that had lost her boots? Started with 'em, finished without 'em? Or a well-dressed young person, like Miss Joanne, that took her boots off special before walking to the river to throw herself in?'

Chaffey looked at him more intently.

'If she'd walked barefoot, Mr Verity, there'd be marks on the feet, which no one says there was. But a body that's drowned don't lose its boots, sir. First thing that swells is the feet. Boots fit tighter in the water. Most times, you have to cut the boots off. Any case, whatever a body's wearing leaves a red impression. Boots most of all. If the boots was lost, you'd still see where they'd been.'

'She had no mark of boots. I saw that for myself.'

Chaffey was mystified, brow furrowed, eye bright with a tear.

'Then,' said Verity gently, 'if someone said her boots were lost by her being in the water, or knocking against bridges or outfalls, they'd be wrong?'

''Course they would!' Chaffey said with sudden animation. 'Who's saying that? Never the doctor?'

'Mr Inspector Fowler,' said Verity grimly. 'Now Mr Chaffey, I ain't no wish to offend nor distress. However, a body that's knocked in the outfall or the river, might it be marked?'

Chaffey seemed to fear some revelation.

'There's always damage, Mr V. Bruising. Consequential on being washed through tunnels or against bridges and ships.'

'So it'll be some comfort to you to know, Chaffey, that your sweetheart had hardly a mark. One that might have been a belt worn round the hip. There couldn't be marks that faded?'

'Marks is apt to deepen in colour after death, Mr Verity, not fade.'

'What I thought, Mr Chaffey. Then she got nothing to speak of.'

Chaffey drained his glass, professional pride overcoming private mournfulness.

'Mr Verity, when ladies drowns, it shrinks them here, in the tips of the bosoms.'

Verity shook his head.

'I never saw. Nor had no wish to.'

Chaffey stared at the long mahogany bar through the smoke-fogged air.

'You saying she never drowned, sir?'

Verity sighed.

'No, Mr Chaffey. She drowned all right, water in her lungs.'

'But not where she was found?'

The sergeant's face seemed rounder and redder in the heat of the bar, while Old Stock's eyes flicked from one partner in the conversation to the other. He wiped a gleam of perspiration from a pointed end of his waxed moustaches.

'Mr Chaffey, I knew before I went there she couldn't drown where she was found. Matter of fact, that's why I went.'

Old Stock gave him an interrogatory leer.

'What you saying exactly, Mr Verity?'

'Simple, Ma.' Verity patted the old woman's hand. 'Flood tide that night was eleven. Your Joanne was high enough on the mud for the outfall to wash her there but too high for the river to take her there on the ebb. But the outfall couldn't have washed her there neither. She was seen alive at two in the morning and the sluices that might have washed her there weren't open again before she was found. I saw her in The Strand at two – in the same black dress and with her boots on.'

'What you saying, sir?' the old woman persisted.

'I'd say, Mrs Stock, she drowned somewhere private. And she was got rid of quick by someone who never bothered over tides nor sluices. Nor boots nor marks.'

Chaffey gave a small sob.

'I was her sweetheart when I had a sov in hand. She got no right to finish like that.'

'Still, you being sweet on her, Mr Chaffey, might count against your evidence.'

Chaffey wiped an eye with the corner of a spotted handkerchief.

'She was a found-drowned, Mr V. Hundreds every year. That's what counts against. A vestry give half a crown to the finders and not much for the inquest. Unless she'd had her throat cut as well, Dr Pargiter's paid just to confirm drowning. If Mr Fowler and the police got nothing to say, there's an end.'

'You think she met foul play, Mr Chaffey?'

The young man looked at him closely.

'You ever known, Mr Verity, a young person that could bear to stoop over a sink with her head in the water until she gave up the ghost? Without someone holding her under? Either holding her under in one go – or bringing her up time to time?'

He slid his legs out from the table and pushed into the crowd of drinkers. Verity polished his hat-brim on his sleeve, staring at the young man who was now out of earshot.

'That's much what I thought, Mr Chaffey,' he said to himself. He turned to Old Stock. 'You'd oblige me, Ma, by not mentioning this to anyone else just yet.'

He got up and went after Chaffey, leading him back.

'You got no notion, Mr Chaffey, how obliged I am. If you and Mrs Stock was able to join me in a further nip of Holland, I shan't distress you. Just a matter I'd like to put to a man of your learning and experience.'

They sat down and watched the aproned waiter refill the glasses. Verity gazed at the young medical assistant.

'How's it look, Mr Chaffey, when a man's run through by a stiletto blade?'

Chaffey frowned.

'I seen one or two, Mr V. Not a usual knife. Hard to tell it's been done. Symmetrical wound. Wedge shape that you'd hardly see. That's how us that practises the medical arts knows it can't be a knife with a back but sharp all round, stiletto.'

He reached thankfully for his hot gin.

'But why wouldn't you see it, Mr Chaffey?'

'With something like a stiletto, the wound closes up as the knife comes out, Mr V, skin being elastic. Hardly a mark to be seen with a blade so narrow. It's damage to internal organs that finishes a chap.'

Verity took his hat off and mopped his face with his red hand-kerchief. Chaffey shifted a little on the tall oak bench.

'Then there's the hands, Mr Chaffey. You ever know a poor devil attacked by a knife and didn't try to push it off?'

Chaffey shook his head, happy to be an authority consulted by the law. He brushed back his love curl.

'Cuts to the hands is usual, sir.'

'They are,' Verity said enthusiastically. 'Why, Mr Chaffey, all that time I was before Sebastopol, you no idea how many of my poor friends was coopered by sabres and bayonets. I never knew one, when he come to the end, didn't fight steel with his hands if he had nothing else. Instinct for life, Mr Chaffey, is what it is.'

Chaffey looked at him uneasily.

'That stiletto blade now, Mr Chaffey. Much blood from it?'

'Skin closes up on withdrawal, Mr V. Don't really bleed then.'

Verity shook his head, marvelling at medical investigation.

'And yet, Mr Chaffey, when Handsome Rann coopered Pandy Quinn, Rann had blood all down his shirt.'

Chaffey's dark eyes went wide and he looked alarmed.

'Blood from the knife, Mr V,' he said quickly.

Verity nodded.

'Must be, Mr Chaffey. Handsome Jack coopered Pandy, then wiped the knife all down his shirt special, so's he could be arrested. Still, I expect the inquest was told all about the cuts that Pandy had on his hands?'

The young man swallowed.

'Not as such. Couldn't use his hands, p'raps.'

'Tied behind his back, I daresay?'

'That'll be it!' Chaffey snatched at the opportunity.

'Then I daresay Dr Pargiter must have told the inquest about rope marks on Pandy's wrists.'

Chaffey made a sound that was just short of speech.

'He didn't,' said Verity helpfully, 'did he? The marks Pandy had were bruises that might come from holding a man down. Now, Mr Chaffey, you ever hear of two men rolling round the floor fighting and one of them – with no help from anyone else – holding the other down and tying him up?'

Chaffey said nothing but Old Stock intervened.

'Play fair, Mr Verity! Chaffey put you straight on Pretty Jo. Ain't that enough?'

Verity's face flushed with resolve. He picked up his hat.

'He might speak for Miss Joanne, bringing the house down on them that murdered the poor little soul. Say nothing, Ma. I'll be back when I know the rest.'

He got up, pushing his way to the cooler air of the summer night. Cat Clare was at one of the tables. She slanted a look of contempt at her natural enemy, thin lips pursed and blue eyes narrowed. Verity paid no attention. He wondered what formalities were required in arresting an officer of a rank superior to his own.

29

'Stand where you're seen, Handsome Rann!'

It was Atwell's voice on the far side of the door, then two of them murmuring together. They could see him through the keyhole or the crack of the door which would show a wedge-shaped section of the room, widening to include the window and far wall. The chair and the mattress were in this section. Only the table with hand-mirror and hairbrush, long strands of a woman's hair twined in its bristles, was beyond surveillance.

He had expected his interrogation to begin at once. Instead, he was left all night, hearing only intermittent movements in the passageway. Perhaps they had left him alone to soften him up. More likely, Brass was asking Policeman Fowler for permission before beginning his lethal work. Fowler might require the silencing of Miss Jolly to make the destruction of the others safer.

That night, half-formed plans for escape filled Rann's mind, each examined and rejected. The room would hold him fast. Next day or the day after, they would choose Maggie or Samuel or Miss Jolly and the screaming would begin, ending each time in death. Even if Maggie or Samuel told all that they knew, the interrogators could not be certain until the final cut.

He could scarcely move from the uneven mattress. Every board in the attic room seemed to creak. Somewhere after midnight he moved softly to the window.

'Back in yer pit, Handsome Rann. I have to come in, you get a smacked head to keep you dancing for a week!'

It was Hardwicke.

'I gotta use the necessary closet,' Rann said brusquely. 'I got the right to that!'

The door was unlocked. He was taken to an evil-smelling drain at the end of the passageway. They brought him back and left him in the dark. The boards creaked as he settled on the mattress again. A ray of light shone through the crevice of the door as they checked that he was there and nowhere else. Then the door was locked and it was dark.

From under his huddled shape, he took the tortoiseshell hand-mirror which he had purloined from the small table, beyond the view of the door, as they shut him in the darkness. In the gloom, he had swayed aside a little and pushed the mirror under his jacket as he passed. It was a simple design, a wooden handle and frame, a thin sheath of tortoiseshell, a round glass six inches across.

A clock chimed three. He drew his finger round the bevelled edge of the glass. The tortoiseshell frame overlapped it by quarter of an inch, holding it in place. With his thumb-nail, he tested this edging, trying to splinter it and work the mirror-glass free. There was a snick as it yielded a fraction and then snapped back into place. He listened but guessed that Hardwicke had heard nothing.

He tried it again, drawing blood under his thumb-nail. He prised it a fraction. The lining cracked and yielded a splinter of thin shell. After that, it lifted more easily from the edge of the glass. With the side of his thumb, he snapped off an inch of narrow edging. By the time the clocks struck four, the smooth bevelled glass was fixed only by the glue holding it to the wooden base of the mirror.

As he had hoped, the glue was dry and brittle. Cautiously, trying not to break the wooden backing, he took it in both hands. Then he lay and waited for an early market-cart in the street below. While the iron-rimmed wheels rattled on cobbles, he forced the glass away from the frame with a muffled crack of wood.

Anxiously he slid his hands over the mirror-back. But the tortoiseshell was smooth and undamaged. Face-down, the mirror would look intact. He waited on the mattress as the summer dawn grew stronger beyond the barred window.

Hardwicke and Atwell came in with bread and coffee. As he heard the door open, Rann got up and let them see him crossing to the little table, its surface hidden from them by his back. They would hardly expect him to work the trick while they were coming in. Hardwicke, burly in his red waistcoat, took him by the arm.

'Get back over there, you lying little toad!'

'I gotta brush my hair,' Rann said, with the woman's hairbrush in his hand. 'I gotta right to that as well.'

Hardwicke spat into the coffee before handing it to him.

'You gotta right to cry like a baby at the things I'll be doing to you, Jack Rann. That's all you got left now.'

Atwell, thin, bald, and humorous, snatched the brush from him.

'Gob in his drink again, Mr Hardwicke, less he should scald hisself!'

But neither of them bothered to pick up the empty tortoiseshell frame of the mirror. It crossed Rann's mind that perhaps a man of Hardwicke's stupidity had no more idea of being photographed as he ravished or punished Joanne than any other dupe set up for blackmail at the introducing-house.

'I ain't a liar,' he said quietly, 'I seen them photographs. You got up in costume with a belt and whip and her tied up. I wasn't there when you did it to her but I can give you all the details. How d'you think I'd know if I hadn't seen pictures? There's a thing like an old pillar and her tied to face it. And now she's dead. S'pose the inquest finds some marks still there on her backside from what you done to her and puts it together? Your game won't be all brandy then, will it?'

Hardwicke snarled at him, 'Get over your side of the room, you evil little monkey!'

But, as with Bragg, a light went dead behind his eyes.

Left to himself, there was nothing but the movements outside the door and the muffled clatter of wheels in the street. Rann walked over to the window, as if placing himself in full view from the keyhole and the crack. To those who observed him, he stood at the bars, the window several inches beyond them, his hands folded across his stomach, gazing wistfully down into Drury Lane, his back to the door.

Between his fingers rested the circle of mirror-glass. Above the street, at the level of attic windows, eastern sun promised a hot June morning. Far below, the first lawyers and traders, stifling in black coats and hats, were walking from the trains and steamers towards the Inns of Court and Holborn. A gravely bearded clerk was about to cross from the far side of the street. Rann carefully caught the sun in the mirror-glass and angled it down. A circle of bright light caught the man's face and slipped away. He raised his hand, as if to brush off a fly.

Rann gave him a moment, then trained the glass again. This time, the man looked round – and then looked up. That was all Rann needed to know. Lying awake in the hours before dawn, he had made up his mind. Today or the next day he would be put to death. Maggie and Samuel would go before him. Miss Jolly might be found at the Chinese Shades. The mirror-glass was the last hope. If he could catch the eyes of a policeman, trying every man who passed on the beat, one of them might have the curiosity to enquire. Failing that, any 'white tie' or 'uprighter' with an interest in fallen women might know the house for what it was and wonder if a respectable girl was not being held captive in its attics.

Bragg and Fowler had counted on Jack Rann's fear of the law. But even if he was taken and hanged, Maggie and Samuel and Miss Jolly would be saved. In any case, Rann decided, he would as soon he hanged next week as cut to death by Hardwicke and Atwell next day.

He watched for a beat officer on the far pavement, where the mirror would reflect the greatest light. A whiskered constable in his tall beaver hat and high-buttoned swallow-tail coat walked slowly past the houses and slum courts. The sun was in a sky of full blue, as the glass caught it. Rann brought the dazzling, dancing circle down. It touched the lower half of the policeman's face but the brim of the tall hat kept it from his eyes. He walked on and paid no attention.

From time to time, Rann went back and sat on the solitary chair so that his interest in the window should not be too apparent. The morning passed. One or two of his targets glanced up but affected not to notice the mirror's brightness, as if scorning a joke.

When the sun moved westward, it would be more difficult to catch it at an angle that carried into the traffic and crowds of the street. Already the girls from the streets north of The Strand were beginning their long hours of solicitation, each on her own stretch of pavement. Some had parades in Drury Lane itself. By evening, they would be jostling for territory. The afternoon trade was less competitive with only a few girls on view.

One or two of the afternoon trade followed a circuit, along The Strand from Drury Lane to Wellington Street, up to Long Acre and Queen Street, down Drury Lane to The Strand again, walking casually, always approachable. Rann picked out several as they walked alone. He made no attempt to attract their attention. The policemen in this division might not be Flash Fowler's but the girls were usually Bully Bragg's. There was one with a veil, sometimes worn in full daylight to disguise the ravages of disease. To some men a veil was alluring and suggestive. The burgundy silk of the dress, in this case, showed a figure that was tall and firm, the rust-red gloss of her hair drawn into a bun.

Jack Rann watched her as she drew level. She stopped. The veiled eyes under the merino hat made an upward survey of the windows, coming to rest on the attic level. Was she one of Bragg's girls, keeping watch on his window and those who waited under it? Or a rival's woman curious at a rumour of prisoners held in the attics?

He knew that she was not Miss Jolly nor any other girl of his acquaintance. None of them had seen him taken by Bragg. If he had simply disappeared, even his penny-dancer would know that a sudden departure had always been part of his plan. Even if they suspected Bragg, he might still have been taken to any one of a dozen houses.

The girl walked on. Rann angled the mirror at the next policeman on the beat but the sun was lower now and it was impossible to shine any part of its reflection under the brim of the tall beaver hat. In half an hour, the light from the sky would be beyond his reach.

Twice more he tried, once with a gaitered clergyman and once with another constable. Then, at the far end of the street, he saw the veiled girl coming on her next circuit. She, at least, had shown some curiosity. He angled the mirror and trained the disc of white light full on her veil. She stopped, her hands to her eyes, shielding them. He let her walk on a little and then shone the disc again. She stopped again on the far pavement, looked up at the source of the annoyance, and lifted her veil. Jack Rann saw only the face of a stranger.

All the same, he stretched his arms between the bars and pressed his palms against the window panes to show that someone was there. The girl continued to look. For good measure, he caught the sun in the glass again and shone it about the casement in front of him, trying to illuminate the close-set iron bars.

The girl walked on. The sun flared along the opposite roofs and vanished. All his cleverness had come to nothing. Even Maggie and Samuel were beyond his help. Only his dancer remained free.

Rann went back to the chair and thought that he had one more chance. It was not a chance of life but a choice of how he would die. He could no longer save himself but, if luck was with him before the end, he might also destroy Bully Bragg, Flash Fowler, even Hardwicke, or Atwell. Even old Catskin Nash.

30

Sergeant William Clarence Verity, Private-Clothes Detail, 'A'
Division, presents his compliments to Chief Inspector Henry
Croaker. The following remarks are recorded for Mr Croaker's
attention and will be forwarded to him in the event of Sergeant
Verity's decease or disappearance. They will be held meantime by a
person of confidence.

Sergeant Verity regrets to inform Mr Croaker that a superior
officer of the Metropolitan Police, Inspector Charles Foxe Fowler of
'H' Division, has apparently conspired with known criminals to
pervert the course of public justice and has further committed wilful
perjury on his own behalf.

In December last, Mr Fowler visited the residence of Lord Seriol
Tregarva in Portman Square, on suspicion of attempted burglary at
those premises. Mr Fowler examined indoors evidence and inspected
the roof. He assured Mr Isaac Kingdom, Lord Tregarva's man, that
nothing was amiss. On 20 May last, Sergeant Verity inspected the
roof and observed in an adjoining declivity the remains of a beaver
hat beyond his reach. He was, however, able to identify this article
as made by James Keller Esq., of St Paul's Churchyard, and as
having been repaired.

While assuring Mr Kingdom that there was nothing to be seen on
the roof, Mr Fowler then visited Mr Keller's emporium, where he

inquired after the repair of such a hat and established that it had belonged to a known housebreaker, William Arthur Quinn, familiarly known as Pandy Quinn. Mr Bertram Manuel of the hatters and his boy are witnesses to Mr Fowler's inquiry. Sergeant Verity respectfully encloses for Mr Croaker's attention records of Quinn's previous conviction and reputation as a garret-thief, entering houses by their attics.

Despite verifying the ownership of the hat on a roof adjacent to Portman Square, Mr Fowler made no attempt to detain or question Quinn in the following month during which the suspect was still alive. Nor did he report the matter of the hat to any other officer, either before or after Quinn's death.

Following the murder of Quinn in the tap-room of the Golden Anchor, premises where Mr Fowler was then in another room, Mr Fowler attended the inquest at Clerkenwell Vestry. Evidence was given that after Quinn was stabbed he was heard to say 'My hat! My hat will be the death of me!' When Mr Fowler was questioned, he twice maintained that he could not say what the words might refer to and knew nothing of any hat. Sergeant Verity submits this as Mr Fowler's first act of perjury.

At the moment of Quinn's death, Mr Fowler described himself as being in another room of the Golden Anchor interviewing a suspect in another matter. He was brought down by the noise and found William Bragg and another man holding James Patrick Rann on the body of the victim. Mr Fowler gave evidence to the inquest and to the Central Criminal Court upon this matter. In his account on oath, Mr Fowler informed the court that Quinn was bleeding copiously and that Rann's shirt was covered in blood from Quinn's wounds. Sergeant Verity begs to draw Mr Croaker's attention to a further enclosure, transcribed from Dr Hoffmann's Pathology. From these observations, it is plain that Rann could not have been covered in such an amount of blood from the wound alone if Quinn was stabbed with a stiletto blade. Sergeant Verity submits that such blood as was on Rann's clothing in contact with the deceased could

243

only have come from some other person or animal, as well as wiped from the weapon used.

Mr Fowler alleged that he had just previously heard some person, namely Rann, leave the tap-room, then unoccupied but for Quinn, as if to drop something down the drain on Hatton Wall. Three weeks since, a stiletto identified as that with which Quinn was murdered was retrieved by Inspector Fowler's intervention from the drain on Saffron Hill and named as Rann's weapon of murder. Sergeant Verity assures Mr Croaker that there is no means by which a knife dropped into the drain on Hatton Wall could be washed down to Saffron Hill.

It is Sergeant Verity's painful duty to ask that an investigation be undertaken in respect of perjury, concealing evidence, conspiracy to pervert the course of public justice, and accessory after the fact in the murder of William Arthur Quinn.

Sergeant Verity further requests that investigation be made into the death of a young person, Joanne Phillips, whose body was found just below high watermark at Wapping Reach on Saturday morning. This unfortunate was inmate of a house of ill-repute whose procurer by the name of Martileau is known to be in the pay of William Bragg.

Sergeant Verity understands that evidence will be given to Shadwell Vestry of this young woman having made away with herself. He therefore respectfully requests to lay before Mr Croaker the following facts.

There were no marks on the deceased consistent with having been washed against bridges or vessels nor through outfalls. The body wore no boots, nor impressions to show that any had been put on. Mr Croaker will know that in cases of this sort boots are not lost once the victim is in the water. Had she walked barefoot to the river or the great drain, the soles of the feet would have been marked. Sergeant Verity was able to see with his own eyes that this was not so. If she wore no boots, the state of her feet was consistent only with her having been carried to the place where she was found.

The deceased was seen alive by Sergeant Verity and others in The Strand, after midnight on Friday, and was found at eight in the morning. Mr Croaker may confirm that the flood tide, which might carry her where she was found, had passed an hour before midnight and three hours before she was last seen alive. Though the body was high enough to have been carried down the great drain by the first opening of the sluices at the ebb, this had occurred at the time she was seen in The Strand and would not have been repeated before noon next day, four hours after the body was found.

Sergeant Verity is therefore obliged to conclude that this unfortunate young person was drowned elsewhere, foully made away with on premises that might be those of William Bragg. He is in possession of photographs, which he encloses, displaying the young person naked, libidinously chastized at the hands of Bragg's man, Hardwicke. Her remains were deposited on the foreshore by darkness, those who destroyed her thinking she would be considered a found-drowned but never knowing the states of the tide nor the times of the sluices.

Sergeant Verity believes that if Mr Croaker should have occasion to read these lines, it will be because the author of them is no longer to be found living. He begs Mr Croaker that further investigations be pursued against Charles Foxe Fowler, William Bragg and their associates. He also urges that justice be done in the case of James Patrick Rann, against whom the evidence cannot show murder, and that the condemned man's life shall be spared.

In conclusion, Sergeant Verity takes his final leave of Mr Croaker in this world, hoping he has always been found every way honest and a friend to justice, commending Mrs Verity and his two infants to the friends of virtue and religion.

W. Verity, Sgt., 8 June 1860

31

Albert Samson brushed the ginger growth of his mutton-chop whiskers and grinned at Verity across the sloping desk.

'What I'd fancy,' he said fruitily, 'is a hiring job. For the summer, to a fine house in the country. Living like a superior servant in the kitchen. Same food and drink as the master but only light work and surveillance.'

'Yes?' said Verity thoughtfully. 'And you know that ain't going to be offered to the likes of you, Mr Samson. But you might be happy instead to walk a beat through the town with yer nose caught in lady's tail.'

Samson slid off his stool, chortled, and reached for his hat.

'And me paired on the beat with a Methodist?'

Verity sanded an ink-blot and closed the ledger.

'Methodists are human, Mr Samson. Sinners like the rest.'

Samson now suspected a trap.

'You got something special in mind, have you?'

Verity shrugged.

'I was only wondering, Mr Samson, supposing I could square it when I come to my diary, if you mightn't fancy an evening at the Chinese Shades. Company of a young person.'

Samson chortled again.

'I got to see this, my son. A Methodist in an 'ouse of sin.'

246

'You got no idea, Mr Samson, how much time gets took up for a Methodist by sin. All this depending on favour-for-favour.'

'Such as what favour?'

From his breast-pocket, Verity drew an envelope.

'You'd favour me by keeping this for a week or two, as a man of confidence. If I was to get coopered in that time, or go missing without cause, you'd hand this unopened to Mr Croaker. If he shouldn't want it, then to Superintendent Gowry.'

Samson grinned, accepted the envelope, and slid it into his pocket.

'You don't half take the cake, my son!'

Like down-at-heel clerks in their tall hats and frock coats, they joined the Monmouth Street crowd, pushing towards the penny gaff. The success of the Chinese Shades had brought such numbers that a uniformed policeman now kept order in the narrow street. A farmhouse kitchen-table on the pavement supported a band of flute, violin, and drum. The light streaming out as the curtain was pulled aside lit the faces of the crowd like a reflection of fire.

The Chinese Shades now occupied most of the performance. There was a comic shadow-play, a patient on a surgeon's table. The victim was opened with a pair of large shears. An assortment of objects was extracted from his entrails: an alarm clock which rang upon removal, a string of sausages, a live rabbit, a rolling-pin, a kettle, and an umbrella. Several times he sat up, to be laid out again with the blow of an iron saucepan to his head. Finally, the surgeon's incision was sewn up with a monstrous needle and thick cord.

The restless amusement ended and there was silence as the broken piano rang out its suggestion of eastern dance.

'Round the back, Mr Samson! Make sure she don't do a bunk through the alley.'

'See the turn first,' Samson said amiably.

'There ain't going to be a turn. You'll see all there is to see in the alley. Get there and hold her if she tries to slip out.'

He stood up and moved in the shadows towards the roughly

constructed stage, leaving Samson to hurry to the alleyway. Behind the calico screens, fierce gaslight shone full on the stretched fabric, casting the girl's shadow. Verity moved behind the lights, where she could scarcely see him. He gave Samson a counted minute. Then he reached for the gas-tap and turned it. The brilliance spluttered into fading twilight, a last glow of red-hot mantels, and darkness.

The audience began to shout its disapproval. A party of costers set up a slow handclap. But Verity knew what Miss Jolly must do. Only one door led behind the stage and she would bolt for it. He was there, seizing an upper arm whose texture might equally have been silk fleshing or cool skin.

'Right, miss!' he said. 'You an' me needs to have a word.'

She let out a wail of terror, more intense than he could account for. Twisting for her life, she broke free and fled, apparently naked, for the alley door. Hearing the cry, Samson opened it from the other side. They were in the passageway of the old warehouse, Verity at one end, Samson at the other, Miss Jolly in the middle.

'Ain't you got more sense?' Samson asked with a smile. 'You can't go out there like that!'

'She might, Mr Samson. Supposing she was in fear of someone that could do worse things to her than the law ever would.'

The tumult among the audience died as Dandy O'Hara appeared with a coster favourite, 'My Long-Tailed Jock'. A large man opened the door between the stage and the passageway. He saw the two policemen with his dancing-girl and quickly withdrew. Miss Jolly dodged towards the dressing cubicle where she had left her clothes. She cried out as Samson followed. Verity motioned him back.

'Now, you listen, my girl,' he said firmly, standing over her, 'we got no quarrel with you, nor what you been doing here. But Jack Rann's another matter. You being his sweetheart.'

'No!' she cried, folding her arms crosswise to cover herself. 'Never!'

'Don't come it,' Samson said, still grinning at her. 'You was his doxy long ago. You'd know where he was, if anyone did!'

'I don't!'

She snatched a bundle of linen to herself.

Verity let out a sigh of impatience.

'We ain't here to hang Jack Rann, but we might save him.'

The look that slanted from her dark eyes made it impossible to tell whether she believed him.

'Save him?'

They faced each other over a distance of three feet.

'Handsome Rann never coopered Pandy Quinn,' Verity said gently. 'He couldn't have done. I know that now.'

Samson looked at him in dismay.

'Draw it mild, my son,' he said quickly.

Verity ignored him and held Miss Jolly's gaze.

'The knife Mr Fowler found in Saffron Hill never came from the Golden Anchor. Drains don't run that way.'

The tight-lidded eyes flicked from Verity to Samson, choosing which to believe.

'And the blood,' Verity said patiently. 'All the blood Jack Rann had on him never come from Pandy Quinn. Might be from another man, or a stuck pig, or a blood pudding. Quinn being cut with a stiletto hardly bled at all. Only way he might bleed was being carried rough from somewhere else. In that case he wasn't cut in the tap-room. And in that case Jack Rann never did it. The tap-room was the only room your Jack was in.'

'Then who?' she wailed.

'Same men as held Pretty Jo's head under water until she died, then left her on Wapping Reach like a found-drowned.'

'But why?' She sat down on a stool in her cubicle.

'Once we find Jack Rann, we'll know. Where is he?'

'He's gone!'

'Where?'

'I don't know!' The eyes went round and the mouth opened in a tragic gape.

"'Course you bloody know!' Samson said irritably. Verity frowned again and waved him to silence.

'Your Handsome Jack got more danger of being done to death by the men who fitted him to Pandy's murder than he ever has of being hanged by Jack Ketch. Don't you know that?'

The first tear brimmed and she nodded silently.

'Right,' said Verity gently, 'you gotta be a good, brave, girl, and help us find him before he's hurt as bad as Pandy Quinn.'

'He'll be took to Newgate and hanged!'

'He won't!' said Verity encouragingly. 'There's evidence to show he never cut Pandy. Any case, wouldn't it be better for him to be in Newgate, with a chance to get a pardon, than in the hands of the villains that's never pardoned anyone?'

She shook her head.

'He's been took by them,' Verity insisted. 'Ain't that what all this is about?'

Miss Jolly stared at the floor beyond her toes.

'Leave him where he is, miss, and he'll die surely as warrant morning at Newgate. Can't you see? You been beaten, hurt, by men of that sort. You know what they can do. If Handsome Jack was free now, don't you think you'd hear?'

She stared with frightened eyes at the same patch of floor.

'Bully Bragg and the others,' Verity added quietly, 'ain't it? The men that held him down on Pandy Quinn.'

She nodded again.

'And Policeman Fowler?' Verity held his breath.

Samson looked aghast and Miss Jolly lifted her face, more frightened than ever.

'Bully Bragg anyway,' Verity said reassuringly. 'Where?'

Miss Jolly put her hands together.

'You'll hang him!' she cried at them.

Samson's face hardened behind the ginger whiskers.

'Hang you, more like! Make Jack Ketch quite frisky. If there's murder and you let it happen, you're an accessory. If you're lucky you'll be hanged; if you ain't, you'll be caught by those that had Pretty Jo, fighting to breathe with your head held under water till you can't breathe no more.'

Verity glared at him but Samson's warning did its work.

'Red-Haired Brigid!' she sobbed, 'that does the Smithfield gaff. I couldn't go where they know me, but Brigid dressed smart in a veil not to be noticed and walked round Bragg's houses. At Martileau's, they had someone in the top rooms working a mirror in the sun. Might be a girl locked up. But it might be him.'

Verity straightened up, hands behind his back under the tails of his frock coat. Victory had come easily. He saw himself before Superintendent Gowry's desk in a few days, receiving congratulations on the arrest of Bragg, the unmasking of Fowler, the discovery of Jack Rann's innocence.

'There's a good, brave, sensible girl,' he said gently. 'You get your proper clothes on. We'll save your Handsome Jack.'

Half an hour later, with Samson escorting Miss Jolly, Verity entered the courtyard off Drury Lane, the soot-grained buildings of a century past towering on every side. Mother Martileau's had been familiar territory to him long before it came under the rule of Bully Bragg. He had arrested a score of its inmates at various times for pilfering the notecases and pockets of their clients, inflicting bodily harm on one another, receiving stolen goods, swearing false evidence.

At this time of night, the house with its porters in coachmen's capes and breeches, its pillars with their torches of gas, was fully lit and busy. One of the doormen took a single glance at Verity, Samson, and Miss Jolly, then disappeared inside. The other man made no attempt to stop them.

Verity led the way into the vestibule, the coloured glass of the skylight throwing diffused reflections of rose and turquoise on the black and white tiling. A bedlam of waltzes and polkas came from the introducing-room to one side with its Broadwood grand piano, its pink-shaded lamps, nude statuary, and large gilt-framed mirrors. Officers, gentlemen, Oxford undergraduates who would graduate only in the *Racing Calendar* or *Paul Pry*, danced with Sarahs, Beckys, and Lottys until they made their choice and agreed a price.

Bragg appeared before him, Hardwicke and Atwell either side. The absurd pile of the Bully's black Pompadour hair was newly arranged, his colour high, as if from a dab of rouge. He was drunk enough to be entirely self-confident as the two sergeants confronted him.

'Evening, Mr Verity.' His eyes rolled and his mouth opened at the preposterous humour of it all. 'Nice new suit that, after your misfortune down Lambeth. You 'ere for a little hocus-pocus, I daresay? Not rumplin' young Suzanne Berry again, I hope. On'y we don't allow that sort of thing here!'

He grinned hugely at his bodyguards on either side. Hardwicke and Atwell stared at the two policemen with as much indifference as if they were not seeing them.

''Course,' said Bragg humorously, 'if you brought Miss Shop-Mouse Jolly here for a hidin', an' all you want is a room to do it to her, that's easy sorted.'

He gave the same open-mouthed grin.

'No, Mr Bragg,' Verity said casually, 'I shan't bother you for a room. I mean to search the premises. I mean to do it now. I'll thank you and your servants to stand clear of my way.'

Bragg shook his head, as if Verity's practical jokes would be the death of him.

'Mr Saward!' he called. 'You hear all that, did you?'

He looked up again at Verity, a hard and triumphant gleam in his eyes. Verity's heart sank. A tall, dark-haired old man, the cheeks sunken and the body stooped, came out of the parlour to one side. His mouth was tightened and pursed as if he had been about to spit phlegm.

Bragg nodded at Verity.

'You tell him, Mr Barrister. You'll do it nicer than me.'

Saward stood before Verity. He sniffed, his nostrils narrowing to little more than bone, and held out his hand.

'Warrant?'

Verity stared back at him and Saward spoke, as if to one of simple intelligence.

'Search warrant, mister. Other words, a legal instrument signed on Common Law authority by a Justice of the Peace, authorizing a named officer to enter, by force if necessary, into a specific house or premises for a purpose which must also be specially described—'

'I ain't got a warrant . . . .'

Saward turned away.

'Then I suggest, mister, that you return when you have one.'

'See?' said Bragg sympathetically. 'Life ain't all *Vingt-et-Un* at sixpence a dozen, is it, Mr Verity?'

Verity glared at him.

'I got reason to suspect that James Patrick Rann, otherwise known as Jack Rann, fugitive from Newgate, is in this house.'

Bragg shook his head, as if to clear it.

'Jack Rann? I don't believe I ever met a Jack Rann. Poxy little name, though, ain't it? Sort of name that needs putting to sleep for its own good. You can't search this house and create a disturbance, of course, Mr Saward just told you that, but wait here a minute.'

The graceful wrought-iron staircase curved up in a series of diminishing ovals. Bragg walked to the first floor and presently reappeared. Verity understood the extent of the disaster. Behind Bragg, in a lavender-grey suit and green stock, walked Inspector Fowler. Verity waited until they were face to face.

'Permission to proceed with search of premises. With respect, sir.'

Fowler looked at him, as if suspecting a trick.

'It has just been done, Sergeant. Two men upstairs are taking the last witness-statement from a young gentleman of Magdalen College, who appears to have lost a diamond cravat-pin.'

'Information as to the person Jack Rann being on these premises, sir. With respect.'

Fowler sighed.

'Two officers of this division, with my assistance as a passer-by, have just searched the premises at the request of Madame Martileau. Madame fears that there may be a thief among her guests. We have searched the attics, the bedrooms, the reception rooms, the basement, the kitchens, the cellars. There is no Jack Rann in the building.'

Verity felt his face growing warm and his heart pounding. Flash Charley Fowler stared back at him. Fowler was a liar and a scoundrel but his rank decided the matter.

'Nossir,' Verity said humbly. 'Very good, sir.'

Fowler sighed again, as if with relief. He was about to turn to Bragg with an apology but first he dealt with Verity.

'Have the goodness to go with Samson. Take this young person and wait outside until I come to you. Understand?'

'Yessir!' A few weeks ago, on the police boat, it was almost impossible to call the newly promoted Fowler 'sir'. Now the compliment came easily from his tongue. With Samson and Miss Jolly, he stood in the lamplight of the paved courtyard.

'Chinese Shades!' said Samson bitterly. 'Company of a young person! We was supposed to be having a bit of roly-poly! Look at this mess! You any idea what Mr Croaker might have to say ...?'

He stiffened to attention as Fowler walked leisurely from the lighted doorway.

'Well,' Fowler said, suddenly amiable, 'I'd say there's no harm done. Madame Martileau's a reasonable woman. Mr Bragg insists he took no offence. An' I hope I'm reasonable. Eh?'

'Yessir,' said Verity meekly.

'What I will do, however, is have this young person in custody as suspect and accomplice in the robbing of visitors to Madame Martileau. Others in the house taking the valuables, the same being slipped to this little piece when she puts her nose inside. Right? She been seen keeping watch on the place. Slip the cuffs on her Verity, there's a good fellow.'

Miss Jolly's face was a parody of terror at being delivered by Fowler to Bragg and the knife, her dark eyes wide and her mouth stretched in a silent scream.

'Nossir,' said Verity quietly, 'with respect, sir.'

Fowler's face creased with grotesque incomprehension.

'No, sir? Meaning what, sir?'

'Ain't possible for you to arrest this young person, sir.'

'Not possible?' Fowler was almost laughing at the absurdity. 'Why not?'

'She been arrested already, sir. By me and Mr Samson. Matter of Handsome Rann and perverting the course of justice.'

Samson stared glassily ahead of him, as if seeing deeply into some nameless horror. But he said nothing. Fowler relaxed.

'In that case, Verity, you got not the least worry. According to the police manual, you now surrender your prisoner to your superior officer.'

'Oh, I will, sir. But it ain't you, sir.'

'By God!' said Fowler, all his assumed amiability gone. 'You shall pay a reckoning for this. That girl is my prisoner.'

Verity stood solidly between Miss Jolly and the inspector.

'Nossir, with respect, sir. This young person is Mr Croaker's prisoner, having been arrested by me and Mr Samson on Mr Croaker's orders. And just as you happen to be superior to us, Mr Fowler, so Mr Croaker happens to be superior to you. And to us, of course. We got to obey his orders, all of us.'

Samson gave a slight gasp, as if of pain, but he still said nothing. Fowler looked as though he might make an annihilating riposte. Nothing came. The heavens would fall on the two sergeants next day but for the moment he was beaten. He turned without a word and was about to stride back into Madame Martileau's brightly lit hallway.

Verity never knew why he asked his parting question. In all the mysteries that had followed the death of Pandy Quinn there was a pattern, after all. Deep in his mind, where he was not aware of it, two fragments of the puzzle joined in certainty. Ten seconds before he spoke, he could not have matched them.

'Mr Fowler, sir!' Fowler stopped and looked back at him. 'When Pandy Quinn was killed in the tap-room of the Golden Anchor and you was upstairs questioning a young person in connection with a petty crime, that young person was never called to the inquest, not having seen nor heard anything. Never named in the police reports.'

He stared at Fowler in fascination, seeing such shock in the blue eyes that he could almost not go on with the question.

'It ain't much, Mr Fowler, but me and Mr Samson was right, wasn't we? The one that never give evidence and wasn't named. She was the one they called Sly Joanne or Pretty-Jo Mischief, wasn't she, sir? The one that was found-drowned off Wapping? It was her, Mr Fowler, wasn't it, sir?'

Fowler stopped and Verity felt like a man who had hit the bull's-eye of a target without taking aim or knowing it was there. But the shock had gone from the blue eyes. It was not dismay, or anger, or fear that he saw in the inspector's face: there was just the flat despair of a man who had run down the ways and turnings of a labyrinth to find, at last, only a blank and pitiless wall.

32

The scream was like a needle of fright through his heart. Worse than by dark, it was horror in full daylight, ringing through the dusty attic sunlight of a warm afternoon. Those who caused it knew their victim would not be heard beyond these rooms. It carried unbridled terror, not pain, the dread of what was to come. They had shown her something as they asked their questions. Some common domestic implement, perhaps, now obscenely menacing. Then came silence, more terrible than the transfixing cry. Rann crossed to the door and beat his fist on it. He rattled the handle in vain, conscious of the mounting toll of seconds that ticked by.

At last came a choking howl and he knew what they were doing. There was retching, another shrill appeal that failed for want of breath. Someone came to him now. The door opened and Bragg stood flanked by Hardwicke and Atwell. Moonbeam was not there. Rann guessed that the unmarked bruiser had been selected as executioner of Maggie Fashion.

Bragg stared at Rann, dispensing a bitter smile under the absurdly piled hair.

'You got something to say, Handsome Jack? Something on your mind, was there?'

'Ask me, not them,' Rann said quietly. 'I know where the dibs is. They don't.'

Bragg lifted one corner of his lip above his teeth, the smile of contempt.

'They ain't been asked yet. Maggie Turnbull with the hard face and big bum had to have a good wash first. Only way to get the truth. Give them a taste of what's coming. Then ask the questions, not before. Saves no end of time.'

'I want an agreement,' Rann said in the same quiet voice, 'that's all.'

Bragg turned to Hardwicke, then Atwell, then back to Rann, his mouth a tunnel of silent amusement.

'Look at 'im! He wants an agreement! Agreement? He wants a good smack round the head! Agreement? Such as?'

'I'm the putter-up,' Rann said softly, 'I know where everything is. You can have it. I'll take you there, show you where. But they don't get hurt. That's the agreement. Once you got the dibs, you let 'em go. And there's no point asking 'em. You know Samuel and you know the girl. They ain't hard as brass, are they? They'd make up any story to stop what's being done to 'em. But since they don't know, it'd just be a story. And it'd be too late for you then.'

Bragg glared at him.

'Too late?' He took the open flap of Rann's coat. 'What the fuck you mean, too late?'

'Tonight,' Rann said, 'it's being fetched. Low water. Tunnels under Shadwell. After the level drops from the flood. Leave it till tomorrow and you can kiss it all goodbye. Suit yourself. Only there ain't no point asking those two.'

'The girl and Samuel been down the drains, Mr Bragg,' Hardwicke said quickly, 'living like Hanover rats.'

'And now we got to take 'im down there?'

'He'd be no trouble in handcuffs, Mr Bragg. With two or three of us. He knows what he'd get!'

'Mr Hardwicke's right,' Rann said simply. 'Bank notes and bonds don't make a big bundle, not even twenty thousand quid. Go easily behind a couple of bricks. The place itself ain't far. Just below where they built the tanneries. Still, you'd never find it on your own. And I can't tell you the exact bricks without being there. No man could describe that without seeing them. That's the truth. But suit yerself. I got no more I can say.'

Bragg turned to Atwell.

'Go and ask Mr Fowler. And see about the handcuffs.' He turned back to Rann. 'What you suggesting, exactly?'

'I'll come with you,' Rann said in the same quiet, indifferent voice. 'You know I won't play up, Mag and Samuel being left here to answer for me. Any case, there's a few of you and only one of me. When you got what you want, you come back and let 'em go. No danger, are they? Hardly run and tell the law, them being the thieves.'

''And you?' Bragg asked contemptuously.

Rann shrugged, as if conceding to Bragg the right to kill him.

'Right, then,' Bragg said, 'so long as that's understood.'

Atwell came back with the silver-metal cuffs in his hand. Rann knew, at least, that Fowler was still in the building.

'Quarter ebb, go down the main shaft from the kiosk near Shadwell Basin,' Atwell said. 'Flood never reaches that far. You can have an hour down there and be out again before the sluices.'

Bragg repeated his half-sneer, half-smile. He jerked his head at Rann.

'I don't like taking His Majesty. What if he was seen?'

'Mr Fowler got a policeman's hat and coat for him. They got no reason to follow anyone dressed like that. He won't be noticed. Specially if the street's patrolled first and hangers-about remarked. And Handsome Jack wantin' to be so helpful ain't going to try hanky-panky. Him being so sensitive to that trollop Maggie and her noise!'

Bragg lifted the corner of his lip again and smiled at Rann, speaking to Atwell.

'Moonbeam,' he said humorously, 'tell Moonbeam to give young Maggie another wash! Just for luck. And smack some sense into that old fool Samuel's head!'

'There's no need for that!' Rann said desperately.

Bragg's lip drew back from his teeth in another grotesque smile.

'I'd say there was need, wouldn't you, Mr Hardwicke? See, Handsome Rann? Mr Hardwicke thinks there's need.'

They stood in the room, Rann held by Hardwicke and Atwell, hearing again the sounds of terror.

Half an hour later, in evening sunlight, the black cab stood where the stable yard of the Hanoverian gentleman's house had been. There was no one to see them as Rann, Bragg, Fowler, and Moonbeam got into it. Hardwicke and Atwell had been left to guard Samuel and Maggie, perhaps to act as executioners when the time came. But that would surely not happen until Bragg returned with the booty. Wild last-hope schemes unravelled in Rann's mind, as they passed through The Strand into Fleet Street. There was no scheme, in the end, only a brief moment of sudden opportunity when he might take Bragg or Fowler with him. He must die at last, but he promised himself he would not die alone. Furtively he tried his wrists in the metal cuffs that held his hands before him. The steel grip was unyielding.

The ornamental kiosk in the docks, by Shadwell Basin, disguised the baser structure of an entrance to the sewers. An iron ladder riveted to the brickwork led down a dozen feet. Moonbeam went first. Rann climbed down awkwardly with his manacled hands. Fowler and Bragg followed.

At the foot of the ladder, they stood in a domed cavern through which the main drain disappeared down a long tunnel. As in all the sewer caverns, stalactites of putrefying human waste hung from the roof. Fowler cursed as the stream in a brick channel splashed his polished shoe and wet the cuff of a trouser-leg. Fowler and Moonbeam carried lanterns and heavy ash-plant sticks.

'If you're having us on, Handsome Rann,' Bragg said softly, 'I'll give your mother something to weep for. Which way's the stuff?'

Rann remembered the plan of the main sewers in this area from his previous journey through them.

'This way,' he said meekly, 'down the high tunnel.'

'Moonbeam goes first. Then 'im. Then Mr Fowler and me.' Bragg turned to Rann. 'I half-hope you are having us on, Handsome Jack. I gotta taste for cutting you. Not all at once but one by one. Dusk to dawn and you cryin' to have it over with.'

'I know what's what,' Rann said meekly. 'I ain't having you on.'

Bragg made a sound of disgust as the tunnel roof opened upwards again and they saw above them the holes of the public latrines near Wapping High Street. Fowler spoke to Bragg for the first time since they had left Drury Lane.

'If he hasn't delivered the goods in the next half-hour, cuff him to a wooden prop and let him wait for the sluices to open, better still for the rats. Either way, he could be another found-drowned skeleton.'

'You can have the goods,' Rann said quietly, 'I got no use now.'

They were level with the side tunnel, above which Samuel had made his makeshift lodging. Rann knew what he must do.

'It's on from here,' he said, 'towards the river a little way.'

Ahead of them, like distant thunder down the dark tunnel, the last of the river's flood tide boomed against the iron doors of the outfall.

'When's the sluice?' Bragg said suddenly.

'Time enough.' Fowler held his lantern to his watch. 'Time enough to go straight back the way we came.'

In the next stretch of tunnel, Moonbeam cursed as he stumbled over a small heap of fallen bricks and tore his coat. They came out into another domed cavern, fed by a dozen side-drains. A family of kitten-sized brown rats scattered squealing into the darkness.

Bragg stopped suddenly.

'What's that?'

Somewhere down the main tunnel, from which they had come, there was a muffled reverberating blow, and then another.

'It's not the sluice?'

261

'No,' said Fowler impatiently, 'not with the outfall doors still shut. They can't raise it till those are open.'

Before either man could speak again, there was a distant crack from the same direction, like wood splitting, then the pattering of fragments, a clatter of broken bricks the size of clenched fists, and the steady rumble of an avalanche. The muffled blows were still audible when the rumbling faltered. The dry torrent came again, closer to them, almost drowning their words.

Bragg's features were rigid with fright. He coughed abruptly as the air of the vaulted cavern filled with a foul and rancid dust. The sound was now a muted but continuous roar, like the breath of a dragon, bricks bouncing on fallen bricks closer still to them. Then, as suddenly as it had begun, the noise ended.

'What the fuck,' Bragg asked, 'was that?'

Fowler ducked back into the tunnel, handkerchief over his face, and walked out of sight. The others waited, Bragg's tongue running on his lips. Fowler reappeared.

'It's gone,' he said stupidly, 'the whole main tunnel's gone. Caved in. There's no way back through it.'

'So how the fuck do we get out?'

Fowler ignored the question and turned to Rann.

'He's not getting out! This bloody little squeak had something to do with it. I'll swear he had!'

'How could the tunnel go? How?' Bragg now foresaw the sequel with undiluted dread.

'I don't know how,' Fowler said quietly, 'but however it was, this dirty squeak got something to answer for. We can't stay here. Get through the outfall to the river foreshore before the sluice opens. That's safe. But let Moonbeam finish him before we go.'

'No!' shouted Bragg. 'We ain't got what we came for!'

'And never will,' Fowler said. 'Ain't it plain? There's nothing here! There never was! It's his trick! But we got to get out on the foreshore. Now! The way we came is blocked. The side tunnels are a maze. The flood comes down some and not others. Can't tell which. The only safe way's straight on, the outfall and the fore-shore.'

'But him!' Bragg almost screamed the words at Rann. Fowler turned again.

'Do him now!'

He handed Moonbeam his heavier ash-plant. Moonbeam looked at Bragg and Bragg, in his fear, nodded. The unmarked bruiser put down his lantern and closed on Rann, who threw up locked hands to protect his head. The first blow missed but drove him back against the wall where a smaller side-tunnel ran off. The nightmare had come upon him, after all, in a stinking brick cavern like a burial vault, the light of two oil-lanterns throwing giant light and shade upon the walls.

His back was in a corner. The hands raised to protect his head left him open to a blow to the ribs, so powerful that when it came he felt numbness at first rather than pain. They would beat him to death and leave him, if he was lucky. At the worst they would leave him half-conscious by the side-tunnel for the flood of sewage to drown him or the rats to find him.

Moonbeam raised the heavy stick to break the fingers shielding the skull. Rann saw the monstrous shadow of the weapon on the wall, saw the giant shadow-hands that held it, saw it swing down. He cried out in a last terror of the sluice, or the rats, and heard the pistol-crack of skull-bone splintering.

But he felt nothing. Before him, Moonbeam went down without a murmur, sprawling across a brick channel. His dead eyes looked upwards at the fetid dome, unconcerned. The gigantic shadow-killer, an iron bar in his hand, was black against the lamplight. But the face, when it turned to Jack Rann, was the face of Lord Tomnoddy.

33

Bragg and Fowler, defenceless but for a single ash-plant against an iron bar, scrambled to the foreshore tunnel.

'Tomnoddy!' Rann held out his manacled wrists. 'We got to have 'em. Samuel and Maggie is still in Bragg's whorehouse. They'll be killed when he gets back.'

'I know,' Tomnoddy said. 'Come down the side tunnels. I can follow them like my own hand in front of my face. And I got the whole story of you and Bragg.'

Rann stumbled on. 'You can't, Tom! How could you hear any of that?'

Tomnoddy shrugged.

'You always was a soft bugger, Jack Rann. You was kind to a poor young washerwoman that lived in Newgate Street. You gave her my name to see she was all right. You was so kind, she couldn't quite puzzle why. Curiosity near killed a cat. So she followed you back to the Granby with her baby in a shawl. Saw you took off by four men. Heard them say Drury Lane to the cabman. She might be a simple soul but she knew trouble when she seen it. She come to me. That house of Bragg's been watched ever since.'

Jack Rann slipped and fell against the brick wall of the narrower tunnel. Tomnoddy helped him up.

'But they was sure it wasn't watched.'

'They would be,' the old sewerman said contemptuously. 'That red-haired fancy-dancer, Brigid, put on a veil and walked about there. They knew her shape wasn't Miss Jolly and they'd got Mag Fashion under lock and key. Miss Brigid was just another bunter to them. So they never bothered. But she saw your mirror flashing, though couldn't be sure it was you. Miss Jolly let on to Policeman Verity. Mr Verity reckons you never cut Pandy and couldn't a-done. He's got evidence. On'y he's singing a solo there. Still, he tried to search Bragg's place last night. Cabman Stringfellow, Mrs Verity's old father, been parked special to watch for anyone leaving that house. Policeman Verity and me was in the cab watching when Fowler and Bragg and Moonbeam came out. And there was another passenger – you – in police clothes. 'Course, we might not have known it was you. On'y Bragg and Fowler was stupid. Mr Verity knew you was never a policeman, for all the clothes. Too small for police. They don't take 'em your size, Handsome Jack. So we reckoned it had to be you.'

They were in the main tunnel, short of the outfall but ahead of Bragg and Fowler.

'Thanks to Cabman Stringfellow and Policeman Verity, you was followed here. Fortunate, seeing you was never meant to come out alive. Mr Verity watched the outfall. I could travel faster through the sewers than him or Bragg and Fowler. I was to drive 'em out by the outfall. I let 'em get through a good stretch of the main tunnel, keeping behind. Then I took the bar to break the roof down and block their way back. They got no chance then before the sluice opened but going on to the outfall. Still I come through the side-tunnel in time to stop your brains being knocked out. We'll get out of the main drain now. This way!'

'I hoped, getting them down here, I could catch them in the sluice,' Rann said.

Tomnoddy straightened up. Moisture dripped from the curve of the narrow roof.

'Listen,' he said quietly. 'They got no idea of the distance to the outfall nor how long it takes. What d'you think that is now?'

Jack Rann heard nothing yet but presently they came to an opening on to the main tunnel again. The iron door to the foreshore had been raised but no more than a suggestion of light carried from it, several hundred yards away.

'Listen!' Tomnoddy said again.

Rann heard only a hollow finger-tip reverberation of water drops falling from the points of rotten brickwork into stagnant pools. Then, far off, there was a sound like traffic in a busy street. A man's voice shouted, a single syllable, echoing and dying along the brick shaft.

'That's them,' Tomnoddy said quietly.

The traffic-murmur was thunder now, a storm in a circle of hills. Then, with a terror that took Rann's breath away, there was a sudden smash of water, a shriek, and the main tunnel seemed swept towards him. Tomnoddy snatched at him.

'Get back!'

There was a human figure ahead of the churning flood. Bully Bragg was trying to run with no sure footing. The sluice-water chased him and caught him. It knocked him down and he scrambled up. It hit him sideways and he spun in a mad dance, hitting the wall and sliding to his knees. He struggled up, waist deep in the flood. The level fell away and for a moment he seemed safe. He broke into another slithering run, striving for the outfall and the safety of the foreshore. But the sluice came like an express train and hit him full in the backs of the legs.

The absurd pompadour hair vanished in the torrent, his footing gone for ever. The flood carried him, arms and legs fighting, like a hero borne shoulder-high. While his head was above the surface he tried to scream but, where the tunnel curved, the force of the water turned him over and smashed him high against the arch of the roof. After that, there was no sound from him. The rising surge beat him against the wall. As the race carried him past the side-tunnel, Rann and Tomnoddy knew that Bully Bragg was already dead.

'Back!' Tomnoddy shouted. 'Further in!'

266

Rann drew away, watching the flood swirl and splash through the low-roofed main channel. Of Fowler there was no sign. Rann imagined him drowned deep in the torrent, beaten beyond recognition by the walls of the sewer.

He was never to know how long he stood with Tomnoddy in the shelter of the side-channel before the swirling of sluice-water slackened and the level began to fall. Then it grew quieter and the water was no more than knee-deep. The current dwindled into ripples and fell until the flow was held in the drainage channel itself.

In his mind, Jack Rann had prepared a death of this sort for Bragg, but the sight left him silent. Whether the sluice had washed the body of Moonbeam to the foreshore, he had no idea. Where Fowler might be lying was any man's guess. A body washed into a side-channel and left would be picked to the bone by the next day.

'The outfall,' Tomnoddy said softly, 'that's our way home. You don't know who might be waiting at the place you came in.'

Rann lifted his hands.

'Get these darbies off me, Tom. Once I get shot of 'em I'm clear. In my pocket I got a handkerchief. Along the hem is five sovereigns and a receipt folded small. A passage on the *Batavia* from Rotherhithe Dock tomorrow night and a bag that's in the shipping office behind Bermondsey Wall. Everything of mine's in that.'

'Let's get you out of here first,' Tomnoddy said quietly.

The thunder of the sluice still rang in Jack Rann's ears as Tomnoddy led the way. The outfall was a pale oval, lit by stars. The tide had withdrawn to a luminous rim of froth in the summer night, its foreshore sleek with the reflection of sky. Dim figures in long toshers' coats and hats, old women with skirts tucked into boots, waded the shallows and scavenged in the mud.

A small group was stooping over an object of particular interest. The torrent of sewage had flowed into the river but bodies from the outfall were usually too heavy to be carried beyond the mud. Three old women began rifling the pockets, stripping the choker and waistcoat from the corpse of Bully Bragg.

No one in authority appeared. Then, from Shadwell Pier, a man's voice called sternly, 'Mr Fowler! Mr Fowler, sir! If you please, sir! Mr Fowler!'

Jack Rann looked up and saw a burly shape against the pale sky, a rusty frock-coat and tall hat of a Private-Clothes jack. There was lamplight on the pier, sufficient to illuminate in shadow-play the firm round face, the dark moustaches waxed at their tips.

'Mr Fowler!' The voice was not requesting but commanding attention. It had not crossed Rann's mind until this moment that Flash Fowler, having hauled himself into the refuge of a side-tunnel until the sluices ran dry, might still be alive, somewhere behind them.

Then Rann saw the figure at whom the Private-Clothes man had shouted. Fowler still carried the ash-plant. The neatly shaven face was smeared and blotched, like an actor painted with a grotesque beard. The linen summer suit was patched by damp and slime. In full view of a brother officer on the pier, however, he was closing on the Newgate fugitive.

Tomnoddy turned to the river.

'Right behind me, Jack. To the very inch.'

'I can't swim, Tom, specially not with cuffs on. He could have me easy with another jack on the pier.'

'He got no such luck,' said Tomnoddy grimly. 'Stick right behind me.'

Rann glanced back and saw Fowler stumbling on the mud but gaining. Tomnoddy reached the tideline, Rann at his back, and waded in. Rann took from his pocket the large cotton handkerchief, its hem containing five gold sovereigns and the shipping agent's receipt. He knotted it round his neck. Before he had followed Tomnoddy twenty feet into the river chill, the current at his knees, Fowler splashed after them.

'Keep right behind!' Tomnoddy said again. 'I walked this river since I was ten years old. There's places you can step easy as on your parlour floor. And places where you'd step and never be seen again.'

'What you going to do, Tom?'

Tomnoddy turned his head, surprised at the question.

'I'm going to kill him, Jack. Same as he would you. He can't let you tell the tale now.'

'You got nothing to kill him with! He's got the ash-plant. He could knock a man's brains out with that.'

Tomnoddy ignored his objection. Rann glanced back again. Fowler's smooth self-confidence had cracked in a look of insane anger, his features distorted by shadow and darkness. Whether or not Rann had it in his power to destroy the inspector, Fowler's expression suggested it. Once or twice he sabre-slashed at the fugitives with his heavy stick but the distance was too great. With the water at their waists, Tomnoddy and Rann were pulling ahead. Rann guessed they were a bridge-span into the river.

He heard Tomnoddy say softly, 'Just here, to the right. Hold my belt, if you can. We got to turn sharp.'

The downstream current washed against their chests, as they turned the angle. Their pursuer had fallen back, as Tomnoddy had calculated he would. But now Tomnoddy seemed to make a decisive error. Fowler saw the fugitives turn and took his chance to cut the corner, bringing Rann into range of his ash-plant. He was only twelve or fifteen feet behind them as he chose his angle of interception.

The manoeuvre was almost complete, Rann within range of the heavy stick. Fowler lunged again, the tide ripping at his waist. He strode powerfully through ten, fifteen, twenty paces. Then he gave a sudden gasp and sank to his shoulders. For two or three silent seconds, his face was a mask of horrified realization, without a scream or sound, until the water closed gently over his head.

'There's places,' Tomnoddy repeated slowly, 'where you may walk safe as in your own parlour, and places where you step once and aren't never seen again. There's a rib of stone comes out from Pelican Stairs and turns. You could walk to the moon on it. Step off

269

it and there's only mud soft as treacle. He might have known if he'd stopped to think.'

He turned back the way they had come.

'I can't go back, Tom!' Rann said suddenly.

'And you can't go on,' Tomnoddy said. 'Policeman Verity knows you never coopered Pandy.'

'None of the others knows! I don't trust police.'

'All right,' said Tomnoddy, drawing Rann reluctantly behind him. 'You'd trust your penny-dancer, would you?'

Rann looked at the pier and saw beside the bulky figure of Verity the trim-waisted shape of Miss Jolly in the glow of the oil-lamps. He followed Tomnoddy to the tideline.

The old sewerman said quietly, 'Don't come no closer, Jack. Stay here.'

Tomnoddy walked up to the pier and confronted the solid form of the Private-Clothes sergeant.

''ello, Mr Verity. You seen anything tonight?'

Verity looked at him without answering. Then he said, 'What I seen, Tomnoddy, is a real 'ero. First I seen Mr Bragg on the foreshore. Then I seen a fugitive, one Jack Rann, chased into the river by Mr Fowler. Me being too far off to render assistance. I saw Mr Fowler keep after him, until they reached the part where the stone goes to quicksand.'

'And then, Mr Verity?'

'And then, Mr Tom, I saw 'em go down.'

He glanced at the figure below him, with the hands manacled, as if he noticed nothing. Rann looked up and saw the girl detach herself from the other two who were alone upon the pier. She walked down to him and stood with the light of the shore at her back. To one side the scavengers were still busy with the body of Bragg, misshapen in wet clothes as if it had been beaten to blubber.

Miss Jolly opened her hand and showed the little key which Verity had entrusted to her. She found the keyhole of the cuffs, sprang their lock, and took them. The light was behind her but the eyes that were hidden from him by the darkness looked at him in a long remembrance. Her hand touched his.

'Goodbye, Handsome Jack,' she said softly, and turned away.

She looked down at him again from the pier as he slipped away towards Pelican Stairs, along a little passageway by the lighted tavern windows of the Prospect of Whitby. Untying the handkerchief which he had knotted round his neck for safety as he entered the water, he worked a sovereign from its hem. Beyond the alleyway, a cab was parked on the far side of Wapping Lane. Rann strode towards it, a single gold coin in his hand.

'Drury Lane, fast as ever you can. An' this is yours if you can do it before the hour.'

The old cabman got down to open the door, his movements lopsided from the gait of a wooden leg.

'Good as there, sir,' he said confidently, 'and as for that sov, you paid your whack already.'

Jack Rann and the cab were out of sight when Verity took the handcuffs that the girl had brought back and threw them clear beyond the railings into deep water.

34

'Let me have this straight.' Chief Inspector Croaker's eyes grew smaller and brighter.

Verity stood at attention, chin up and shoulders back. In the light of the next summer evening he faced three of them, seated behind the desk of Superintendent Gowry's office, the grandest of all the rooms in Whitehall Place.

'Straight!' Croaker glared at him. One of the other two was an out-of-area Inspector of Constabulary in black frogged coat and military breeches. At the centre sat Gowry, forehead and cheeks brick-red from Indian service which had turned his fine moustaches and abundant hair pure white. Gowry had fought in the relief column from Jalalabad to Kabul, after the slaughter of the British regiments at Gandamak. He had been an infantry major in Sir Colin Campbell's advance on the Sikh artillery, saving the day at Chilianwalla. Unlike Croaker, Verity knew him as a real soldier.

'As I say, sir, I was on the pier when all this was happening below.'

'Alone on the pier?' Gowry enquired gently.

Verity met the keen blue eyes with a feeling of regret.

'No other officer present, sir. And having no idea of Mr Fowler nor Rann being in the outfall . . . .'

'Let me have this straight, Sergeant!' Croaker was back again, bitterly encumbered by the presence of Gowry and a senior official. 'While Inspector Fowler, regardless of his own safety, plunged into the river in pursuit of an escaped murderer, you were content to stand upon the pier and watch?'

'Yessir.' He caught a movement of Gowry's eyes, sorrow at trust betrayed. 'Only it wasn't just like that, sir, with respect.'

'Oh? Was it not?'

'You have to remember, sir, that it was dark and all this happened very quick. I never thought Mr Fowler'd chance going in the river, sir. Knowing how many have gone down there.'

Croaker's mouth twisted with contempt.

'Indeed, Sergeant. But there is some difference in moral calibre between yourself and Inspector Fowler, is there not?'

'Oh, yes, sir. Most definite, sir.'

Gowry came in again, quietly. 'What exactly, Sergeant, did you see?'

'Rann vanished, sir, and so did Mr Fowler. Straight down. One minute the water was just at his waist. Next minute he dropped, sunk, clean gone. Must have stepped off a stone ridge into soft mud. Like quicksand when the ebb begins.'

'Do you say, Sergeant, that Mr Fowler and Rann were both lost?'

'Lost to sight, sir.'

'At the same moment?'

'Near enough, sir. 'Course, it was dark.'

He stared firmly into the evening sky beyond the window and wondered whether his answers had yet crossed the threshold of a painted 'Commandment Against False Witness' in the Cornish chapel of his childhood. The Inspector of Constabulary intervened, a hard quizzical face that had grown used to lies.

'Bragg lay dead on the foreshore. That right, Sergeant? Caught in the main drain by the sluice and washed out?'

'No doubt of that, sir.'

'The fugitive Rann and Mr Fowler must have come out alive? So

273

Rann, Bragg and another man whose bones were found eaten clean were in the sewer tunnels with Mr Fowler in pursuit?'

Verity's forehead creased.

'How it must have been, sir.'

'It argues great courage on Mr Fowler's part, does it not, to tackle three such dangerous men in the confines of the sewers? But when the moment came, you were content to stand and watch, as Mr Fowler went to his death.'

The broad window looked out clear across Lambeth and Bermondsey. A dying sun shone red-gold on the pale classical spire of St John's, Rotherhithe. Under its elongated shadow, the squat hull of the *Batavia* had been winched about until she lay with bows downstream. Several passengers were at the stern rail, taking a last view of the towers of Westminster and the Pool of London. By midnight, the vessel would drop her pilot off Gravesend. Tomorrow she would enter the open waters of the Western Approaches, lost to the world until she docked ten days later at New York.

The questioning had lasted a full hour. The Inspector of Constabulary looked up at the plump witness.

'You may leave this inquiry, Sergeant. It does behove you, nonetheless, to reflect on the part you have played in the loss of a dangerous fugitive and of a most gallant officer. You may also reflect upon your debt to Inspector Croaker.'

'Sir?'

'Your folly in attempting to search the premises of Bragg in Drury Lane has been redeemed. On hearing of your failure, Mr Croaker obtained a justice's warrant and led a party of twelve uniformed officers with Sergeant Samson at dawn today. Two persons, Hardwicke and Atwell, were arrested in possession of a large amount of money in bank notes and bonds, suspected as being the greater part of the proceeds of a fraud now known to have been committed upon clients of the Cornhill Vaults.'

'Sir?'

'Two other persons, a young woman that was known for previous offences, and a man Samuel with a conviction for dishonesty, were detained but released. They claimed to have gone to the house together merely for immoral purposes, an assertion against which there is no evidence. As a result of Mr Croaker's diligence, some four-fifths of the proceeds from the Cornhill fraud appear to have been recovered.'

'Glad to hear it, sir. With respect, sir.'

'Your gladness, Sergeant, is neither here nor there. You would do better to thank the good fortune which has placed you under the command of an officer of such courage and resource as Chief Inspector Croaker.'

'Yessir. Thank you, sir.'

As their eyes met, Croaker was favouring him with a tight reptilian grin of triumph and promise.

'Eyes front!' Gowry said quietly.

The Inspector of Constabulary talked on. Verity wondered how much the final missing fifth of the proceeds amounted to. He gazed solemnly at the window, where the last of the sun on a stretch of cloud above Rotherhithe was turning to the deepest gold. The passengers at the rail of the *Batavia* made their way below, as the light faded and the vessel moved slowly downstream.

Half an hour later, in the sergeants' room, among tall sloping desks and stools, Samson said, 'Had your roasting, then?'

Verity glowered at him.

'Why was you with Mr Croaker down Drury Lane?'

Samson flushed. He brushed his mutton-chop whiskers on the edge of his hand.

'Fair's fair,' he said reasonably. 'You'd had your chance. And Bragg was gone off with Handsome Rann.'

Verity took a step towards him and Samson took a step back.

'I want to know, Mr Samson.'

Samson shrugged.

'Disturbance outside Ma Martileau's. Forty or fifty cabmen and

275

half-a-dozen reverend gentlemen, all swearing a pure virgin been enticed into a house of sin and imprisoned in the attics. Mrs Verity's old father seen rioting! They was going to have their way in with staves and cab-whips to rescue the doxy.'

'And Mr Croaker went down for that?'

'Not exactly,' Samson said self-consciously. 'We heard that bugger Rann been mixed up in it, no one knowing yet he couldn't be because you seen him sink in the mud. Still, it had Mr Croaker off like a greyhound. We got in there with a warrant. Had to fist one or two. Bragg's footmen. Virgin turned out to be Mag Fashion, that hasn't been a virgin since she knew she could be otherwise.'

Verity looked uneasily at his companion.

'Who said about Jack Rann being there?'

Samson beamed and worked his knuckles reminiscently.

'Joker. Told someone he was Rann and if we wanted him he was living on the top floor of Mother Martileau's. By then, of course, you'd seen Handsome Jack in the mud. All we found was Soapy Samuel and Mag Fashion locked in the attics, with Hardwicke and Atwell downstairs counting the money.'

Samson snorted derisively and continued.

'When Bragg went off with Rann, I reckon Hardwicke and Atwell were left behind, to snuff Soapy Samuel and Mag Fashion. Hardwicke and Atwell say otherwise, of course. They swear Samuel went willing to Ma Martileau's, asking for their help, saying he can tell 'em where to fetch more money from the Cornhill Vaults than they ever imagined. Down the Ratcliff Highway, under a floor.'

'Where?'

'They couldn't say,' Samson shrugged, 'some old tosher's place. I reckon Hardwicke sees how they might get the money and skip before Bragg comes back. If there's no money down the Highway, they can always do Samuel and Maggie for having 'em on. So Atwell guards 'em and Hardwicke goes to find the money. The tosher weren't there, them working at nights. Hardwicke comes back with thousands of bank notes, bonds, and sovs, which he swears he only had because they meant to have it off Samuel and the tosher to return it to the lawful owners.'

'What's Samuel say?'

'He don't know a thing about the money. Him and Mag Fashion just went to the house for a bit of a time. No witnesses to say otherwise. Hardwicke and Atwell were downstairs with the money in their hands. Makes them primo for the Cornhill Vaults. Inquiries been made about that today. Seems Lord Mancart had a bill for a thousand sovs dishonoured yesterday.'

'What time was you and Mr Croaker at Bragg's place?'

'About four in the morning. Hardwicke and Atwell never knew then that Bragg and Flash Fowler were dead. I'd say they was about ready to snuff Samuel and Maggie, then off with the money. But they was still there when Mr Croaker came to join the fun. Anyhow, while you was giving evidence just now, Hardwicke and Atwell been charged with doing the Cornhill Vaults.'

'Hardwicke and Atwell couldn't do a china pig!'

Samson grinned hugely.

'And you'd know about that, would you? You was the bright spark reckoned Handsome Rann never done Pandy Quinn. But he did.'

Verity stared at him.

'Who says?'

'Mr Home Secretary. He been through the case. Been through this so-called new evidence. Knives and drains. Nothing but nonsense dreamed up by you and old Baptist Babb and Chaffey, scrubber-up at inquests. So the Home Office still says Handsome Jack was well due for stretching. Only you reckon the bugger saved 'em the trouble, out on the mud.'

They climbed back on their stools and opened their diary ledgers.

'It is true, isn't it?' Samson asked presently.

'What is?'

'Handsome Rann. You saw him sucked down like Charley Fowler?'

Verity stared at him, as if thinking of something far beyond.

'Mr Samson, have I ever lied to you?'

They went back to their chores. Samson looked up again.

'Any rate, I suppose you can have this back now,' he said.

It was the envelope in which Verity had sealed his posthumous memorandum to Croaker. Until Samson tossed it on to the desk, he had forgotten it. He picked it up.

'You bloody opened it!' he said. 'It was to be handed unopened to Mr Croaker if the worst should happen to me!'

Samson shrugged.

'But the worst didn't happen to you, my son. Only to be unopened if handed to Mr Croaker, supposing the worst happened. Nothing about being unopened if the worst didn't happen. Lot of rubbish about Handsome Rann not doing Pandy Quinn, which Mr Home Secretary says he did. Sly Joanne being snuffed when even the inquest said found-drowned. Still, I liked the last bit – commending Mrs Verity and her infants to friends of virtue and religion. Rich, that was!'

The outrage was so absolute that Verity was lost for words. He tucked the torn envelope into his pocket. At last he said sadly, 'You ain't a man of confidence, Mr Samson. Not a man of confidence at all.'

It was rare for Chief Inspector Croaker to address the Private-Clothes Detail on parade but he did so on the following morning in the yard of Whitehall Place. Verity found himself in the front rank, almost face-to-face with his commander. The day was cool with a breeze from the river, whipping and snapping at the flag, lowered to half-mast.

'In Charles Foxe Fowler we mourn the passing of a senior officer and a gallant comrade.' Croaker was shouting a little, as if to make himself heard above the breeze. 'We mourn his passing but treasure his example.'

278

'Example, my arse!' said a quiet voice behind Verity.

'The easiness of his manner concealed a . . . .'

'... bloody robber,' said the quiet voice and someone sniggered.

'... dedication, loyalty and feeling ...'

'...up a dollymop's skirt ...'

'Silence in the ranks,' said Croaker firmly. 'We do our late comrade disservice by allowing even our murmurs of grief to disturb the discipline of parade.'

At dismissal, Verity turned aside and faced Sergeant Alford.

'Seen the new roster?' Alford asked cheerfully. 'They put you back in uniform all next quarter. Waterloo Road, waving traffic about. Someone don't love you, old cock.'

That night, in the ancient brass bed with the two cradles at its foot, Bella said, 'But if this person Rann never went down in the mud, Mr Verity, you could have took him. Now you gone and told untruth.'

Moonlight through open curtains illuminated his round face on the pillow, dark hair flattened on a head that was hatless at last.

'Your old father done a great thing, Mrs Verity, getting them cabmen together.'

'Only 'cos you let Jack Rann go free and then told untruth.'

'I never told untruth, Mrs Verity. I told the inquiry that he and Mr Fowler both vanished. So they did, only different directions. And when Mr Samson asked if I really saw Handsome Rann go down in the mud, all I did was ask Mr Samson if I'd ever told him a lie. Ain't the same as untruth.'

Under the sheet, Bella stroked his leg with her toes. The doubt on her face added a new dimension of prettiness.

'It's not what you was taught in chapel,' she said quietly.

'Ain't it?' he said thoughtfully. 'We was Methodist and Radicals. My old father and my mother was married when the Reform Bill was in the 'ouse of Commons. I was named for it. William Clarence for old King William that was Duke of Clarence and wanted the reform. I was taught justice. How we got to break the power of the squirearchy and the established church. Even Handsome Rann got a right to justice. You know they was still going to hang him if they caught him? Mr Home Secretary decided. Even after Bragg and Fowler and the knife and the drain! Thanks to what I let 'em think, they ain't even looking for him any more.'

Bella turned on her back.

'Then you saved him.'

'Not really. You was right, Mrs Verity, when you said there's lots of good ordinary people in the world, them that never give a tinker's cuss for Home Secretaries, nor Mr Croakers. You know who saved Handsome Rann? He got saved by a poor starving washerwoman and her baby in Newgate Street. And an old tosher down the Ratcliff Highway. And a penny-dancer from a Monmouth Street gaff. And an old cadger dressed up like a parson. And a young medical chap that could never pass to be a doctor. And an old harlot that watches fallen creatures so they don't run off and sell their fancy clothes. And if Handsome Jack did the Cornhill Vaults and got clean away with his share, they'd dance to hear of it, and bust theirselves laughing.'

Bella giggled.

'You ain't never going to let fly with that down Paddington Chapel, Mr Verity!'

He turned on his side and put his arms round her.

'P'raps I won't, Bella. But ain't it true? Handsome Rann's the only one got away with his share. His Miss Jolly's back to showing you-know-what down the Chinese Shades. Mag Fashion'll be kneeling to gentry and ladies in some mourning draper's again. Soapy Samuel got to be nothing but a trick-parson. But don't Rann deserve what he got? After all what was done to him? But they'd hang him still! Thank God I never took him on the mud.'

Bella sighed, as the breeze across the rooftops of the little streets ruffled the curtains at their open window. Then she was confidential again.

'Even supposing,' she said quietly, 'you was sent for ever and ever down the Waterloo Road, just to wave the traffic about, we got so much to be glad about. We ain't starving. We got a roof. There's even a bit put by.'

'There's that,' he said philosophically.

Bella drew him closer.

'And s'pose you was sent to do nothing but *sweep* the Waterloo Road the rest of your life. Even then, William Clarence Verity, you'd still be my good brave sojer!'

He chortled self-consciously.

'I don't know about all that, Mrs Verity.'

'I do,' she said.

>>> If you've enjoyed this book and would like to discover more great vintage crime and thriller titles, as well as the most exciting crime and thriller authors writing today, visit: >>>

The Murder Room
Where Criminal Minds Meet

themurderroom.com